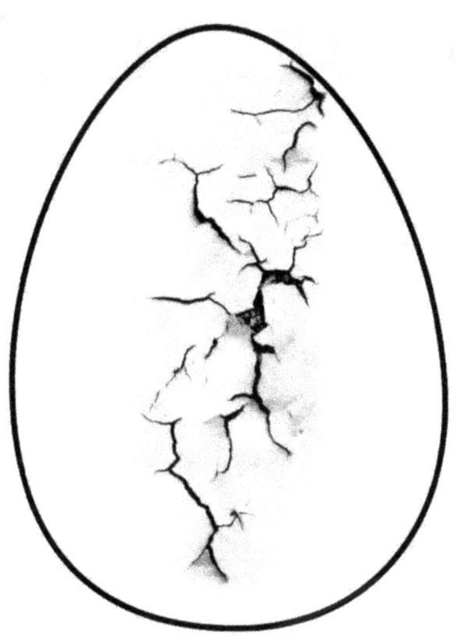

(Working Title)

Don Bronco's

"DON'T LET THE BUSINESS
TARNISH THE ARTISTIC."

--> DON BRONCO

(Working Title)

Shell

A novel???

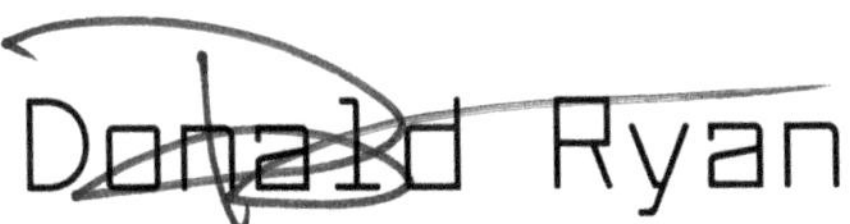

Side note: the ISBN is 9781088068441

Ebook available at the publisher's website.
Cover design by David Wojciechowski
Typesetting by Alan Good

Published by the one and only Malarkey Books!

malarkeybooks.com

To my wife,
my family,
and Philly B,
who found $20 then caught on fire.

"I'm a failed poet. Maybe every novelist wants to write poetry first, finds he can't, and then tries the short story, which is the most demanding form after poetry. And, failing at that, only then does he take up novel writing."

—William Faulkner, The Art of Fiction No. 12

Chapter 1

Zeek found the first piece of eggshell in his High Country omelette. Not mentioning this to Sally, he slid the shell past the hash browns to the edge of his plate. He did, however, say, when Sally finally asked how everything was while refilling his coffee, that everything was great, as always, and to be sure to give his compliments to Sal, her husband, the six-foot-six short order cook. To point out the shell was pointless. Zeek ate there, at Sal's Counter (which Zeek and only Zeek called it, likening it to being a 70s sitcom set in the 1950s) four to six times a week and, being particularly fond of breakfast, felt no need to call attention to himself or the shell. You can't make an omelette without breaking a few eggs. These things happen. A little shell never hurt nobody.

He paid at the counter, waved goodbye to Sal through the window, and with his brown leather briefcase headed off to the bus stop, leaving behind a hefty tip as always.

The corner of Alabaster and MacDade was as uninhabited as usual. Zeek made himself comfortable on the bench, sandwiched between an ad advocating Homes for the Homeless, a dollar donated for every photographic upload, #housenation, and a poster for the most delicious gross-out comedy of the year, *Cooking*..., a load served up hot and steamy this fall. He would wait for the film to stream in 4K to avoid attending the theater alone, opting for the comfort of his own home, seeing how the tiny seats were tight against his rounded frame, anyway. Across the street the man with thick-rimmed glasses was opening the convenience store. The bus would be arriving any minute.

The driver looked as asleep as the dude sprawled along the back row's four seats, his hand tucked down the front of his gym shorts. Zeek picked his usual seat on the otherwise vacant bus, in the middle, on the right, as always. He enjoyed gazing out the window, like it was an oversized television where he could relax his brain and vacation his thoughts, a morning meditation of sorts. That, and the aisle seat was less constricting. The roar of the engine drowned out the dude's snoring between stops. Zeek combed his hair to the side through his fingers, using the window's reflection as a guide. His mustache was straight and well trimmed under the misdiagnosed bulb of his assumed twice-broken nose.

They were approaching The Bolster (which Zeek and only Zeek called it, likening it to being the thin-walled, dimly lit hourly rate joint the husband, wife, and adorable kids enter in a shock of stained sheets and broken box television before cutting into the crisp, white wonder room with a view in those fun-filled, family pack vacation ads) located between the fourth and fifth stop. And even though the bus didn't pass along the front of the motel, crossing the backside where the neon sign didn't glow, this was, hands down, the pinnacle of Zeek's morning commute. Here was the only place in the city with an outdoor, in-ground pool. At this generally empty hour the pool laid still, the occasional exception being an early riser exerciser swimming laps. Zeek waited for this angle every Monday through Friday morning. So while not being particularly fond of pools, and more specifically pool attire, he liked imagining children running, laughing, as boisterous as their neon floaties, their mother relaxing in a one-piece behind oversized sunglasses and layers of lotion. A father charring up some dogs. Otherwise, they'd be having packed sandwiches and waterlogged chips. Zeek enjoyed this idea of sun, this idea of fun.

But every Monday through Friday morning, the gray line Bus 12, would pass bleakly by, a few strangers getting on, a few strangers getting off, Zeek on his way to the office.

George Gilliam (which Zeek and only Zeek called it, likening it to the uniformed monotony before the mold is shattered, the day to day shook up, the bleak remembrance and gray tedium of how could we live like that before) was housed in the pristine cylindrical high rise overlooking the city through its curved, mirrored glass. The company, renowned for its micro-innovations and hip office décor, oversaw the managed production of the small parts for the large parts used in the larger parts of things. A facet of the grand scale. Zeek worked on the sixth floor, the lower levels reserved for office spaces and cubicles, the upper for acronyms and conference rooms. And although he shared an office with Dave, he had his own desk and his own computer where he read emails and responded to emails making sure other employees read their emails and responded to emails in between the onslaught of daily meetings. Zeek was never thrilled about meetings, finding the chairs, while well cushioned, a bit snug, preferring his Office Lounger 2970 behind his desk. But all in all, on any given day, it wasn't a bad gig. There were definitely worse jobs down below.

Zeek found the second piece of eggshell at his desk. He said good morning to his receptionist, Matte (Dave and Zeek adding the e because he was so damn dull), like he did every morning as he passed the entry desk and was greeted with the slight, same as ever nod. Dave's Office Lounger 2250, which inspired Zeek's own, sat tucked under Dave's desk, his computer screensaver still flying the windows he downloaded as pastiche to '93, the desk still bare of any and all personal effects save the framed photograph of an attractive blonde woman jostling with two playful, blue-eyed blond boys in the professional, soft focus woods of autumn. Zeek called out through the open office door, asking if Dave had been seen and/or heard from yet. The receptionist buzzed back with a no. Odd, not unheard of, but odd, this being the second day in a row without Dave.

The inner workings of Zeek's digestion imploded anxiously like the discomforted pit of an x-rayed stomach as seen on TV. He took a candy bar from the stash in his briefcase to fill the void. On his second bite, a rounded point crunched against the roof of his mouth. He dug into the masticated mess like a surgeon playing Operation and pulled out the tiny, white shell. In all the bars, no matter the candy, Zeek consumed in his lifetime, he had never once come across an eggshell. But, to be fair, he justified not knowing the ingredients of nougat against not knowing anyone who did, feeling safe enough to assume eggs were involved in that tradition over the chocolate, caramel, or peanuts. These things happen. If this was a game show, it was Zeek's luckiest of lucky days. But, it wasn't a game show. It was 10:44 a.m. with still no word from Dave.

2 meetings, 164 emails, 1,942 clicks across the internet, and 1 Candy Bar later, Zeek was back on the bus, closing the route to his 1 bed/1bath single unit apt (please no pets). It had been a bustle of a day. He was more than welcome to be home, opting for Chinese delivery over takeout (min $15 order), and while waiting watched nothing in particular on his UXHD microplasma cored 77" Kyoshiri, as always.

Chapter 1

Zeek found the third piece of eggshell in his coffee. He sat at Sal's Counter's (which Zeek and only Zeek called it, likening it to being the quaint Mom & Pop for those oh to feel young again elderly couples in pharmaceutical ads) literal counter under the false morning of fluorescent bulbs, the sun waking up on the dark horizon. Sally asked if everything was okay this morning as she refilled his cup, and not just with the food, mentioning casually in passing how he only ordered a half stack of pancakes with his Hearty Morning Platter. He said everything was perfectly in order, just like his breakfast, as always, give his compliments to Sal. She smiled down at him, warmer than the rising sun, but Zeek still noticed her disbelief by how she showed too much teeth.

He poured a steady stream of sugar into the topped off cup, allowing the new heat to melt it into the toasted liquid, before topping it to the rim with the six to eight tiny cups of Picturesque Farms, those complimentary only-ever-found-in-restaurants brand half-n-halfs, to flavor it the right shade of beige. He gave the creamed coffee a gentle stir with his spoon, careful not to spill too much, the little he did caught by the napkin used as a coaster. He hated Sally having to go behind him. But, in the delicate whirl created, he noticed a white fleck along for the ride. He spooned it out and poked it. The tiny piece of shell stuck to his finger. He brought his index towards his face, like a cinematic close-up, blurring out all the rest, but Sally moved into the soft rack focus of his peripherals, so with a quickness he hid the curiosity in the napkin under his mug. He saw no need to bother her with such a trifle, as it most likely fell from one of the six to eight creamers. The Picturesque Farm obviously had picturesque chickens.

He paid at the counter, waved goodbye to Sal through the window, and with his brown leather briefcase headed off to the bus stop, leaving behind a hefty tip as always.

He sat alone on the bench at the corner of Alabaster and MacDade, his briefcase at his feet. He quietly watched the man with thick-rimmed glasses open the convenience store for the day. In the distance he could hear drumming, a spastic tic-tic-ticking against the steadiness of bass. Zeek looked down the flat street for the bus, seeing instead the sun's reflection on silver, rhythmically flashing a faint glare in front of a blur of blue and a tinge of yellow. Or was it gold? He'd have to wait till they were closer. All in due time. Time they were keeping overlaid with snares. The man with thick-rimmed glasses watched from behind his glass door. Zeek checked his watch. The bus should have arrived by now. He'd have to explain his tardiness if asked. No one would.

The drumline was now close enough where Zeek could make out their blue and golden yellow trimmed uniforms, with a banner to match, leading the "Inner Mid-Land Recreational All Drum Marching Band, Chapter 2AA, 'Can You Feel The Beats.'" The street overflowed with the river, a current of snares and toms whitewater rapidly clashing against the cymbals, washed under by the bell-bell-bellowing bass. Sticks tapped the drums' skins, the drums' chrome, the drummer in front of drummers, banging on the trashcans, on the streetlights, the curb and grates, the quiet street where Zeek sat every Monday through Friday morning becoming a rhythmic chaos, a melodic mash of clank-knocking rap-tap-tapping. And bringing up the rear, The Grey Line Number 12 pulled over and slid open its doors with a whimper.

The driver, half asleep as always, seemed unaffected by the parade, and the dude sprawled across the back row literally slept through the ruckus, hand tucked down the front of his gym shorts, snoring off tempo. Zeek shambled his weight halfway down the bus and situated himself in his right side aisle seat. He checked his reflection in the window, smoothing his already straight stache.

The bus creeped, stalking the band. Even with routine stops it remained never far behind like an anticlimactic coda. Like the victim of happenstance, as the band marched the grey route, turning down Henry, right on Jones, left up Indiana Ave, until veering off the beaten path into the back lot of The Bolster (which Zeek and only Zeek called it, likening it to the ideal cinematic hideaway for those needing somewhere to go, for a respite away from their onscreen world at large, whether for aesthetic or budgetary reasons). One of the bannermen held open the pool's gate with his bannerless hand, marching in place, keeping the banner taut and in tune with his companion, creating a makeshift wall, damming the flow of drummers into the pool area. Zeek leaned closer to the window, squinting a bit as an ineffective visual focalizer and/or to clarify actualization. One by one, the band marched into the pool, dropping into the water their four:four beat. Snares and feathered caps leveled with the concrete. Basses and uniforms disappeared below. The last cymbal crashed into the crowded water and was followed by the banner. The gate closed itself behind them. Zeek rubbernecked across the empty seat, his large forehead pressed onto the window, trying to see what all he could and infer what all he could not as the bus pulled away from the fifth stop.

A throat cleared behind him.

He removed his head from the smudge he left on the window and shifted his weight back into his aisle seat. An elderly woman, not much taller than he was sitting, even slouched, peered down.

"I don't think you'd mind."

"I don't—" Each syllable a question matching the look Zeek was giving.

"Very good then." She scooted into Zeek's knees blocking the path to the window seat. The bus rocked forward. Instinctively, Zeek caught the woman. He could feel a frailness under her wrinkled skin.

"Can I help you?"

"Thank you, but I'd like to take my own seat." Her voice was firm. Exact but not rude, like a studio star past her prime in the golden age of Hollywood. Zeek looked at all the other vacant options. "And he won't make for good conversation," she continued, answering what his expression was asking. Zeek opened a path without standing as in what good was arguing? She dragged her oversized bag across his belly and sat in her own seat, where she situated herself with a little wiggle as if the seat, which engulfed her attenuated-with-age frame, was too small, and tucked herself under her unnaturally large purse.

"Dolores Fry."

"Excuse me?"

"Dolores Fry. But the friends that I do have call me D. That's a capital D. While the friends that I don't have call me Small Fry. Don't call me Small Fry."

"Yes, Ms. D." Zeek attempted to laugh the words in a lacquer of friendly nonchalance, but his voice quivered into intimidation, like he'd been scolded for something not yet done.

"And—" The mid-Atlantic elongation ended abrupt.

He held on his face those straight lips of neutral cordialness.

"Your name. This is where you introduce yourself." Her expression remained that placid pushiness of the elderly. Her varicose hands remained curled on her purse. It was only her voice that registered a crisped twinge in remembrance of the bygone days of yesteryear.

"Yes. Right." He stuttered to recall "Ezekiel."

"Are you quite sure about that?"

Zeek watched her eyes scan every oversized inch of him.

"Fairly."

"Then it's fairly nice to make your acquaintance, Mr. Zeekeal." She didn't shake his hand, which was probably for the best. The idea of crushing something so fragile in his gentle mitt terrified him, even if he couldn't rationalize the fear or understand the calm. Ms. D looked forward, unfazed by the world around.

The high rise of George Gilliam (which Zeek and only Zeek called it, likening it to a lustrous colony of organized normality, a central metabolized system, an oblongata for the medulla) dominated up ahead, standing tall in the city's sky. Zeek looked past the old woman and at his own reflection. He combed his already straightened mustache with his fingers.

"Have a good day," he said, not wanting to be rude.

"I might. I might not."

He gave a smile, quaint if it wasn't all so terribly awkward. And even after stepping off the bus in front of the cylindrical high rise, felt compelled to look back and give a small, fidgety wave he hoped to all mercy Ms. D didn't actually see.

Chased by embarrassment, Zeek hurried into the sanctuary of the office tower, hiding behind the thick glass door as the bus rolled off to the next stop. He turned and read without reading *"Hard work is the salt of life. Persistence is the pepper." — Theodor Dupox*, the oft reputed father of the first hand-held electric pepper mill, painted underneath the world clocks hung above the lobby's information and securities desk, as he did every Monday through Friday morning on his way to the elevator.

Zeek got off on the sixth floor, as per usual, and said good morning to Matte (Dave and Zeek adding the e because his personality lacked any ounce of luster). "Is

Dave in?" He continued to his office, stuck his head in, checking for himself, and saw two empty Office Loungers and the multicolored, coin-sized windows flying across Dave's otherwise blank screen.

"No." Informative.

Zeek set his briefcase on his desk, the leather's dull thud louder than intended. He nestled himself into his Office Lounger 2970 and awakened his computer. Emails wouldn't check themselves. He peeked over his shoulder. The room had been so quiet without Dave's faint tappings on the keyboard. Zeek wasn't enjoying the hum of silence. He tried suppressing the desire for a Candy Bar so early, but what better way to break the silence than by crinkling a wrapper? So why wait? He didn't, and then responded to the first of 187 emails.

He found the fourth piece of eggshell atop a pepperoni, nestled by a mushroom. With the last email sent and more piling up, virtually overflowing his inbox, Zeek was relieved Ms. D wasn't on the evening bus. He was done for the day, overdue for checkout, his eyes and attention strained from staring at his monitor since that morning. All he wanted was to go home and rest both by watching some television. Order a pizza. Pizza was consistently the best idea. So he spent his evening watching nothing in particular on his UXHD microplasma cored 77" Kyoshiri, getting up only once to answer the door. With the box in his lap like one big plate, unbothered by the grease because that's where flavor congregated, he lifted the cardboard hinge to find the fleck of white set on his supreme. He picked it out and held it delicately in his fingers in the light of the screen's flickering. Briefly, he thought about calling and complaining, but what good would that do, honestly? It probably fell from a bag of cheese. Or maybe they used an egg wash like he saw on a cooking segment once. Either way it wasn't the pimpled kid making minimum wage or the chain's manager whose salary wasn't much more than the kid's fault. The circumstance found him. These things happened. So Zeek placed the shell on the coffee table, swapping it out for the remote, and began flipping channels between slices.

Chapter 1

He found the fifth piece of eggshell in a napkin. Zeek buried his face into his beiged coffee. His head was heavy, weighed down from the bags underneath his eyes, hovering over the counter at Sal's Counter (which Zeek and only Zeek called it, likening it to one of those hidden gems tucked away on The Food Channel late at night). He was tired. But from what? It was just one of those mornings to be shrugged off, cast into the past in lieu of the afternoon. Yet so far the day wasn't looking so bright, the sun taking its sweet time rising over the horizon.

Sally set the Hearty Morning Platter in front of him. She had skirted the please no substitutions with French toast for pancakes, so he at least had that going for him. First and beforemost, he poured syrup over the toast, watching it spill down the plateau cliffs of Texas crust. Syrup needed proper time to soak. Zeek cut a corner, prodded it with his fork, and pushed it around the puddles, actions rendering a giddy oui-oui yeehaw. But en route to his face a bulb of syrup drizzled onto his shirt's rounded protrusion between his jacket and his tie.

He put down his fork, bite intact. The metal clanked against the plate, breaking the placid atmosphere of the breakfast bar, an unwelcomed reminder of the chaos the day would bring.

"Everything alright, hun?" Sally asked, refilling his coffee.

"Yeah. Yes." (Oui-Oui.) "Everything's great." (YeeHaw.) He reached for a napkin from the metallic dispenser between the salt and ketchup.

A tiny piece of eggshell fell from the inter-fold of the napkin he pulled. He wadded the paper, staring at the white fleck no bigger than a key on a keyboard. His head cocked, tilting further the harder he looked, like a confused puppy that understood words but couldn't put together the sentence, giving the syrup time to soak.

"Don't go smearing it in. I'll check the back for baking soda. We're bound to have some." Sally walked off before Zeek could say thank you, assuming Zeek was even going to say thank you, his mind solely focused on the shell.

Zeek pressed the shell onto his forefinger. Slowly, as to not startle himself, he held his finger before his face, beseeching it for answers but concluding he didn't know the question.

"Dab at it with this." Sally, placing the ramekin of white powder and a cup of ice cubes on the counter, interrupted his amateur analysis. "Grandma swore by it."

"Sally?" Zeek knew what he wanted to ask but couldn't articulate the how. The unsure and unsteady words "Have you guys had any problems with eggshells?" sounding as crazy out loud as actually finding them.

She responded with a bend in her brow, picking up his disconcerting inflection. "You find some in your toast? Because I'm always telling Sal, 'You've got to be more careful,' but he can be so blasé, always saying things like 'A little shell never hurt nobody.' But you're loyal and Sal's lazy, so breakfast is on us."

"No, no. I mean—"

"No, no. I insist."

"I mean, shells in general. Like in Candy Bars or napkins."

"I'm not following you."

"I'm not either."

"How about I get you some more coffee?" She ignored the fact his cup was full. Coffee was the ultimate excuse. So he downed what he could before she turned around with the pot.

"You know, I've never caught your name." She polished the words as to not tarnish her tip.

"Ezekiel." He was trying to sound put together, but the appellation wobbled on the caffeinated second syllable. With the amount of Monday through Friday mornings he'd frequented this particular establishment, Zeek realized this was the longest conversation he'd had with Sally. Everything previous, although cordial, remained strictly professional. In a word: business-as-usual. However, this was all back mere minutes before, back when he considered himself a regular rather than irregular due to a single question.

"Everything is great, by the way," he mentioned to flip back to the familiar.

"Including the shell?" The redux of banter.

"Especially." He smiled, his lips too tight for either's comfort.

He tried paying at the counter, but Sally still insisted no, so he left a hefty tip as always, including gratuity to cover his meal, waved goodbye to Sal through the window, and with his brown leather briefcase headed off to the bus stop.

The convenience store on the corner of Alabaster and MacDade was an unusual bustle of commotion. Zeek watched the man with thick-rimmed glasses open the store, as per usual. But then he saw a customer. A lone man in a black jacket entered the store with a twitch to his step, leaving the empty street empty. Zeek looked down the way as if he'd find the path the man came from, but there was no hint, no trail cut into the damp air. And then there was the car. It pulled in harsh and with a halt, parking angled at the front side of the building. A woman, not heavyset but top heavy, rushed out and into the store as if she was destined to be late as the second customer.

The hum of the street lamps bowed to the sun, the gray clouds quilting the sky, heavy, blanketing the morning, an agitated songbird gave up on its dream of hitting it big in the city, the man in the black jacket stormed through the glass doors and paced the brick storefront before turning and storming back in. And Zeek sat like a blip in the universe, slouched between an ad for Project Rainwater (TEXT 27722 to donate) and a poster for the third season of *Cop Drama* (starring two-time Academy Award nominee Martin Hearty as "an average cop solving above average crimes, Tuesdays this fall").

A backfire interrupted the quiet whisper of dawn. But the only car in sight was parked crooked and vacant. The city seemed deserted under the morning fog and the smell of exhaust. A backfire shot off a second time. The popped layers reverbed from somewhere straight ahead, somewhere in the direction of the store, muffled in the distance by the building. The man with the black jacket, not necessarily rushing but more anxious in determination, seconded his exit. He crossed the street without looking, straight towards the bus stop. Zeek looked for anything to avoid eye contact and somehow settled on the sidewalk. He wasn't in the mood for cordialities about the weather or apologies for his lack of loose change. However, Zeek couldn't avoid the sound of the footsteps getting closer.

Or the whistle.

A psst Zeek answered.

Their eyes met. He appeared younger without the distance, maybe, the harsh lines from harsh lines possibly misread made it hard to tell. Not knowing if he should flash a smile or look away, Zeek did neither. The man tossed something, a little black ball, towards Zeek without breaking the pace of his jolted steps. Reacting without direction, Zeek caught it and was now in possession of a double double chocolate muffin wrapped in cellophane. He eyed the muffin like he'd never seen this style of pastry, like the concept of a double double chocolate was new. He tried saying thank you(?) or what's this (questioning the obvious), but neither came out in the huff. No matter. The segment ended. The man in the black jacket had no desire to be recognized as he plowed up MacDade like rushing the wrong way into a destination nonexistent.

He found the sixth piece of eggshell on the muffin. Zeek examined the wrapped pastry at hand, rotating it to all sides, the morning sun glinting off the cellophane like a crystal ball. To the best he could tell, there were no cons. The sooth saying it was just a muffin. Basically a puffy cake. And Zeek was quite fond of cake. He unwrapped the tangled mash of plastic, delicately and slowly with bomb squad precision. Yet, he stopped, muffin in his palm, cellophane draped over his hand. On the mound, decorating dead center like a cake topper, was a dime-sized fleck of shell. Zeek pulled it out. He could feel the brittleness of the edges but the sturdiness in its curve along his finger.

Agitation formed like pinhead bubbles in his naturally chilled pot of existence. So he flicked the shell. Flicked it with every newton of force his forefinger could muster. And the fleck soared, literally as if it had sprouted wings. A graceful trajectory that met an abrupt end on the side of the bus, which opened its doors with a whimper.

The driver was hunched over the wheel as if actually sleeping. Zeek stepped into The Grey Line Number 12 and sauntered to his right side aisle seat, briefcase in one hand, muffin in the other. Zeek didn't check his reflection in the window, didn't finger-comb his comb-over, didn't smooth his already straight mustache. Instead, he sat face forward. And he watched. He saw the curved ads bordering the roof peddling their cheeseburgers and cheeseburgers and dot-coms, saw the windshield sucking up the road under the bus, saw the stagnant, artificially cooled air stifling the rows of empty seats. But to an observer seeing him, his numbed stare was blank. His mind closed to the world. He was neither part of this reality playing before him nor the reality pressing play. He just was. A plaything, cheap and hollow. A forced commodity. A small cog. A doodle on paper. A character in a role.

Harsh rapping in the divot of his shoulder tapped him back to his senses. He blinked, startled. The cognitive perceptions of the setting reappeared. His deep thoughts now buried and forgotten, like a dream where the resonance lingers but the conclusion no longer nears the surface. His feet were back on the proverbial ground, his awareness planted in the seat. He reminded himself he was content. Irrevocably content. And if he had to be anything, content wasn't the worst thing to be.

He felt the harsh rapping again. Over his shoulder was a face he didn't immediately recognize. But there was a familiarity below the backwards snapback and underneath the unkempt beard. The dude usually asleep was awake, holding the overhand bar, and hovering over Zeek, rattling along with the bus.

"You're not going to eat that?" He pointed to the unwrapped muffin. His voice was smooth without being rich yet still not like poverty. The inflected consonants cut a bit sharper, foreign to the region.

"I—well, no." While taken aback, Zeek was more than happy to rid himself of the muffin. It felt nice to help.

But then again, Zeek was slightly disappointed when the dude didn't appear overly grateful. Instead, what should have been gratitude took the form of a monotone "Obliged," before he returned to his sprawled position across the back seat. And without trying to stare, aware of not wanting to be rude, Zeek was nearly positive he wasn't even eating his muffin. He looked out the window in contempt of his good deed going unnoticed, otherwise what's the point, to see The Bolster (which Zeek and only Zeek called it, likening it to a jewel in the jungle brush stumbled upon by an explorer for a humorous but well needed night's rest) had already passed, his favorite part of the commute missed like an opportunity.

A throat cleared behind him.

"Yes," Zeek pointed.

"Were you expecting someone different?" Ms. D rebutted with a complete nonchalance as if it were some scripted repartee they'd shared for seasons.

"No. It's just been a different sort of morning."

She scooted by, dragging her oversized handbag across his belly. "All mornings are the same. What differs is how you play them out."

Zeek's response involved silence and stillness.

"I've seen enough mornings come and go. Day by day, in fact. The sun comes up. The day begins. The creator creates. And out of all these consistencies, are you or are you not the same difference?"

"Well, this one's not the same kind of different," he said.

"We have an optimist."

"More realist."

She choked on a scoff. "Questions are the only things that can be considered real." She resituated under her oversized bag, which to Zeek's amazement wasn't crumpling her like a dried leaf into dust. "I work at the shelter. The animal shelter. I volunteer. Most domesticated animals are far superior than that animal Man. But there's what they refer to as an overpopulation. What they should call it is an inconvenience. All this means is humanely, the irony of the word, putting down dogs and cats to maintain a population below an arbitrary figure some man behind a desk created. There's no reason outside control. So the question is where the truth lies. Why let the arbitrary dictate the day to day?"

George Gilliam (which Zeek and only Zeek called it, likening it to a company not built for people but around people by people, an emerald beacon of hope paving the golden way through the stresses of distress into the human root of humanity like there's no place like home) couldn't arrive fast enough.

"Astounded?" she said, her voice content by her own speech.

"Yes, ma'am."

"And what is it you do with your time?"

"Oh. I'm a technological task point managing specialist and multi-unit cross personnel overseer technician."

"Poppycock. What is it you do that's you?"

Zeek thought about himself, who he was, "I correspond with and connect varying levels of communication throughout the company, mainly using emails as a primary means," and found it wasn't necessary to explain and justify his hard work.

"Sounds like your soul overfloweth."

"I make a living."

"But are you alive?"

Somewhere between the muffin and the inquisition, Zeek had finally had enough for one morning. As cordially as possible, he picked up his brown leather briefcase and stood at the front where he waited for his impending stop. Moments later the bus jolted to a halt. Zeek clumsily held the bar, maintaining his balance like a pendulum. The doors, thankfully, opened with a whimper, but before getting off Zeek made the mistake, the fool, of looking back to see his muffin, uneaten, on the floor.

Those small pinhead bubbles were becoming pearls. He knew it was pointless, beyond pointless. Stupid, really. But that unsettling heat of provocation still boiled inside him. He brewed, percolating the already running hot reminder he didn't care about the muffin. He didn't care about eccentric old ladies. He didn't care about drumlines or eggshells. He related to simple. To breakfast, television, and the way he liked things. He even cared about his job for forty hours between Monday through Friday and Dave whenever he was there.

He got off the elevator and, without saying good morning to his receptionist, went straight to his office. There was no surprise. Dave wasn't in, his Office Lounger 2250 tucked under his desk, his desktop screen swimming with nostalgia.

"Meeting at 1:30," Matte (Dave and Zeek adding the e because he lacked the pizzazz to ever take the three-odd steps to the door) called out.

Zeek didn't bother to respond. Why should he?

He found the seventh piece of eggshell in his keyboard. His email load that morning felt heavier than normal even though the ballpark 150 was the general average, so he tackled the day as always from the bottom. But, of course, the day would keep weighing down. He had plenty, daresay, more than enough to do before the scheduled disruption. And to add insult to injury his button b-twixt his W and R, crucial to his day's work, was sticking stock still, rndring it uttrly uslss. He continued poking the key as if it would fix itself, as if it was spring-loaded and would click itself into application like an ink pen. It did not. He copied and pasted an E from previous emails, but the incessant right-clicking caused more interruptions than flow. So, grudgingly, our main protagonist would just work around his hiccup, insouciant to syntax and form.

That was until he took a pair of scissors from his desk drawer, the kind ergonomic for a child's tiny hands and safety with its curved tip and pink plastic handle, too thick for Zeek's equivalently thick fingers. He pried at the E. His goal here wasn't necessarily to remove the key from the board but loosen it. Give it a nudge. But it clicked and popped through the air. He picked the letter off the floor. Nothing was visually askew with the hollowed cube. He leaned over the keyboard to give it a blow, that old time-tested technique for reviving plastic technology. And this was when he saw it. Small, off-white, and crammed into the square where the key should sit flush. He used his scissors, delicately this time, to lever the shell enough to pinch it out.

He leaned into his Office Lounger 2970 while taking a deep enough breath to cool his frustrations. From this point on he could no longer rationalize these things happen. These things don't happen. Or, if they do they've never happened to him. However, with his weekend already booked he chose the active role of least concern. So tonight he would sail off with a little television, do as little as physically possible on the good ship Staycation, and mentally nullify the registration of the week's accounts. But before he could pose the shadow of being homeward bound he first had emails to answer and a meeting to attend. He replaced the E key which now typed like a charm.

Chapter 2

Staff,

Kindly follow company policy apropos company standard:

~Staff must look at company inbox (daily).
~Staff must look at all and confirm looking at all company mail.

Miscommunication from floor to floor is 1) without confirmation or 2) "lost."

Our company's wish is providing top quality for all. In doing so, all staff must act as a part within a singular unit via CPU mail throughout all positions (from top down).

All staff should look at this company's handbook for validating CPU mail functions.
(https://www...)
Kindly confirm this CPU mail following standard protocol.

Ezekiel Douglas Macrae
Technical Task Point Managing Specialist
Multi-Unit Cross Personnel Overseer Technician
Level 6

Chapter 3

He found the ninth piece of eggshell in a menu. Zeek woke up well after noon. It was his day off. The key words here being his and day. And he tended to execute his days off by staying up until the wee, pre-morning hours flipping through channels, eventually nodding off in his black leather Plushbottom, and on this particular day waking to a news doc on industrial farm factories ("the future of food") and a microplasma full of chickens.

On his days off Zeek didn't have to shower, shave, even brush his teeth. Again, it was his day. His pantsless day if he so desired. He could amble around, doing nothing, and love every second of it. The sounds of the television, somewhere between ambiance and conversation, were cozy in the background while he made himself a cup of instant coffee. He rummaged through a stack of delivery ads he'd accumulated with various meals in search of a post-breakfast fast-breaking lunch. He thumbed over a pizza ad, considering but not set on it, and found a trifold menu for the wing joint a few blocks over. It had been a while since he had wings. A few weeks. Maybe more. Remembering didn't matter now. The craving set in. The course was set. He opened the fold to browse Wing It's 37 sauces when it slid out from between the first crevice and into the open drawer. An eggshell, quarter-sized, the largest so far. Zeek picked it up, but in doing so it cracked in two brittle pieces he caught in his palm, which he stared at without realizing, his body frozen, his vision zeroing in but unable to read the situation at hand. He wasn't losing his mind. There was no way. He was tangibly touching shell. Figments of imagination can be grasped but literally not like this. He had had enough. Or had he had enough? He'd yet to question the possibility of someone toying with him. But maybe because the answer was inconceivable seeing as he didn't know many people, let alone anyone with the skillset or intelligence, to pull off an endeavor this fine-tuned and spectacular.

He blinked himself back into the reality of his kitchen and brushed the shells onto the counter. He had decided on chicken wings. Plotting the course. But first needed to put on pants.

Zeek lived on the left hand side of the bottom floor, the apt moniker BL, of The Family Mansion (which Zeek and only Zeek called it, likening it to the nicely dilapidated houses ghoulish families established as residence in those string of successful B&W TV series before his time, that even without the tangled, creaking gate delineating the property and the fact it was painted an awful Easter egg yellow, when the moonlight hit it just right the dark shadows were effectively gothic) which consisted of a Victorian style house divided into five living spaces, two on each floor, one in the upper peak, on the corner between a studio gallery and a downtown department store marketplace. Zeek didn't personally know his neighbors other than a who's who of recognition, or his neighbors him, but everyone keeping to themselves was cordial and quiet enough to be considered quite neighborly.

He found the tenth piece of eggshell on the sidewalk. Or, for that matter, whether considered a part or a whole, the tenth piece of eggshell found him. Zeek left Wing It with the It Platter's 32 wings, 4 flavors, and a Sip It Super Large Cola, and since sitting with the acquainted strangers on television made him feel less alone than the empty booth of a fast food joint, was heading home. On foot, surprisingly enough. And of course this wasn't Zeek's optimal mode of transportation, preferring most, if not all, other less physical forms, but being only a few blocks around the corner the walk wasn't too detrimental in the waves of shade breaking from the sun's peek-a-boo with the clouds carried by the breeze. As picturesque as the farm, if Zeek was into that sort of thing. The bottom of his super large plastic cup echoed a chilled emptiness between the bare ice and the straw at his lips, pleading for refill, when an egg landed just before his stride. Zeek stopped. He searched skyward, past the bare lines of telephone wire towards the empty mosaic of gray puffs on blue. Not a bird in sight. Zip. Nada.

He craned his neck over the...egg? If egg was accurate. There was nothing gooey. No whites or yolk. Nothing. Zilch. Only sidewalk and shell. And not even a complete shell, but rather the small tipped-top half above a cracked edge. He tapped it with his shoe. It wobbled on its broken curve. Zeek reexamined the clouded sky, searching for what exactly, if anything? He didn't know. But he did note a cloud that looked like rain and another that looked like a jovial mink. The ice again echoed from the straw perched at his lips. He rattled the cup as if it would magically refill itself, or at least melt the ice into something drinkable.

"I'm glad to have been of service" pulled Zeek's head from the clouds. The dude, the slacker who sleeps on the bus, who ungraciously took Zeek's muffin, hung a telephone on the cradle after effectively talking to no one. The line connecting the receiver had been snipped and dangled a metallic tail in front of the archaic payphone box. Zeek was under the impression the city had removed the system. Obviously they missed one rogue, lone survivor.

"How's it going, man?" The dude greeted Zeek with that chummy recognition on a personal level.

"I don't have any change." A guttural reflux.

"What? No. I know."

Was Zeek aware he was ever so slowly moving the hand with the plastic carry-out bag of chicken wings behind his leg in an attempt to use his body as a sort of shield from the guy's presumed hunger or was it purely instinctual? It's not like Zeek was avaricious. He was as fair as he was polite. He just had his heart set on those chicken wings with the foreknowledge of how to appreciate them. This dude, on the other discourteous hand, let his free muffin collect filth like greed on the bus floor. Zeek lived by that golden aged code: fool me once, shame on me; fool me twice and I'll be cordial but that's all you're going to get. It was the natural balance of human nature. A universal abide.

"I think you dropped something," the dude said, demonstrating the least concern for Zeek's bag.

Zeek moved his foot to feign the examination and discovery of the shell beneath him. "No. It's not mine," he said.

"You sure?"

Zeek wasn't. But more over the insistent question of being sure about the shells than the shell itself. Sure there was a chance he'd possibly figure out the significance of the shells. But now was not that time. His chicken wings were losing the steam depicted on the ad. And he was falling behind on all his previously recorded must-see television events his day allotted. So what else was left to say but "I'm sure."

The dude's shrug said, "Anyway," but what he physically said was "Then come find me when you're not and have the time."

"Excuse me?"

The rusted payphone rang. Zeek jumped in his own skin, acute and uncomfortable, and landed feeling silly at the height of the start.

"I'm so sorry, I have to take this." The dude lifted the disconnected phone mid-ring. The piercing rattle stopped. "Thank you for calling Pelican Informational, this is Don, how may I be of service?"

Zeek took this opportunity to sneak away with his bag of probably now soggy chicken wings, leaving behind the shell and whatever the hell else was going on.

He walked at a quickened pace, like running without picking up his feet or really bending his knees, as fast as his disproportionately thin legs could carry the rest of him. A few blocks shy of his East 1Oh3 apartment, he leaned as he veered the corners. He momentarily considered continuing down to the department store marketplace, but instead decided against this decision he'd likely live to regret. He had a lot on his plate. Or, at least would once he got all thirty-two wings to a moderately oven-toasted pizza joint faux-crispy. And given the events gradually postponing his weekly lunch date with his microplasma, it was the best he could do.

He hit the steps leading into The Family Mansion (which Zeek and only Zeek called it, likening it to a manor the deep south gentility passed down from generation to generation, which eventually and reluctantly falls into the hands of the spoiled loafer son whose unquenchable indulgences broke the family home into a house), and entered the bare, white-walled foyer lit by its tainted yellow light bulb shoved uncovered into the ceiling. He wiggled the key into his BL apartment lock, yet didn't turn the bolt. A voice, an unusually familiar voice reverberating down the upstairs hallway into the downstairs lobby as sounds do with nothing to stick to, caught his attention. Normally, Zeek would quicken his slip into the safety of his apartment under less inklings. It wasn't like he had a problem with the neighbors, and he wanted to keep it that way. Plus, to reiterate, chicken wings. But the voice rang so familiar he felt compelled to wait and confirm his suspicions. He couldn't care less about what was being said, the obscene "Oh don't you fret that sweet ass. I'll pump it full of inspiration." It was the inflections, how the voice threw sentences on a curve rather than a straight line.

However, after a momentary reconsideration, Zeek stuffed himself through the door of his apartment at the sound of the footsteps on the staircase. Just for safe measure, as in just in case he misrecognized the voice as Dave's. He left the door cracked enough to investigate, and sure enough, as the owner of the voice passed he recognized the sheen of the slicked-back hair, the upright posture which held tight a firm gut on an otherwise thin frame, the gold chainlink bracelet on one wrist, and the gold-strapped, square-faced, high-end-businessman-trafficking-cocaine-in-a-film-from-or-about-the-80s watch on the other, he was right.

"Dave." Zeek spoke the name softly like a question already good and well knowing the answer.

Dave turned around, and Zeek noticed, first, Dave was caught off guard at the sound of his name, and two, just how much he missed Dave around the office. It wasn't like they were close or anything. But they did develop a bond that basically remained in a single office on the 6th floor of George Gilliam (which Zeek and only Zeek called it, likening it to being innovative in prioritizing business and interpersonal ties through tech between faceless coworkers and customers). But seeing Dave outside the office blazed in him a backdraft through the doorway contained by a wry smile.

The word nice came to mind, as in it was sure nice to see him.

"Zeek, Buddy Boy, what're you doing here?" Dave elongated his reach and shook Zeek's hand like it was nothing.

"Ezekiel. I live here. What are you doing here?"

"I've been spending some extra personal quality time with the girl who apparently so happens to live upstairs. The artist." There was a pause for recognition Zeek didn't give. "She's a damn good one, too. And not just when she's on top getting off on her game." Another pause sans recognition. "You ever been with an artist?"

Zeek could positively say with assurance he had not.

"Then let me tell you what, Buddy Boy. You're not alive."

Zeek invited Dave into his apartment, a rare occurrence considering all the company he never has, trying to link the picture on Dave's desk with the girl upstairs with any answer other than affair. Maybe his wife was an artist? He'd never met her, therefore couldn't cast stones.

Dave sprawled out at the kitchen table in the chair closest to the door. "It's all a ruse, Buddy Boy. That picture came with the frame," Dave said as if reading Zeek's expression like the previous paragraph. A statement that followed continuity, especially considering the lack of personal details attributed to the family, including but not limited to their names. "And take it from me, Zeek, you should especially consider getting yourself a stock family. It really builds character around the office."

"Ezekiel."

"I'm well aware, Buddy Boy. But it fits you like that mustache."

Zeek did take pride in his mustache.

"Want some chicken?" The inside of the lid was dripping with condensation, and as expected, the wings were tepid. So he peeled back the lip to the dipping sauce and searched for the subtle nuances of cold chicken without bothering with the oven in front of company.

"Sure, let's see where the night takes us. What's this one?"

"Mango Tango Habanero."

"Ooh."

"So where have you been lately?"

"Told you: Upstairs."

"For three days?"

Dave shrugged with the smuggest aura of self-pleasing glory.

"We were worried when we didn't hear from you, you know."

"Oh. You and who?" Dave leaned forward over the table.

"Well, I was worried about you."

"It's good to have a buddy." He metaphorically slid back into his satisfaction.

Zeek helped himself to another ramekin of sauce.

He found the eleventh piece of eggshell(s) painted on a canvas in the gallery next door. Less physically, more metaphorically: you'll see. Since Dave didn't seem to have anywhere to be but Zeek's kitchen table, despite the previously perceived assumption of his leaving, Zeek learned the artist upstairs, Shellie La Dop, was an up-and-comer (1:), who he braggingly claimed was madly in love with him (2:), had an unpoppable bubble of a "tight ass" (3:), and about the overall sheer mastery of her work (4:).

1: Whether in the art world or solely in Dave's concupiscent opinion was never made quite clear.

2: While not readily admitting the inverse was exponentially true through witticisms such as: "If I were an artist, Buddy Boy, she'd be the muse."

3: He spent days trying to "pop."

4: "A goddess with acrylics."

"I can show you some of her work, it's hanging all over next door. And trust me, Buddy Boy, you need to see it. It'll change your life. She's going places. Plus, I need to step out for cigarettes."

Zeek finished his chicken wings, tied the scraps of trash in the bag, and left it on the counter by the can. Who was he to stand in the way of Dave's excitement, a spark, which flickered deep in him like a pilot light he'd never seen before in Office Dave? Okay. Honestly, he'd rather be catching up on TV including the TV he just missed while he ate. But in the grand scheme, what was another hour when the commercials can be skipped? A: Forty-Two minutes. And there was still that whole eggshell bit. If that persisted it would probably need his attention at some point.

So, basically, all that was to say Zeek locked the door behind them, and they left the BL apartment.

The gallery next door had two large, rectangular pillars by the storefront window where they hung teasers to the showcase inside. Zeek freely glanced in passing at what they were offering from time to time but never paid much attention. But standing there with Dave, Zeek couldn't help but stare, jaw loose, and head cocked astonished. He accredited this to the paintings cracking open some inner emotion, something usually reserved for heartwarming fluff on the news or talkshows or final episodes of long-running sitcoms where the cast says goodbye to the audience, their characters, and each other. He was in awe. Connected. Reality stripped and stretched in a blur of white like a blank canvas. There was only Zeek and the paintings. The left one was an egg on a blue background that faded from a midnight to an afternoon from corner to corner. The egg occupied most of the canvas, and didn't tilt, wasn't resting upon anything, was just a perfectly perpendicular egg composed from deliberately curved swashes of off-white paint floating in the space of the canvas, seeming to pop out through the use of heavier swoops rounding the edge. A piece of the shell was missing from the top side, completely absent in the reality of the painting. And this space was filled with space, no longer made of paint, but an existence like literally looking up through a crack into the universe: stars and exploding suns, galaxies in wispy clouded clusters, swells of nebulas. If not for the weight of gravity Zeek would have been sucked into the painting to endlessly float aimlessly through the black hole into the depths of infinity. The right painting was a series, comparable to the left in size and scope. An egg, again, framed from top to bottom, centered and perpendicular in the canvas. However, the background's palate faded from a midnight black in the bottom corner to an overcast afternoon gray at the top. This egg was missing a piece of shell identical to its counterpart, the same spot on the top side, the same fragile cracked boundary, the same actuality existing inside the crack, except this egg looked down through the clouds, some wispy, some thick, swirling cool and damp, towards a collage of blues and greens and browns. Buildings and trees pointed towards the heavens like expressed swatches of impressed paint. Choreographed specks danced around the plane, some colliding, some repelling, some serenely still. Zeek's feet were still firmly planted on the sidewalk, but that didn't matter. He too was a floating speck falling between the maze of city. His bird's eye view narrowed on two figures staring into a window. A breeze chilled across his face. He watched it pick up and replace the hairs combed over his bald spot. A car rolled by jarring a soundtrack of heavy drops and rattled windows, effectively pulling Zeek's attention out of the painting and back to the gallery's storefront. Back to the city around him.

"I have to meet her," Zeek said low, to himself, forgetting Dave was present in any way other than physically.

"Told you, Buddy Boy. Told you."

But first they had to go to the marketplace on the other side of The Family Mansion (which Zeek and only Zeek called it, likening it to that habitat for a motley crew of inner-city dwellers who have nothing in common except not knowing each other who would band together in one of those way-after-hours B movies to ward off mutant rats or redundant virus zombies or whatever other low-budget teenage goregasm) for cigarettes, Dave's initial goal. The store appeared misleadingly bigger on the inside than it did from the outside, with rows and rows of shelves that should exceed, with any logic, the brick-walled perimeter. And this was just the ground floor. Yet the breadth of the marketplace maintained an air of coziness, blanketed in a fluorescent glow, air conditioned to a customer satisfaction guarantee, the smell of flowers and coffee welcoming as a grandmother's cottage. The two didn't venture, staying direct to the cigarette counter, but if they did wander they would have found anything they wanted and more they thought they needed. While Dave made his transaction, Zeek watched people scurry up and down aisles with careless speed, their carts overflowing like this was the first and only time they'd ever, ever, ever, go to the store. Zeek, too, could have used a few items. Necessities actually needed, which were essentially just a surplus of Candy Bars. But now was not the time, with Dave and all, so he bought a soda to make up for the one he already drank.

"I didn't know you smoked," Zeek said as Dave lit up while walking back towards the apartments. He tightened the screw lid back onto the bottle and licked the wetness off his stache.

"I don't always, Buddy Boy." A thin veil coated every word. "Just from time to time when the urge strikes."

Zeek nodded like he understood, like he was interested. In actuality, he wanted another sip of soda.

Dave posted up on the stoop like he was waiting for his crew. Zeek stood awkwardly on the sidewalk, shifting his weight side to side. A most dynamic duo.

A cawing chirp baited Zeek's attention. Perched atop the black barred metal trash can on the street corner was a pelican, its wings folded back, its oversized beak tucked to its chest, its beady, unblinking eyes level with Zeek's. They stood frozen towards each other like gunslingers at high noon. Zeek wouldn't qualify the city as coastal by any means. There were beaches, sure, huge touristy spots either too rich or too crowded, but they could only be reached by a few hours drive in any direction but west. And not being keen with the city's geography listed under other, there might be a lake or pond or swamp or bog in the general vicinity, but if there were Zeek wouldn't know. Therefore, his understanding stopped with the pelican being a waterbird without water, much too far from home.

"Well I'll be a biscuit," Dave said.

The bird arched its neck and expanded its wings, stretching its dark-tipped feathers, and shook off the city breeze ruffling its down, eyeing the street like a Rorschach or a watchman. Its throat sac quivered to its bark, a screech like fingers on wet glass. And with that, the bird took flight, shot off by fright from that bus-lounging, muffin-stealing, payphone-attending, who was this dude?, crossing the street in his same ratty gym shorts and red plaid shirt.

"Shouldn't we go in?" Zeek hit the steps with anticipation.

"All in due time, Buddy Boy. What's the rush?" Dave held up the half-lit cigarette.

The dude wasn't lured by the gallery, drawn to the eggs, obviously not a fan of art.

Dave dragged long and slow as if deliberately taking his sweet time.

Unlike Zeek, who had hurried to the entryway. But not to his apartment. Instead, positioning himself behind the jamb, as much as would allow in an amorphous-cartoon-character-hiding-behind-a-pencil-thin-tree sort of way, and peeking through the frosty glass, posting up to see exactly what this shirker was up to this time around. Zeek wasn't in the mood for conversing with relative strangers.

But of course, Dave was. Zeek could hear nothing clearly but a mumble while watching Dave get into a conversation in Dave's own way, by means of seeing him generally acknowledge the existence of another and offering the dude a cigarette, which he went for but declined. This didn't stop Dave, though, who transferred the flame from the previous butt.

The dude pointed up and down the street.

Dave nodded and pointed up and down the street.

Their conversation was visually pleasant, cordial, only awkward for Zeek. He was antsy, more restless than agitated. That impatient irk of a child sharing his favorite toy but immediately wanting it back. Yet he wasn't about to go outside and play. No way. What he would do was wait. Keep an observing eye on things. Make sure Dave didn't do anything as irrational as inviting that dude in. It's not like Zeek was rude. Remember, he had freely proffered his muffin on his own accord. And it was the lack of gratitude that merited some bad effects after he'd already certified himself publicly as a good Samaritan.

The conversationalists shook hands, and the dude wandered off towards the department store marketplace, leaving Dave at the bottom of the stoop to finish his umpteenth cigarette. He'd be done any minute and meet Zeek in the bare foyer.

"You skippy up in here, Buddy Boy?"

"Just time to come inside."

Dave tilted his head with the right amount of nod that agreed without question and headed towards the stairs. Zeek followed, also without question.

They walked down the second-story hall towards the arched window converted into an arched doorway. Zeek had never ventured upstairs, and for a reason unbeknownst, was surprised to learn this hallway was just as awfully bland. This basic simplicity, the off-white walls, and three plain doors, TR, TL, and number 3, strangely comforted Zeek.

Behind one of these doors lived an impressively unshaven old man whose gray Medusa hair made his already unusually large head larger. Zeek had seen him two or three times, no more than a handful, and never without gold-rimmed glasses that took over his face and headphones that engulfed his ears and parted his hair like the sea. Behind the other lived a couple, possibly young, thick accents from somewhere that wasn't the city. Zeek heard them on occasion passing his BL apartment, sounding in the midst of a heated argument then laughing exaggerated pleasantries. Door number 3 was either a storage closet or a maintenance room or possibly both. Any other knowledge pertaining to occupants or doors extended beyond Zeek.

He found the twelfth piece of eggshell, an extension of the eleventh really, you'll see, at the top of the winding, metal staircase at the end of the hall. At some point, the old fire escape was converted to an entryway leading to a third level. Zeek followed Dave over the ledge of the windowless door onto the enclosed platform and up the stairs recommissioned with a twisted finesse, which moaned under their weight. Dave, without bothering to knock, opened a door leading to another hallway, which was more a tight space like a closet. And dark. Plain. Windowless. A strip of blank house. Zeek's eyes adjusted accordingly to the gentle sashay of light swaying across the floor at the end of the short way but was still unprepared for the surge of white before Dave.

"Knock, knock," Dave said as he disappeared into the cascade.

Zeek reached out and parted the wooden beads hanging in the doorway, squinting as he stepped through. As his eyes widened and his pupils tightened he noticed jeans running up a pair of legs, holes split at the knees, racing into an oversized V-neck intersecting low enough to where Zeek politely assumed no bra was supporting the perfect perkiness while narrowly contouring the subtleness of her neck and shoulders, accented by the light radiating around her braided hair bundled under a sash tied round her forehead, highlighting the sultry innocence of her dark eyes and high cheeks. So this was Shellie La Dop. A flawless beauty speckled in paint, tainted by Dave's beastly frame, she latching her face onto his, he tightening her onto his gut, closing the gap by palming her ass, she dipping her fingers into his greased-back hair.

And then there was Zeek, awkwardly awkward, standing in front of the swaying beads. He glanced around the bright, white loft, light pouring in from the circular window tucked under the curved ceiling and the skylights cut into the slopes, one over the kitchen, a wraparound counter with a sink, cluttered with coffee cups, a coffee machine, and coffee rounding into a fridge pushed under a cabinet Zeek assumed held more coffee mugs and bags of coffee, and another over a fireplace, more so an extension of her mantel, stacked full of books. A mattress was at some point dropped on the floor and never moved again, off-center and crooked, now topped with disheveled blankets and pillows. On the far side, the floor was used as a nightstand, see more books and coffee cups. Closer, there was an easel. And on this easel was a canvas. And there were canvasses hanging on the walls, canvasses leaning on the walls, canvasses in the kitchen, canvasses in stacks on the floor. Canvasses filled with ovals and eggs. Some lifeless shapes. Some clustered in nests or lined in cartons. Some sat around on barstools, others in line for the barista. There were eggs poised in Office Loungers, eggs daydreaming behind restaurant counters, eggs inspiring other eggs cracked open like nesting dolls. The canvass propped on the easel was a pencil sketch WIP, singular and still like the two hung in the gallery, the negative space filled with red. The one below leaning on the leg had an egg surrounded by a pearly white and cracked open with a red flickering around orange and yellow strokes of fire. Zeek's brow dampened as the flames turned blue, blazing into the heat of darkness. Not black. Dark. Dark like the stench of fear. Zeek couldn't see himself in this darkness, couldn't see anything. He felt its presence. Being burnt alive without igniting a spark. Could smell his flesh singeing from his bones, his guts, his soul fizzled out and forgotten, not achieving even ash. Zeek was merely an observer. A passive vessel. Depersonalized. In essence more quiet than silence.

"So, Buddy Boy," Dave's voice, a reminder of time and place, brought Zeek back into the white walls of the loft, "if you haven't discerned from the allure, this is Shellie La Dop." His arm was unnecessarily around her as if trying to convince their mismatched pairing, Dave, no offense, like a perp in *Cop Drama*, striped button-down, gold chain peeking, rolled cuffs just above a gaudy real time imitation watch, honestly looking like a step-father too old to be taken serious as a lover, and she, well, was the petit portrait of perfection.

"Ezekiel." He stepped forward and took her hand. Its cool smoothness shivered up his arm and sped his pulse.

"A pleasure."

"Buddy Boy here is a fan of your work downstairs."

"Just downstairs?"

For no conceivable reason, Zeek blushed, now more embarrassed than embarrassed. "These are nice, too."

"These aren't finished."

"You'll come to learn she's never finished." Dave plopped down on the mattress and propped himself on an elbow like college dorm room seduction.

"Someone distracts me easily and often."

Dave shrugged, it's true.

"But, please, please. Find a spot. Get cozy." The words flavored the melodic sweetness of her voice, not saccharine like some model's walk-on role or that saccharin zeitgeist fatale, but genuine. Real. "I'll make coffee."

Zeek balanced himself on a barstool at the jutted counter designating kitchen. It was either the stool or the beanbag chair, a relic Zeek had never seen used outside a screen, but now his weight was drooped and toppling over the skinny legs.

"So, Zeek—"

"Ezekiel." He felt like a mushroom.

"—how do you know Dave?" She set three mugs on the counter as the machine percolated into the room the sharp yet soothing aromatic pot.

"Oh, from work. We work together."

"I see." She looked towards Dave.

Dave nodded, also true. "Buddy Boy here is the lord of the emails."

"Is that so?"

"That's what he says."

Dave laid on his back. "Your humility means nothing here."

"He's right. Even passivity, at the end of the day, should dictate presence." She poured three cups three quarters full. "Cream or sugar? Or, cream and sugar?"

"And, please. And how do you know Dave?"

"You know how the usual goes. You ditch one pretentious asshole in an uptown bar to find another in a sleazy dive. It's the same old classic fairytale. Fine with vanilla?" She held up the creamer bottle like a model on a game show.

"That's something you have to ask yourself," Dave said to the ceiling.

"Please." Tell him what he's won.

She placed a mug on the counter next to his soda and carried the other two to the mattress. Zeek wrapped his hands around the mug, the warmth extending through the glass, prickling his fingertips. He read, "Someone's got a case of the Mondays," scratched like a cat across the cup face. The afternoon was too warm for coffee, even inside the apartment, but Zeek sipped anyway.

Shellie sat quietly next to Dave, cup to her lips, looking around her exhibit like a critic's artful contemplation. Zeek followed the directions of her eyes leading to the question: "What's your take on the eggs?"

Now, at this point Zeek could tell her what her paintings spark inside him, the sense of being a speck in the universe, the sense of the universe being a speck in him, the ineffableness of something bigger than himself, of fate or sentencing, of wonder and wondering, on creating art for the artless, not kitsch or pastiche but creation that resonates in the world, that shifts a perception into a reality, that clicks on in the real, consciously or unconsciously, that pricks the soul, a reminder of that childlike credulity, a scientific proof of this is, that pushes to an answerless question of greater understanding, whether up, around, or within, why here, why now, why not eggshells, but all Zeek said was, "I like them."

"You're sweet." She sipped with slow precision.

"Naysayers of the egg be damned." Dave still hadn't touched the mug on the floor. "A true up-and-comer."

"Again, Dave?"

"I'm insatiable."

"Be polite. I have company."

"He's my company. Buddy Boy, ask her why eggs. It's the best part."

"I shouldn't."

"Go on."

"I'm sorry."

"No, no," she said, "people ask. It's what makes us human. Answers on the other hand..." her voice faded out as if someone was slowly turning down the volume, her eyes off somewhere in frozen deliberation, focused on the everything of nothing.

She tuned back in with a blink.

"We all need a muse, whoever you are." She motioned towards a painting discarded near the fireplace. "That was an early one. One of the first, really. I had just moved to the city and was living across town in a little rough n' tumbler. City life was all I wanted, to be a part of something, sync with the bustle. And I had it all figured out. Find myself, find inspiration, find art within. Done deal, albeit a bit naïf. I couldn't find a job, couldn't find hope, couldn't find a single connecting soul in the grand collective. The romanticism of it all began fading away with a quickness. I was fading faster than my dream, my heart hardening like my hopes. But one morning, on the cusp of packing it in, there was this sharp chirping, so much like a cry for help that when I peeked out the window I thought I'd find an old lady being mugged. On the side of my rented room, in the middle of the dusty, dirt yard, was the old, wooden pieces of a toppled shed the crackheads had never repaired although tweaked up and raging. From the slope of what was once the roof, a craned neck and bucketed beak peeked over the picketed fence of dry rot siding, arching its largely disproportionate head back and screaming to the sunlight. Now, I'd never seen one in person, but I knew a pelican when I saw it. I went outside thinking the poor guy was lost and trapped in the jagged remains, but as it turned out I was off on all accounts. She was right where she needed to be, making the best of that shit heap, turning that pile of junk into a home with every egg she laid. And she sat there, on the eggs or perched over them, occasionally flying off to come right back. I'd leave out bits of bread from time to time, not knowing if pelicans even ate bread, but generously offering what little I could afford so she wouldn't have to leave her nest for too long. Yet, when she did succumb to the urge to scavenge I'd sneak over and look at the eggs nestled in the depression of broken shed fortified by twigs and moss. They were about the size of my hand, a dingy white, with small strokes and smears of brown like a Monet. It was art in nature,

nature in art, truly one in one and the same. So I began painting the eggs, being as true to nature as nature was to me, trying to capture the details of the overlooked, the earth's impressionism, the creator's subjective expressionism, the magical realism of nature in and of itself. All the while the bird's steadfastness against the crackheads, against their taunts, screams, and cans at all hours inspired my diligence. She stayed with her eggs like I stayed with my paintings, at times frightened but fighting to completion, incubating a small part of me into something new. I'll never know what brought my pelican so far off from the ocean, never know what brought her to my back yard. But I felt she was there for me as much as she was there for her chicklings. Over time, her eggs hatched, and she nurtured her children to flight, so I too knew it was time to nudge my paintings from their nest. I began exploring new possibilities for my eggs, personifying them into bar rats, home bodies, office drones, pushing them out into the real world, so to speak. Into something alive to fly off with the small, hatched parts of me."

She let the air of the final sentence ebb, and she sat there, looking intently into the rustic hardwood, silent in the wake of her own story.

Zeek didn't interrupt her, taking a small sip of coffee, allowing the words to wash over him. The response didn't connect on a personal level, despite seemingly having his own eggshell narrative, but it did move him, flowed through him a current of pragmatic competence.

"That was beautiful bullshit, babe," Dave said, not getting up.

Shellie's cheeks widened with a smile her eyes tried holding down with modesty. "You don't think it's too long-winded? Too exasperatingly cliché?"

"È perfecto."

"As in gallery ready so le dilettantes will buy this shit?"

"Serve it to them hot, babe. They'll eat it up."

Zeek looked at the paintings, the painter, looked around the room for something honest. The paintings matched the story even if the story didn't match the paintings. Then he looked at the one on the easel. What lie attested in the crack? These paintings were more than just strokes of paint, more than just the artist. Should he see strokes of genius? They did move Zeek, molded his soul into something potentially profound. Yet if it meant nothing to the painter should it mean nothing to him? There was value entertained in fetched veracity. But maybe she did care. Maybe the paintings meant more than she was willing to admit, a shell for the vulnerability she willingly put into the world, save a slice of something private for herself. But...

"Did you say something?" Shellie said.

Did he? Or should he?

"What about the cracked paintings, I guess?" All these questions spewing forth, Zeek had no idea. "I don't think you mentioned them."

"Oh, those? People seemed drawn to them for whatever reason, and I got to eat."

And that was good enough for Zeek.

It also seemed good enough for Dave who sat up on the mattress, quick, as if the answer literally moved him. He grabbed his untouched coffee and quaffed it with a serious vigor while maintaining the finesse of not letting a drop dribble. "You know what this coffee needs? A cigarette." He put the drained mug back on the floor with no need for a rhetorical answer and stood.

"And speaking of food. I know a quaint little place with the best if not the only quiche in town," Shellie answered.

"What are your thoughts, Buddy Boy?"

Zeek was looking at the window, unable to actually see through it, and shrugged like a caged animal inured to the zoo conditioned to the world around him. "Sure." He wasn't the type to turn down a meal.

Zeek found the thirteenth piece of eggshell on his person, in his pocket. The trio gathered and exited The Family Mansion (which Zeek and only Zeek called it, likening it to being the proverbial house on the hill, a matte painting periodically lit by lightning hung behind an oversized gate with a small sign reading "Keep Out" or "No Trespassing" which didn't detour guests from keeping out or trespassing), cutting left up the block. Zeek's steps became casually slower as they passed the window of the gallery, dropping back enough while keeping up with the group.

"Glance, but don't gawk," Shellie said, but Zeek noticed her peek towards the window, that kind of sideways glimpse of someone passing their reflection, which questioned the intended recipient.

The quaint little place with quiche turned out to be Sal's Counter (which Zeek and only Zeek called it, likening it to the small town diner where all the locals drank strong black coffee and there was always freshly baked cherry pie for the detective from out of town). This marked the first occasion Zeek had been to the restaurant for anything other than breakfast, although the sun's early descent, adorned in purples and reds, was the processed negative to its indigo green rise, equally picturesque through the diner's wall-sized windows. Zeek conceded from sitting at his usual spot behind the counter to the booth with the party. He slid in the best he could, utterly lost to the appeal, the table pushing into his stomach thus forcing the bench to uncomfortably correct his posture.

"Miss La Dop and Zeek."

Zeek turned his head, one of the few parts he could move, towards the all too familiar voice sounding day-worn as opposed to the usual drowsy morning-chipper, to find Sally looking down at the table, apron shifted and stained, pulling a blue pen from her tussled mess of hair.

"Quite the surprise. I wasn't aware you were acquaintances."

"Neither were we." Shellie's voice rang musical even in the simplest of sentences. A portmanteau of giddy and sultry.

Dave stretched his arm across the booth, securing his spot at the right side of greatness.

Zeek said, "Ezekiel."

"What can I get for you? High Country quiche and coffee?"

"Is it that predictable?" Shellie said with a smile.

Zeek flipped the menu over, frantically studying before his turn. He never considered a lunch, let alone a dinner menu, at breakfast, generally sticking with the side he practically knew by heart. And lo and behold, they did in fact serve quiche, listed down in the bottom corner of the menu: itemized standards and a quiche of the day. Sal's quiche and its apparent popularity were new to him.

But the panic of ordering shifted into a panic of place. A customer entered the restaurant, virtually undetected in the corner of Zeek's eye. Just a glimpse of gym shorts and plaid passed with a casual ease that caught his attention. But it was as if the ungrateful muffin sponger knew exactly what he was doing when he sat at Zeek's spot at the empty counter and folded his hands to patiently wait for service, like he was toying with Zeek, wanting Zeek to watch him.

"And for you?"

Sally's expected question caught Zeek off guard, so he flipped the menu over then over again as if shaking out his order and stammered, "I'll have the same."

"The same as..." Sally let the question trail off into an elongated "as," forcing it into an answer.

"Uh. What they're having? Please."

"Who?"

"Both?"

She made a note on her pad.

"Alrighty. Two quiche, two burgs, two hot coffees, two iced Colas," she repeated to the table with breakneck habit before yelling it out to Sal in the kitchen and returning to her enclosed habitat behind the counter.

Dave and Shellie were talking low between themselves, maybe to Zeek, maybe not. They didn't seem to mind. And neither did he, seeing as he was busy, doing what he did best. Watching. Observing. Not planning a course of action, per se. But if events did unfold he'd at least see them happen.

"Can I get a cup of coffee?" the dude said to Sally, hands still folded.

"We can't keep doing this."

"I've got money today." He sounded almost shocked.

"One cup. Maybe two." She reached behind her for a mug and the pot. "But you can't stay here all night. We have actual paying customers."

"I won't."

Sally cut him a glance as she poured.

"I won't," he repeated an octave up into honesty. "Promise."

"But don't you think he will, Buddy Boy?" Dave's commentary cut into the scene.

"I don't know what he'll do. I don't even know the guy."

"Thought you were a big fan of *The Show*."

"What show?"

"*The Show*."

"Oh, yeah. Right. Who isn't?"

Shellie shrugged. "It appears to evenly appeal to all demographics."

"Precisely," Dave emphasized the "pre." "I don't watch much TV—" which Zeek understood as *I watch an exceptionally average amount* "—but that show, my friends," Dave tapped the table with his index finger, "is ahead of its time. Can you smoke in here?"

"It doesn't smell like you can," Shellie said of the tangent.

Zeek tuned back in to the dude sipping a coffee. He never once turned to look at Zeek, continuing to look straight ahead with such deliberate intensity, that even without the satisfaction of acknowledgement, Zeek felt toyfully played with, like a cat's metaphorical prey.

Sally stepped into his line of vision with their drinks in hand.

"Excuse me," Zeek said.

"Yes, hun."

"Who is, uh," Zeek felt it necessary, though the place was otherwise empty, to indicate a direction by pointing behind his open palm to hide his accusatory finger, "who is that gentleman at the counter?"

"I don't think I can answer that question from a legal standpoint and still retain my position." She giggled and slapped his shoulder with true southern charm before Zeek could look at her with a squinted expression. "I'm just yanking your chain. Straight faces was never my specialty. But him? Don't rightly know. Just some guy that comes in from time to time but only pays periodically. He comes across as a nice enough fellow, bless his heart, but this is still a business."

"So that means you don't know who he is?"

"Am I supposed to?"

Zeek exhaled from his nose and would have slouched if the booth permitted. While the city they shared was considered large both via topography and the census, the coincidence of people coming in contact with the same people on an unconsciously regular basis wasn't far-fetched by any stretch of the imagination. This dude just so happened to ride the same bus, walk the same streets, dine at the same restaurant as Zeek. A happenstance coinciding with living in the same city rather than their daily existence within the city.

Then why on earth did it irk him so much?

"No, I guess not."

"Your order should be up any minute."

"Thank you," Dave said and waited till Sally was back behind the counter before continuing. "Everything on the hunky-dory there, Buddy Boy?"

"Everything's fine." He grabbed hold of the table and began shifting his weight out of the booth. "If you'll excuse me."

Zeek entered the quaint bathroom, a single row of sink, urinal, stall. He checked his reflection in the mirror and used his fingers to comb his hair disheveled by the day's activity back over his bald spot. And, while in the privacy of the room, he leaned towards the mirror, top lip stretched, and checked up his nose before smoothing his mustache.

The door swung open behind him accompanied by the squeal from its elbow hinge. Zeek, in a panic of doing no wrongdoing, flipped on the faucet and stuck a hand under the running water to effectuate a justifiable reason for standing in the bathroom other than just standing in the bathroom. He tried correcting his posture into something more casual, but the act became rigid in the awkwardness.

He looked into the reflection to see who joined him.

But of course.

Why wouldn't it be him?

He positioned himself at the urinal.

Zeek, whose charade now involved soap, was rinsing diligently pretending he didn't notice the dude's trespass over the privacy divider.

"I need to ask you something."

Zeek hurried for a paper towel. "I'm sorry. I don't have any." His automated response.

"I haven't even asked you yet."

"Right. Sorry."

Stop apologizing.

"I was just wondering if you now had time for change? See, I've got just enough to cover the coffee but kind of wanted to leave a tip. There, I said it. Now you can tell me you don't have any."

"I don't have any." The low humbleness in his voice surprised even Zeek. He should be angry, or annoyed, or confrontational, exude some level of confidence. Not humility. The muffin con should have maxed out humble.

He reached for the door handle but didn't open it. Instead, he pulled something from deep inside him. "Why are you following me?"

"Am I? Are you sure about that?"

"You're on the bus every morning."

"So are you."

"And at the payphone."

"Had business that needed attending."

"The phone wasn't plugged in."

"Minor technicality."

"And what about walking down the street earlier?"

"What street when?"

"Earlier. I saw you."

"Sounds like you're the one keeping tabs on me." He smiled, benign and inviting. Zeek welcomed this like the plague. "Maybe you came in here in the hopes I would follow."

"That's absurd," Zeek said, suddenly unsure.

"No, you're right. Much too convenient. A bit too deus ex machina."

"Too what?"

"Doesn't matter." The simplicity of the words didn't match the dude's expression, his gaze veering off slightly to the side, his eyes and lips tight like deep in thought, but quickly loosening back into the reality of the bathroom. "Back to it, you one hundred and ten percent don't have any change?"

"I already told you..." Zeek reached into his pocket to validate his statement but trailed off upon finding a thin, coin-sized lie. He pulled out an eggshell and held it gingerly between his fingers, yet before that node of realization could set in the dude plucked it from his pinch with a:

"Thanks, man. I really appreciate this. I'll be seeing you," scooting past Zeek and out of the bathroom.

In Zeek's true and authenticated style, he stood frozen in contemplative thought, a duration somewhere between a nanosecond and an hour, long enough to rationalize without comprehending the eggshell, like why was this happening, where were they coming from, and how did it get in his pocket. These things didn't just happen. Or do they and he'd been oblivious? No. That was absurd. He would have noticed eggshells on, in, or around things other than eggs at some point in his existence prior, now wouldn't he? Unless... He blinked himself back, his still fingers still held up and pinched together coming into focus. He considered splashing water on his face like main characters do for clarity when confronted with the unanswerable while standing in a bathroom. But there was no time for faucets.

Zeek hurried from the bathroom. Dave and Shellie sat in the booth, table now covered in plates, which any other time would have been ideal, to return to the meal on the table. Sally stood behind the register flipping through and straightening a wad of cash, her head bobbing in time to the count. The thick porcelain mug, wisps of heat still dancing, remained on the counter surrounded like a sacrifice by strewn, unopened creamers. But this time, the dude was gone.

"Where'd he go?" Zeek said, seemingly out of breath, which shouldn't be the case even for a man of his size.

"Hey, Buddy Boy, the food here is Queen B," Dave called out around a mouthful of burger.

"Who?" Sally didn't look up from the cash she was flattening.

Dave answered incorrectly, mininterpreting, thankfully muffled by the mouthful of food.

"I'm not really sure who. But that guy. Drinking coffee." Why did Zeek sound so frantic?

"Him? Don't know. Don't usually keep tabs on people's affairs outside of this place, but for him I might start making an exception. Left one hell of a tip." A smile beamed.

"I think I need to step out," Zeek didn't quite finish the thought before hitting the door. He felt the cool evening air brush his face.

"Where you going, Buddy Boy? Your food's getting cold."

Minute fact, he was wasting a meal. Second-guessing he turned, unwinding before he unraveled. "I may need to start a tab."

"It's all taken care of, hun."

The door closed behind him.

But now what?

He scoured up and down the sidewalk, but there was no sign of the dude under the searchlights of street lamps. So he did what came natural and turned with the wind, towards the bus stop and his habitual route, pacing quick without running with his hands buried deep in his pockets, brisk as the chilly air.

"Where you off to in such a hurry?"

Zeek stopped, and there he was, posted up on a stoop Zeek safely assumed wasn't his.

Well, that was easy.

"I'm not sure."

"Then by all means, don't let me hold you up."

"No. It's not as you make it seem." Zeek stood like the Webbster definition of awkward, n., looking at the sidewalk, shuffling his feet, the polar antithesis of the dude's casual lean on the steps. The words, "It's more I'm not sure why you took it," stumbled from him like a burden.

"Excuse me?"

"The shell. Back in the bathroom. Why did you take it?"

"You offered it. I distinctly said 'thank you.'"

"Doesn't much answer the question."

"True."

The dude looked up, and instinctually Zeek followed his line of vision skyward but saw nothing above the row of mock Victorian brick buildings. Not even the stars glimmered beyond the street lamps. Maybe it was too early for stars, maybe they hadn't been put to bed in the velvet blanket of sky.

"Look, I'm sorry to bother you," Zeek said, turning to go back to the restaurant. He wasn't as far down the block as he imagined post haste. He could make out through the glow of the window the flickering of two bodies' silent movie mannerisms enjoying the food and each other.

"You're not the main character."

Zeek shut his eyes and inhaled deeply in quick contemplation of ignoring this versus the "What are you talking about?" that came out.

"What if I told you you're not the main character?"

The street lamp flicked.

"And I'm supposing you are?"

"Not necessarily. I'm more of an imitation."

"Right. I have to get back, see."

"I don't think your friends mind."

Zeek looked back at their silhouettes of enjoyment. "I need to pay my bill."

"It's all taken care of."

"I thought you didn't have any money."

"You're welcome."

"Well, I need to—"

"Left a hefty tip as always, so you're running out of rational excuses."

"I'm not," Zeek admitted accidentally, recovering with, "I need to say goodbye."

"You don't."

"Excuse me."

"Fine. Here's your excuse. It's obvious you left and they'll catch up later the next time you see them." He stood up and brushed off the seat of his shorts. "C'mon. Take a walk with me. No more no."

"Who do you think you are?" Zeek said, low and to himself, but loud enough for the dude to hear the tone of eyes rolling.

"Where are my manners?" He descended towards Zeek, hand extended. "The name's Don Bronco."

Zeek looked at the hand. Grabbing it would indicate a commitment to the dude's existence, an acceptance of his nonsense, a path Zeek seemed to already be on where forwards and backwards lead in the same direction. Yet he shook it anyway, compelled to be polite. It was his nature.

"Now let me introduce you to the director," said Don Bronco.

Zeek found the fourteenth piece of eggshell in the bar. Don Bronco began leading Zeek up the way, reeling him in with a sideways nod and a smirk so pleasant as to not be completely trustworthy, as if implying he had no choice but to follow. They walked along the mostly residential section of town, passing the occasional small lamp boutique or sandwich window, heading towards down town downtown. Zeek trailed behind Don Bronco, barely carried by shuffled feet. The cause to the effect outweighed his reluctance, for once not motivated by the television. One, speaking of which, he should be at home watching. At least from his Plushback the missed adventures could be taken in comfort and easily explained in less than two hours, give or take the decade. And let's assume Zeek almost immediately regretted the decision to follow this Don Bronco character, which rationally he had no business doing, again from the Plushback he could easily skip ahead or better yet change the channel. But instead, here he was.

"Where are we going?" Zeek panted the words, not accustomed to such long distances on foot, while watching the street lamps flicker as they passed as if settling in for the evening.

"To see the director."

"I got that much out of this. But where are we going?"

"Few more blocks."

"Stop. Just stop." The light hovering over Zeek fizzled to dark. He leaned against the pole, breathing towards the sidewalk. "Can you please tell me what's going on?"

"That I don't know."

"What do you mean 'I don't know?'"

"Exactly. I only know as much as you do. Not much more, but not a thing less."

"But you do know about the eggshells?"

"Yes."

"And that's why you took it?"

"No."

"Right. Then what about this director of…?"

"It's just an idea."

A breeze ruffled the bit of hair folded across Zeek's head. The late afternoon was transitioning a chill into night. Not cold enough for a jacket, per se, but enough nip to reestablish itself as fall. Don Bronco continued against the breeze as silently as the air around him. Zeek again followed. The effect of his reluctance no longer needed cause, even if he was replaying key events and conversations like reruns over and over in an attempt at understanding why walking down a dark street with this muffin-wasting stranger was a legitimate way to spend his day off. On Saturday nights, the only thing that should be this worn out by now was his remote. And he was hungry, running out on a late-snack-early-dinner like some fool just because he found a few eggshells. Whoever made that decision, he wasn't himself. He admitted, what was he thinking? It wasn't as if the shells were off-putting to the point where he couldn't handle their spontaneous existences. Sure, they were a bit unusual. But realistically, while mildly inconvenient, they weren't harming a thing. Not a thing but his Saturday.

At the corner the duo turned right onto a street that for no reason whatsoever seemed darker, and passed a fenced-in, overgrown vacant lot towards the humming pink and blue glow of "Fellcws," seeing as half the o's tube expired, hanging from a windowless brick wall. Don Bronco pulled the door heavily chipped with green paint, tucked into the wall as someone inside pushed. Loneliness creaked, just needing a little something on its hinges to get it through the evening. A man with a chest-length gray beard hanging off his oversized head hiccupped, "My pardons, good sirs," while Don Bronco stood there propping the door with an outstretched hand. The smell of hard drink and hard times wafted to Zeek who took a step back allowing the stranger, or did he look familiar?, to pass.

Don Bronco coaxed Zeek with that signature sideways nod and entered the bar.

Zeek followed. He'd come this far. But also because he didn't know where he was and/or how to get back.

The open room was dimly lit, a few scattered tables strewn between a wall of dark stained booths and the bar. The amount of empty seats greatly outnumbered the patrons, a few of which looked up and divided their attention between their drinks and the door, as hushed as their whispers to their liquor.

Don Bronco ordered something as he sat one stool down from an older gentleman, whose thick, dusted white hair was in direct contrast to his deep burgundy jacket, the tarp-like fabric cut for members only. Zeek scanned the single shelf of dusty bottles backed by a mirror tinted with time, cracks of black fragmenting, not looking for any brand in particular. Not being a big drinker, he feigned it well enough at office parties thanks to classy old movies and classier ads but couldn't tell one from the other any which way. He said, "Same," as the safest course of action as he sat up on the high-backed chair, hoping he just ordered nothing stronger than a beer.

Don Bronco greeted the gentleman at the bar with a silent nod. The old man gave his attention to the pint nearly full even without the dissipated head, which osmosed time into sweat around the glass. Some yup down at the corner of the bar slammed a shot glass upside-down which startled around the hushed room like a liquor-soaked backfire. Zeek wouldn't admit he jumped at the sound, using the bartender setting a full rocks glass in front of him as a means of playing it off, as if physically preparing for his drink with a shimmy. But it didn't matter how uncomfortable Zeek was. No one noticed. Not here, the people drowning out their own problems. A deeply personal experience.

Zeek pulled the drink closer to himself, leaning forward to take a sip through the vastly undersized pinhole straw without picking up the stout glass. Soda. A plain Cola, skimped on syrup. Zeek actually would have preferred the beer, unsure of which was more dissatisfying, the flat lack of bite or its being possibly diet.

"So, how are things?" Don Bronco asked, indicating the man in the burgundy jacket but in a manner anyone was free to answer. He took a sip of his Cola. "Good, that's good to hear," he responded to the silence. The man hadn't moved from his position over his pint glass.

"Who, Zeek?" Don Bronco continued, pointing past his shoulder to Zeek with his thumb.

"Ezekiel," he corrected, but low like he was missing something, not sure if he really wasn't hearing some drunken mumble. He spun the thin straw between the ice along the edge of the...wait, earlier? Or ever? Had he introduced himself?

"No one really," Don Bronco continued as if Zeek wasn't in earshot at the bar and/or as if the man in the burgundy jacket, who hadn't turned his hanging head from over his beer, was very much into this conversation, "just some guy I've come across. Buddy Boy here's been having the, you know, the problem."

Zeek stopped spinning the ice, for sure for sure something was amiss. That was what Dave and only Dave called him likening it to—well, Zeek had no idea why it stuck with such consistency. It's not like he was even a huge fan of nicknames, but he let it ride because it was Dave and it was just the type of thing Dave did. It was in his character. But honestly, he didn't know where it came from or why. He heard it one day and knew it was in reference to himself. That was how names stick. Granted, on some small scale it was by and large better than other names he was generally called.

And yet, when this Don Bronco character said it he liked it even less. Zeek didn't know who this dude thought he was, but whoever it may be it sure wasn't Dave.

The man in the burgundy jacket picked up his beer and took a long, smooth sip. "I was once a captain on a warship, the Sea Fox. She was as big as she was beautiful. It was the great war, World War II, the greatest war man will know, the type of sequel that surpasses the original by leaps and bounds, and my crew and I were skidding water in the Pacific, full sail to the heat of battle. Pure heat at the edge of the world. Due to a miscalculation petite involving French sailors and their c'est terrible navigational skills, the Sea Fox plowed into what was left of a French carrier, a lifeboat of four sailors, one soldier, and a war criminal. We managed what we could, pulling all but a single sailor from the rising waves." He ran his finger down the sweat of the glass, causing a single droplet to trickle into the pressed paper coaster, and rubbed the dampness between his fingers. He continued to the glass, "Communication was limited, our ship's translator volleyed German, but words weren't necessary in recognizing we had evil, a step down from pure, on board. Joe G. hisself. Never once making a sound. The hate in his eyes was loud enough." Beat. "Now, we understood the terms of war, and the French soldier, a surprisingly rugged young man, made sure of that through a series of pointed gestures and sharp glares, no being a universal communicator, but that didn't stop most of us from wanting to rip out Old Joe's throat."

Beat. "We posted the soldier in a wardroom away from the men, Joe G. lassoed to the steel workings. Frenchy refused to leave the room. Both silent. Too silent. Neither made a sound. The only thing in the air was the eeriness that accompanies silence that silent. Needless to say, things were going to hell on deck. We were splitting into factions: order in the present vs. order for the future—the commanding officers abiding systems in place, the rules of engagement, a saneness to the chaos, the men, led by the ship's cook, CS Whip(ped Cream), a mass of muscle and gut, projected any future without Joe as greater than a future with, to not squander the opportunity God has put in our hands. And as Captain, I sat on the fence, the most monstrous amongst men." The captain in the burgundy jacket rotated the thick bottom of the pint glass on the coaster, spinning the beer inside, watching as if his memories swirled in the tide. "Tensions reverberated through the ship with the rhythm of a bass line picking up tempo (bum-bum, bum-bum) coming to a head in a clash of strings and horns (da-na-na-Naa-na) as the men, led by Whip, stormed the officers' quarters looking for blacked blood. Some officers upheld their duty and stood in their way, but most turned when the men, not outwardly assisting but quietly condoning the lesser of two evils, a hushed wrong to lead towards a brighter right." Beat. "And me? I stood back and observed." His beer disappeared in a swallow. Clichéd and dramatic, but effective for his plight of memory. The bartender swapped the glass without indication. "Picking the wrong side can be shit, but not picking a side—that is weakness. And once that chain is weakened, there's no soldering it back." The man in the burgundy jacket, hunched over his fresh beer, took a sip through the foam.

"Chin up, buck-o," Don Bronco said, a jolt into the bar's accustomed hush, his pitch startling the air. "We all know how it ends." Bending the thin straw over the rim of his glass he took a sip of his Cola, an homage of sorts to the old man in the burgundy jacket's story. "The crew barges in. Scared lil' Joey antagonizes. The soldier gives a soul-drenched morality speech. Blah blah blah. Cold War implications. The audience eats it up. You win Best Director 1962, snag an award for screenplay, yet still snubbed Best Picture."

The man in the burgundy jacket neither confirmed nor denied Don Bronco's accusation of awards, staring into his beer as if he was not only lost in it but trapped by it.

And Zeek? He sat there sipping on his Cola, baffled as to why there wasn't a television, not even an old aesthetically fitting box TV, in this establishment playing some sort of staticy sporting event or 24 hour news programming, and what it was people could actually do in here for hours on end when it clicked. The Sea Fox, the soldier, Joe G., he'd seen it all before, late one night or early one morning, when The Vault Classic Movie Television channel played something a bit more risqué, something post Hays. He caught it as the title announced the film in big military style block lettering, *THE SEA FOX* (© MCMLXII A Bucking B. Production LTD. All Rights Reserved) and stayed through its seasoned use of damns peppered with sons of Bs, a few Ss, a blatantly implied F-bomb, the first implication in cinema history which Zeek would have found amusing had he known, and a surprisingly bawdy fist fight. He enjoyed the film well enough, rating it somewhere between having no desire to watch it again having seen it once and still recommending it if it ever arose in conversation.

"And what of the time," the man in the burgundy jacket said like a counterargument, low and to his beer, "I was an Arkansan farmer whose son returns home years after his release from a stint in the federal pen down state with a lascivious siren on his arm? And me being the hard-drinking, Sunday-going man without convictions like I am, I lust after the bombshell, and she welcomes it, seducing my touch right under my boy's nose, he all the while remains shut off and shut out like he was still locked up, like they never did release the boy that went in."

Zeek listened to the man reminisce. Sort of. As in he heard the life's sentences being spoken without quite parceling out the words. The majority of his concentration was on why his glass could not sit flush on a particular spot of the bar. To the right or the left of this spot the glass sat on the cardboard coaster and the cardboard coaster sat on the bar just fine, but the particular spot raised the absorbent piece of cardboard ever so slightly which in turn ever so slightly tilted the glass. And yet when he rubbed his fingers across the bar Zeek felt nothing abnormal along the polished surface.

"What of it?" Don Bronco said while Zeek continued his bar examination. "It was critically and commercially a flop. Your first, at least in terms of critical disdain, which, let's be honest, generally doesn't account for squat with the general public."

Zeek's eyes narrowed into a squinted focus. He had found with his thumbnail a small speck protruding from the varnish.

"Don't get me wrong," Don Bronco continued, "casting real Arkansan farmers as father and son was a strategic move, their performances were raw and real, and against Dolores "Dorothy" Chip's sublime subtleness," he leaned back like sinking into a cloud of confidence, "was naturally visceral. It's a shame it marked her only big screen appearance, a blip on the radar before obscurity. So while the screenplay could have benefited from some editing, the direction was precise and the New American way it was pieced together innovative." He shrugged.

The man in the burgundy jacket sipped his beer without a sound, stock still with the exception of the muscles involved in consumption.

Zeek picked at the bar.

Don Bronco returned to a forward lean, shaking his head no to emphasize the negativity of "But the real downfall was the affair."

"You leave her out of this."

"It was just so trite and clichéd. Even Predictable found it predictable. There was sprinkles of passion in the lust but there was no chemistry betwixt the seasoned man and the starlet. The surface dialogue just thin enough to get by, drudging on and on, scene after scene, like you were trying to convince yourself rather than the audience that it was a stroke of genius rather than just stroking off. Tell me, what ever happened to the lovely Miss Chip once you rolled off and rolled the credits?"

At this point, if Zeek had been paying any attention he would have seen the tiniest ripple of honest emotion coming from the man in the burgundy jacket. The man's lips tightened to his teeth, his nostrils flared to the inhale of oxygen, his brow furrowed, his grip tightened knuckle white around the glass sweating like he was wringing it out. But with Zeek it was the flake he'd picked through the varnish that occupied his attention as he chipped at it with his thumbnail. In the scheme of things, or when it came to dislodging things from the bar, Zeek was making decent headway, all things considered, enough so the generationally appropriate dime/chip-reader-sized piece of off-white was free enough to show its natural curl upward from the wood, a curl curled enough to pinch, which he did and to his surprise tugged free from its lacquered encasement. He held it in his palm, feeling accomplished somewhere between his diligence of task and the inadvertent destruction of property, yet upon flipping over the prize the self-satisfaction swelling inside him fizzled flatter than his Cola. On the back were four letters, typeset in black: a capital z, lowercase e, lowercase e, and lowercase l intersected by a cut off horizontal lowercase v. Zeek.

He also did not hear Don Bronco's continued antagonization nor see the man in the burgundy jacket's continued muted spiral into anger. He was more looking to share the mystery concerning the token in his palm along with the twinge of excitement that came with it. Things happen, but not usually things with Zeek's name on them, even if the zeal was implied and misspelled.

"My friend here knows Ms. Chip, alive and well, living of all places here in the city," Don Bronco said, self-gratification rolling off his tongue.

Zeek wasn't aware he knew the Ms. in question.

"I don't give a damn, you son of a bitch," the man in the burgundy jacket growled. "I'm hearing clearance to land a blow that'll take off that shit-eating grin. Does your friend know that you imperious f—"

"That's our cue," Don Bronco said, springing from relaxed to standing before the short sentence's completion. He reached back and tapped Zeek's shoulder. "Now's about that time we should be leaving."

Hearing the words like music, Zeek slammed back his drink of mostly ice and followed Don Bronco promptly towards the entrance underneath a busted sign with a singular, red lit X.

"What about the bartender?" asked Zeek with the stiff lips of a ventriloquist as a means of keeping a semblance of cool to their unrehearsed but seemingly choreographed departing, like the good cop/bad cop detecting duo found prime time on Tuesdays, Wednesdays, Fridays, and most everywhere else on syndication, since Mondays were reserved for sports, sing-offs, and other reality-based competitions, and Thursdays for comedy.

Don Bronco responded with, "He's been fully compensated," without turning, focused out the door.

They crossed the street from *Fellcws* where Don Bronco stopped and faced the bar, arms crossed, straddling the line of shadow the streetlamp draped on the pavement.

"With a minimum of 20%?" Zeek, uncomfortable in the spotlight, moved to the dark side of Don Bronco.

"That's what you really want to know?"

"It's just anything less isn't industry standard."

"Heard. Move on."

"I didn't hear anything."

"And you won't with this banter stalling."

"I thought you said we were leaving."

"We left, right?"

"We didn't get very far."

"We're far enough, literally. And we'll go further. But that's on you, my friend."

"When?"

"That's relative."

"What do you mean?"

"That's more like it." Don Bronco never took his eyes from the bar. "Rhetorically, what time you think he leaves?"

Zeek opened his mouth as if to attempt a pertinent guess, however his brain mired between who was the he in question and if that he leaving meant him getting home.

"Basically never," continued Don Bronco. "He's there, in that bar, beer in hand, perpetually. Before and the during and the after. In a sense, always. That's why we had to set a trap, lay the bait. No one ever simply complied because you showed up or asked. So we good cop/bad copped it. I know you watch at least one of those detective dramas. They're on every night."

"Was I the good cop or the bad cop?" Zeek interrogated.

"Bad cop, obviously. And you played the part with gusto."

A tingling sensation zigged from his gut to his stache, exiting as a self-satisfied "Hmm." He liked this idea of bad cop, assuming he'd automatically default to the starched-shirt good cop role. But now ugh, anxiety, this meant he had to be the one in the perp's face on the other side of a two-way mirror, slamming his...

"I'm sorry. I can't. I've exaggerated liberties. You're actually neither cop. But you're doing fine. Just keep doing."

What was Zeek's role then? He hadn't the foggiest. Yet still a feeling zagged like lightning from his stache deep into his gut, striking in the darkest pit a spark, an inkling of being a vague participant in something outside his routine.

"So then," Zeek said slowly, enunciating each syllable without poetics, awkwardly segueing into "What exactly am I supposed to be doing with this?" as he held out the piece of shell in his palm.

"What about it?" Don Bronco's eyes, fixed like an addict on the bar door across the street, didn't shift attention.

"Do you at least now know what's going on?"

"Specifically?"

"Specifically."

"In a way of sorts."

"And nonspecifically?"

"Nonspecifically? Then, yes. I know."

"And..." Zeek said by elongating the n and trailing off into the d, hoping Don Bronco would pick up where he had not continued.

"And it's nothing specifically. Yet. We're nearly halfway there."

But like a thunderstorm, the illumination was gone before being sound.

He shrugged the whole thing off. Bad cop.

Zeek found the fifteenth piece of eggshell on a pizza. Again. Before asking what exactly he was nearly in the middle of, the man in the burgundy jacket crept out from the bar. At first there was merely a sliver between the door and the frame, a narrow crack misperceived as a dusky illusion, but then a head appeared like an apparition detached from a body, looking this way and that, up and down the sidewalk, searching for some big danger in the nothing of the night, before disappearing back into the bar, then reappearing and disappearing and reappearing in no specific incremental pattern, until finally the door swung open wide enough for the old man to shuffle out. His steps barely cleared the ground, a trundle of scraping pavement, an anatomical feat of forward progression without bending the knees, his staggering pace further muddled by age, drink, and/or apprehension. No cars came through as the old man crossed, *Fellcws* not being a prominent local hotspot tourist destination, but if by chance there was the driver would have surely slammed the brakes and screamed a poetic slam of obscenities muffled by rolled windows.

Under the glow of the lamp, the yellow-tinged shadows deepened the wrinkles lining the man in the burgundy jacket's face. He looked older, hunched, weathered from the uncertainty of being away from the old world he had become accustomed to knowing.

"Something I can do you for?" Don Bronco said, arms still folded, feet still planted, still playing whatever game with the old man in the burgundy jacket he was playing.

"You have my attention." He stood toe to toe with Don Bronco, not quite erect enough to be considered eye to eye, but eyeing him down nonetheless.

"Me?" His tone elevated the word into a disyllabic question, the second beat acting as a digit fingering himself. "No. Targeting me as having something of yours is close but apologetically misdirected. My distracted companion however," his sentence trailed off into an ellipsis.

To an nth degree, of all the modifiers possible for his companion, Don Bronco chose accurately. As a nonsmoker Zeek was considering now was the time to light up, let the brief, exaggerated spark flicker intrigue across his face, allow the hovering scintillation of the long, deliberate drags hint at his presence in the darkness like those long-coat detectives in B&W noirs nostalgically parodied on 90s sitcoms and cartoons where carrots or tails were standard stand-ins to save the children or by those gruff but fair, tough-as-nails detectives who lawfully broke the law for the betterment of the city's streets with an eat shit smirk clenched around passé implications of gum, a toothpick, or a straw in a paper cup. This internal amusement played out behind his set eyes, which if not for the night, the old man in the burgundy jacket would overtly misconstrue as a cold stare and grounds for a direct, more aggressive confrontation to Zeek's bad cop persona.

The old man cleared his throat with a "Well?"

"Well," Zeek waded into the gap of silence, the novelty of the cigarette burnt out. He was ready to go home with or without answers. It wasn't terribly late. He could catch up on an episode or two of *The Show*, thanks to Dave's reminder, and make it to bed at a decent enough hour depending on the number of episodes he ended up watching. He could just as easily worry about answers tomorrow after breakfast. He rubbed his hand over his belly. As far as he could tell he hadn't withered. But that didn't stop him from mapping the places in the vicinity of The Family Mansion (which Zeek and only Zeek called it, likening it to being the ill-lit homely inn for weary travelers at the start of their grand adventure, never to be returned to again) where he could pick up a quick meal-sized snack.

"Sass like that means you think you're some sort of badass, don't you? I'll have you know I've seen things, scrounged things, created things out of my own powerless being. More than I've ever put out which is more than you'll ever understand."

The old man in the burgundy jacket was right. Zeek did not understand. So he took the path of least resistance when confronted with the hard-boiled confusion of the previous generations' irritation towards the lazy and lackadaisical modernity, and agreed with an easily palatable "yes" coated by a tranquillizing "sir."

"Don't go soft on me, sonny."

"Ezekiel," Zeek said like a rhetorical question.

"No one's going soft." To Zeek's relief, Don Bronco finally decided to reestablish his presence in the scene. "Or hard. Or side up. Or any variation of which. We're merely having a friendly conversation amongst friends."

"All my friends are dead." The man in the burgundy jacket wasn't a fan of mediation.

"Not all your friends," said Don Bronco unreassuringly plain.

"I'm tired of you two, and I'm incredibly thirsty. So how about we stop yanking my old shriveled. Do you know who I am, big man?"

Zeek looked at Don Bronco, his face contorted between not knowing who the big man in question was and looking for his out. It started with his brows bunched to the middle of his forehead, one slanted, the other arched, because although he was the bigger of the two from the old man in the burgundy jacket's hunched perspective Don Bronco could be considered equally big in stature. Then the slanted brow lifted and his eyes squinted as they rolled to the right where his mind's eye saw Shellie's kitchen counter in the remembrance of where he left his bottle drink. He too was incredibly thirsty. But that drink was probably trashed by now, gone and lost like him. Oh well, neither mattered anyway, Zeek's countenances unseen in the dark.

"Of course not. You're too young. Let me tell you something about who I am. I am nothing. Almost literally. I am a name without embodiment, associated with award ceremonies, director's credits, and the glory days of west coast scandal. I was happy then. I was something tangible in spirit. Untouchable in body. And to prove it I had more accolades under my belt than pounds under a fat, rich Limey's. Also had a wife, that saccharine bitch, she was an empty, candy-coated shell of a woman, but she was hang-on-to-your-dicks beautiful. A national sweetheart. She was America's as much as she was mine. And then there was our daughter. Now she was the best part of me, body and soul, and more beautiful than her mother, if you can believe that. The single greatest thing I'd ever produced, greater than all the films on my resume, and not only the critical darlings that made my career, mind you, but the still underrated classics, with all the accolades tacked on weighing them down. But while she was my body and soul, my mistake laid stake in where I put my heart. Enter Dolores Chip, a plain girl known as Dorothy where she grew up in Lee's Summit, Missouri, just south of the true Kansas City, as she'd always suffix, hinged with the faintest twinge of twang, liker her petite mouth was formed around the drawl. She stumbled into my existence, quite literally, when she fell as a chorus girl for a minor background scene in my Neo Americana take on the noir, *Dusk City*, a film meant to push the boundaries into the gritty truth that the line between laws and crime is violently blurred. I personally went over to berate the young girl, already annoyed with the fact my second unit director dropped out and I was stuck filming the driveling screen filler. Yet, seeing her on the floor, the way she turned up towards me, her soft, auburn curls springing off her cheek, I saw a sinking in her golden doe eyes, a fear quivering on her pouted lower lip, my red hot fury boiled over into passion. I'd see to it no harm ever came to this creature. I invited her out to be a part of this new project I was developing, something natural, sowed from the roots of southern culture, on location, real people. The salt of the earth kind of people. And even convinced the studio head, personally, to give the lead to this unknown, but all that breath spent on realism being authenticated by the creation of a new star couldn't shine a light on her veracious innocence. The affair predicated as naturally as the summertime, warm and free as a breeze. A holiday away from the day to day, the drudge of what had become, the sprinkle of higher truths and happiness, pure love and life into the sands of time. Like the first time we were close enough for our lips to touch. I remember the nerves. Can you believe it? I was nervous. Not from the rush of adultery but because I knew if she were to kiss my core, that tiny universe inside me would explode into the heavens, a high I'd never return from or reach again, my heart chanting to light the fuse. And it lit, blazing nights to days and days to suns. But then came the omniscient press. They ran headline after story after column: lusty mogul seduces (yet another) harlot starlet, a flop in the bedroom turns into a flop on screen, oh poor boohoo America's sweetheart. The backlash turned something so precious, so beautiful, so full of life into a wasteland. Physically. Emotionally. Bleakness. My wife left, which was to be expected, no harm done there. She bathed in the attention, the national outpouring of tears became the lacquered coat for that empty shell. However, she took my daughter, took all custodial rights. I fought against this, was in and out of courtrooms for years, the judges siding with my ex-wife, too busy fantasizing about fucking her, ruling how could I tarnish someone so perfect? The bastards. The whole lot of them. Hard under their robes. But even through all of that, Dolores, my Dorothy, remained by my side, a pillar, a staff, a rock, whatever trite but true metaphor you deem worthy. She hated the negative spotlight. She tried acting like it shone right through her, for me, for my sake, but I could tell how it refracted off the small dimples of her tarnished innocence. I wasn't the easiest man to deal with, but she did everything in her small-town know how to stand by her man. Then the accident happened, my ex-wife's young, hung playboy and his hotrod took my little girl away from me. And I lost it. Why the bitch would ever let my little girl in the car with that meat-headed ass I'll never understand. Even now. At first I believed it was some sort of penance, some black hole in my soul needing to expand outwardly through my body and consume all the light around me. I purged myself into darkness, feeding it the small stars that gave me being. And like the damned fool I am, I sacrificed my films, sacrificed unto it my Dorothy. And for what?" The old man in the burgundy jacket answered his question with silence. "And now I come here, hidden in plain view. Masked without a mask. A nothing. Spending my days or time or life trying to drown out the black bleakness, speckling the infinite hollowness with the memories of once was. I relive the past. Literally. Without boundary. An albumen of thoughts around a yolk of remembered bliss. Fickle but unhatched, nevertheless, fluid and soured. Every day the same. So please, if it has come to this, please, if there is any chance..."

Zeek listened to the puzzle but still wasn't sure where exactly he fit. Maybe it was true, maybe he was indeed too young. Guilty as accused. He looked to Don Bronco for direction, but he had that same wide-eyed anticipatory stare as the man in the burgundy jacket, so that was useless. He was the one who got him lost in the first place, anyway.

"A chance of what, exactly?" Zeek finally said, arcing the question and tilting his head. Just because he was unsure as to why Don Bronco dragged him out here didn't mean he couldn't be respectful of the old man in the burgundy jacket's plight, seeing as it was quite personal.

But the softened plea in the man in the burgundy jacket's voice ramped back into frustration. "A couple of dicks. That's what you two are. Bags of dicks."

"Now, sir, I must object." It wasn't the oddly investigatory insult that roused the objection but rather the tone, like a dog comprehending the voice rather than the words. "I've had a long day, and as it's progressed I've grown increasingly hungry on top of not rightly knowing why we've all been dragged out here."

"For serious? Not a clue? Not even a stab?" Don Bronco sounded more frustrated than the man in the burgundy jacket.

He shrugged while racking his brain for some answer, expressly the correct one for the fast track to getting dinner, getting home, getting out of these trousers and getting into his Plushbottom. As far as he could recollect he had never seen the farm movie about farmers, but was more than willing to put it on his ongoing mental list of movies to catch up on. "I don't concentrate well when I'm hungry."

"The bus lady. You know, the lady on the bus."

"Ms. D?"

Don Bronco's quick "Yes" was a tonal jump-for-joy and a sigh of relief. "Small Fry."

"More about this bus." The old man in the burgundy jacket weaved impatience with excitement.

"I don't know much about her, honestly, except she's rather intrusive."

"Let's get back on the bus."

"Yeah, Zeek, the bus."

"Ezekiel," Zeek said like a subplot.

"Is that the line?"

"Is my name the line?"

"This is absurd," said Don Bronco, commentator on confusion.

"Where can I find the Ezekiel?"

"I'm Ezekiel."

"So you're the driver?"

"Merely a passenger on The Grey."

"Seriously? This is the trip we're taking?" Don Bronco, chiming in, before mumbling something about building attention.

"When?"

Zeek questioned the sanity of the situation and why he stopped avoiding Don Bronco in the first place, but answered the old man in the burgundy jacket. "Bus 12's any given weekday. 7:20 sharp-ish."

"Ha-ha-hot damn." If the man in the burgundy jacket was younger he might have danced. "I'll be seeing you two then, you beautiful dick bags. Bright and early." And he'd continue dancing all the way across the street and back to the bar instead of shuffling at his everyday old man pace thus leaving Zeek and Don Bronco out under the streetlamp, separated by light and shadow.

"Well," Zeek said, a single, drawn-out word with a single clap, that nuanced pairing used universally as a precursor for saying farewells and have a wonderful evenings.

"That's it?"

"I should probably be going."

"I was expecting so much more."

"Have a wonderful evening."

"That's all you have to say?"

Zeek pretended to watch the toe of his shoe scuff atop the sidewalk. "Farewell?"

Don Bronco ended the combined sound of a sigh/dying animal with, "What horseshit."

Zeek shrugged. He thought so too. Not because he couldn't possibly be more polite than that, and honestly, who could, but rather because he didn't know which direction would lead to his apartment preferably with takeout along the way. Pizza came to mind, but anything would do.

Headlights cut into their conversation and pushed the chin of Zeek's squinted face further into his neck. Don Bronco stood motionless as the car pulled up, crossing into the oncoming lane. It parked at an angle, where Zeek could make out the lit car topper of a pelican outlined in a bold navy blue, a bright red pepperoni pizza hanging from its beak, hovering over PELICAN PIzzA, the z's lowered to compensate for its wing.

"Won you guys 'Buddy Boy' Zeek Macray?"

"Ezekiel," Zeek answered reflexively.

"You're 'Buddy Boy' Macray?" the voice said as crisp and cool as the evening.

"Yes?" he questioned in case he shouldn't be.

The compact lemon's door flung open, caterwauling on its dented hinges, and Don Bronco stepped out, balancing the insulated pizza jacket, not bothering to cut off the engine, prefiguring the speed of the drop.

Zeek took a double take.

Well, maybe not Don Bronco exactly, but the driver did look doppelgangerly similar in an untidy navy pants/red shirt uniform. His standard issue navy hat with an emblem matching his car's was pulled dangerously low over his eyes, which possibly led to Zeek's dead-set comparison. This other Don Bronco slid a box from the bag and handed it to Zeek.

"I'm sorry, I didn't order this."

"It's all taken care of. Receipts right here: 'Ate your quiche, thanx for the meal. Ordered you pizza. Hope that compensates. If you get it.'" He gave Zeek the receipt with a "you welcome" and got back into the car.

"How did you even..." Zeek let the question fade into the strangeness of holding an unordered pizza.

"Some guy said an xtra 50 if I could find a mustachioed Matt Foley with a guy who looked like he might live in a van down by the river. Thought whatthe hell, I could make that happen. But who would of thunk it."

"I'm sorry, did you say Farley?" Zeek misheard simultaneously with Don Bronco's "Impossible." But neither mattered. The junker sped off in the opposite direction it had come.

Zeek held out the box. "Pizza," he offered in a way that stated the object.

"Sure. Why the hell not?"

The box top flipped open across the shadow and the light glistened across pepperonis and cheese. An oldie but a goldie of classic flatbread cuisine. But sitting at the convergence of the eight slices, where the three-legged pizza table should be, sat the rounded tip of an egg's shell holding the cardboard from the cheese. Don Bronco snatched it and tried palming the small dome around curved fingers with the poor execution of an untrained street magician.

"What was that?" Zeek asked, steadying the unbalanced box on his beefy fingers.

"Nuffing." Don Bronco stuffed the pointed end of a slice into his mouth, folding the crust around his finger like a northern tourist.

"That was definitely something."

Vigorous chewing responded to the observation. Zeek watched Don Bronco's mouth chomp, grind, and mush the avoidance of topic. He grabbed a slice for himself, careful not to topple the box, and took a ravenous can't beat 'em join 'em bite. As it turned out this bite became one of the best decisions Zeek had made, thus far, all evening. Even if the pizza was terrible it was still pizza, and this couldn't have been more true, with the minor exception being this was the best-tasting pizza Zeek had tasted to date and, without debate, probably the best-tasting pizza he'd ever taste. Period. End of sentence. He gladly took a second, larger bite, propping the slice flatly across his fingers. The proper proportion of crust:sauce:cheese smoothed the balance of his palate: the crust neither crumbly like a cracker nor doughy, a perfect depth to bake in a delicate crunch while thick enough to be a sanctuary for the sauce balancing the punch of tomato with garlic, oregano, basil, and natural ingredients both sweet and savory, was that a hint of rosemary he tasted?, all topped with a layer of a mozzarella blend browned carefully as to melt evenly but not overly char. And if this wasn't enough, there were the pepperonis, small discs of pepper-cured meat, the beloved pinnacle of pizza passed down the generations of joints and eateries, mamma mia, wading in the thinnest layer of grease.

"What's this?"

"Delicious," Zeek said, snagging his next slice.

"What? No." Don Bronco lifted the cardboard lid on its bent hinge. "This."

There, written in thick, industrial-sized sharpie, was the address for 1111 W Ebb Ave above "2 4 a $" with "free w/ box and a friend" scratched thin underneath in a hurry.

Zeek said, "Never heard of it," around a mouth full of half-masticated heaven.

"It won't be far from here."

Zeek nodded, or appeared to because of his voracious chewing.

Zeek found the sixteenth piece of eggshell in the dirt. Don Bronco picked up another slice, folded it, and turned to walk back the way they had come. Zeek looked up and down into the vacantness of both directions, into the unfamiliarity of this side of town. He also grabbed another slice for good measure and flipped the box closed while following suit till something seemed, at the least, recognizable.

"About that thing in your hand. I'm pretty sure you're not about to tell me yet, are you?" Blindly following, which couldn't get any more directionless, he figured it wouldn't hurt to ask direct. One last shot in the dark.

"It's nothing."

"It's literally something," Zeek felt the need to point, "in your hand."

"Then it's literally figuratively nothing." As if to emphasize his point, Don Bronco tossed the eggshell with a flick of his wrist towards the overgrown, vacant lot on the other side of the street they were passing. Zeek tried following the trajectory of the object but was sure he never actually saw the shell hit the ground, thinking instead small wings bowed from the sides, stretched out, and flap flap flapflapflapped in opposition of gravity to coast on the safety of air. But who knew for sure? Under the influence of night, anything was possible in the shadows.

Moreover, there was not a moment to hunt for remnants of anything left behind at the rate Don Bronco moved. He walked as if he was late for the biggest event of his life, his power strides longer than Zeek's hefty legs could stretch. They passed the street on the other side of the lot the pair originally came down, continuing straight, assumedly further away from the peace and comforts of The Family Mansion (which Zeek and only Zeek called it, likening it to being a haven away from the outside world, a bunker of solitude and safety when the end should be near but the destructive invaders, whether terrestrial or extra, were shifting the midpoint of the plot and dragging out themes). With each block they crossed the city streets appeared lighter. But the semblance of brightness had no basis for the night. The street lamps didn't increase. Traffic remained nil. Row houses and duplexes began popping up amongst the run-down, commercial sector of small, out-of-the-way warehouses and factories, the ones not abandoned and heavily tagged turned into mom-and-pop post-postmodern start-ups along the outskirts of town. But their lights, though chic and hip, were too dim to be considered illuminating.

And, of course, Don Bronco weaved further into the quiet and farther away from the places Zeek knew.

On the hazy night sky overcrowded with clouds loomed an electric tower, the steel lattice sketched like a penciled stencil on a gray canvas. A small church consisting of a single sanctuary sat haphazardly halfasserdly angled from the gridlock street in the otherwise empty, adjacent lot. Its steeple paled from the heavens in opposition of the tower. The cross at the apex, undeterred, still grasped skyward. The surrounding lawn was mowed low. Across the street, trees grew in the ordered chaos nature intended. Branched in clusters of trunks and shrubs, some planted roots in the openness outside a concrete skeleton. Others burst forth from the windows and roof, walled in by the remains of what once was a masonry, the painted logo a fading reminder, its final headstone.

Inside, other markers were scattered amongst the overgrowth, many ornate with crosses and praying hands, outlines of rosaries and baroque boarders, but all of them nameless and without dates, timelessly unclaimed. Zeek could see none of this through the brush, following Don Bronco around stones.

What he did see through the brush was light being flecked into a hundred tiny suns pushed into the space by cluttered noise. Where the back wall should have been was an opening, a hole knocked out by time and teens, now an entrance to the radiance and sound. A bonfire raged in the middle of the yard fenced in by the doorless overhangs, once industrial sheds for brick palates and unprocessed stone now displays for dust and debris. The exception being the largest single unit on the right, housing the rock-refining equipment of drums and amplifiers. And people. They filled the lot between the trees and the fire, the voices individually indistinct blending into the murmur of community.

They walked up to a foldout table made of pressed wood. The kid sitting behind it had a nose ring dangling like a non-anthropomorphic bull from an animated serial. So, Don Bronco stepped up with the matador confidence of the anthropomorphic rabbit or mouse. Zeek, laggard, behind.

"Ticket," the kid said, monotone from repetition, his knob knocking his upper lip.

"Hand him the box."

Zeek did so by extending his arms at length, give or take three feet from the table, then slid it with a finger thus adding a few inches, on the off chance the bull would charge.

The kid opened the box and took the last slice of pizza Zeek had been saving.

"He's the friend." Don Bronco pointed to Zeek with his thumb.

The kid's teenage apathy motioned the companions in, pizza dangling from his mouth, and frisbeed the box into a pile of tickets, a trash heap of boxes, bottles, and paper bags, no two brands the same.

Zeek followed close to Don Bronco, because like it or not, he was the only person he knew in the vicinity and questionably why he was here. So apologizing profusely in a continuous mumble, his thick frame overstepped its bounds through this minefield of strangers.

The bonfire burned bright towards the sky.

They made it to the farthest side from the entrance. Don Bronco turned his back to the fence and faced the crowd.

Zeek did the same and watched the people being a crowd.

He wanted to ask where they were or, better yet, why they were where they were. But Don Bronco beat him to it.

"Don't you ever ask yourself why?"

"What?"

"Don't you ever wonder why you?"

"In what regards?"

"Choose one."

"Like why'd you bring me here now? Or why don't I know where I am? Or why drag me through all that business with that old man? Or why can't you explain anything about all those eggshells so we can call it an evening?"

"I distinctly said one."

"Buddy Boy!"

Dave's voice punched through the crowd like the exclamation to the point. One arm extended, the other wrapped around Shellie La Dop. "We didn't think we'd be seeing you again after you ran out on us. At least now we can say thanks for covering dinner." He pushed a fist into Zeek's shoulder, one of the oddest social gestures of gratitude.

"That wasn't me."

"Thank him for the pizza," Don Bronco interjected, not turning from the crowd.

"What pizza? Who's your pal, Buddy Boy?"

"Him? Who I shared the pizza with."

"Aww. Charity," Shellie said flatly, questioning clarity through dazed eyes.

"Might as well be with my writer's budget."

"Painter," she responded in her own way.

A hush swept over the crowd, the conversation in the corner the decrescendo. Four guys, each differing in manners and dress but manifesting as a single unit, congregated around the drum kit. Electricity buzzed and clicked from the amplifiers. And then music, strikingly melodic, thunderously rhythmic trash, recycled like the ticket heap. The crowd went as wild as the fire, a blazing mass of hand-raised energy. Zeek stood solemn but inside burned bright. He was the blue ember under the flame.

"Well I'll be damned," Dave said slowly, emphasizing every word like a supporting character's first on-screen glimpse at the mystery off-screen to prepare the audience for what was to come. At the front of the band, leading with the microphone, was Matte (Dave and Zeek adding the e because of his unpolished personality) the secretary. And he shone. The brilliance of his voice accenting the melody with juxtaposed harmonies. His shirtless body language charged with passion, a conflict as aggressive and smooth as his vocals. If Zeek was an ember on the edge, the secretary on stage was the sun that consumed the world with fire. It was beautiful. "Who would have thunk it." Dave finely concluded his astonishment aloud, which he deemed necessary.

And just as it began, so it ended. The show was over. Dave and Shellie cheered with the crowd. Zeek smiled.

"We are Twenty-Four A Money. Goodnight." The microphone was placed carefully back onto the stand, the most anticlimactic of all the rock star moves, but the crowd ate it up to the rafters.

The band left the stage. It was over. There was no sweet second course encore. And yet the people in attendance were satiated, the droning murmur returning to the static white noise of humanity.

"I believe it's getting late," Zeek said, interposing his own voice into the hum. "It's probably best if I get going."

"What are you talking about, Buddy Boy? The evening may be quelled to rest, but the night is just beginning."

"I assure you, I'm alright."

"Are you trying to tell me you didn't just witness what the hell I just witnessed?"

"You mean Matte?"

"It was such a good show," Shellie offered in between Dave saying: "Of course I mean Matte" and "What kind of coworkers would we be if we didn't make obvious our show of support?"

Zeek heard Don Bronco's voice in his head urging him to go. But when he looked for confirmation, Don Bronco was standing as stoic and silent as when they had arrived to this spot. So he naturally reevaluated the urge to the murmur of the crowd and its influencing mentality, shrugging off the misinterpretation of sounds, which Dave promptly interpreted as agreement.

Dave lit a cigarette. "Let's do this."

Reluctant but abidingly, Zeek put one foot in front of the other, looking down and carefully watching to verify he'd actually stepped again in the direction of questioning his judgment. "What about Shellie?" he asked to cover his tracks as he turned and saw her sit on the grass.

"She's a big girl," Dave said, not looking back. He cupped his palm around the hot end of his stick and entered the crowd.

Zeek's compliance flashed to his 77" Kyoshiri UXHD microplasma, tuning into nothing in particular except for the vague notion of what he was potentially missing in contrast to what he was doing, a visual metaphor for his evening, and began again with his profuse apologizing behind Dave.

The pair bumped and coerced their way to the makeshift stage-less stage and rounded the corner of the doorless frame. "Hey, man, can you help me out?" Dave asked the first guy they came across, some tall dude covered in sweat and tattoos, leaning against the hanging wall. A longneck bottle dangled from one hand, drumsticks were fidgeted in the other. The guy looked over from his conversation with some young girl, who appeared innocent yet old enough, perched on a rock. His eyebrows arched into the curved displeasure of the interruption. "We're looking for Matte."

"No dice. He's already skipped."

"For the night?"

"Can't ever tell."

"What a shame." Dave snuffed his butt into the dirt. "Guess we're stuck catching him at the office. Anyway, thanks. You guys put on one hell of a show."

"Yeah." Deadpan. He knew.

It was Zeek who didn't know. He wasn't paying any attention. His focus was solely on Dave's shoe. Or, at least, the earth beneath it. So for the sake of not pushing Dave uncharacteristically out of the way, he carefully watched the spot where the cigarette fell. It might have been the way the lit end reflected its small glow that attracted his focus. A signal of sorts. Inversely, it might have been nothing. A trick. A false flag. But one never knew the distinction for sure until the moment passed, and even then found questions in the reflections, so Zeek waited patiently, passively watching, as he would for anything else as natural as another featured episode.

Dave nodded while looking around, plotting an exit, which exquisitely climaxed with, "Right," and with a single step away, Zeek swooped into the moment with a speed not normally exceeded by his physical form, the velocity pummeling his belly like an avalanche towards his chin. A force major. In a slow-motion replay his fingers would be seen pinching one of two broken pieces from under Dave's foot while his own feet lost traction and scooted crossways over each other just before his body hit the ground like another boulder in the yard. Meanwhile, back in real time, Zeek picked up the second half while the girl on the rock laughed her girlish giggle.

He held them out in his palm. "Ma" on one half, "ya" on the other.

"You alright there, Buddy Boy?"

"I'm fine."

"What's that?" Zeek looked up at the guy not offering to help him to his feet. "In your hand. My sister wants to know."

"Haven't the foggiest," Zeek responded in earnest, considering how embarrassed he should be.

"You sure went for it with a quickness."

"No. I just fell."

The guy scoffed.

Dave extended his hand.

But Zeek was already pushing himself up on his own accord, gracelessly managing a bottom-up inverse of the fall.

"Let me see." The guy stepped forward.

Zeek, without qualm, handed over the bits and used his free hands to brush himself off.

"This some sort of trick?" His squinted concern didn't match the anger in his tone.

"What trick?" Dave asked in defense, regardless of his cluelessness.

"Her name."

"What name?"

"Right here."

"What's there?"

"Maya."

"Is that her name?"

"What the fuck are y'all on?"

"Woah, Hoss. Let's simmer back a degree."

The guy cooled with the last of his longneck. "Right here." He returned the pieces as his sister asked to see them, her voice bathed in a Zen as collected as she was beautiful. The guy twisted in an awkward pivot of too late, acknowledging he heard her but not quite comprehending fast enough, and the shells dropped into Zeek's hand. Zeek, ever the gentleman, walked over and handed them to her. An odd, confusing interplay of characters all the way round.

Her reaction was quiet as she studied the pieces, and Zeek was sure whatever conclusion she derived would be the one he, with a lack of a better option, would agree with.

"Where did they come from?"

"Over there, I guess." He pointed to the spot of dirt.

"You think I can keep them?"

"Finders givers."

She smiled her calm smile, face down, eyes up, the contained gratitude distending the illusion from beautiful to gorgeous.

Zeek smiled back, his lips constrained and straight, reeled tight into his cheeks a bashful you're welcome.

Digging around in the Styrofoam cooler, the guy offered out beers over the cold shifting of compacted, tiny glaciers, to which Dave obliged.

"I guess we started off on the wrong foot."

"Stranger things have happened." Dave popped the cap with his lighter, the bottle's light hiss beckoning with a secret. He tilted the long neck towards the purveyor in a customary salutation.

"I can be a bit on the protective side." The guy snapped the bottle cap with a perfect arch into the open cooler. "I guess it comes with the territory. Most guys aren't as," there was a beat in his cadence as he silently tapped his drumstick to his thigh, a measure for the right word, "polite? See, her and that kit are all I have left. I'm kidding. That's way too melodramatic. But she does mean more than the world to me. She believes in me. Sometimes it takes that ounce of faith to runneth over, you know." Dave removed a cigarette and offered about, returning the favor to the only taker. The drummer had his own white lighter. "So you said you worked with Matt?" the guy went on, making conversational amends. "He can be a real cocky asshole. Which fits, since it seems all he ever wants to do is drink and—" ("Be nice," Maya's sweet conscience chimed in.) "Facts aren't rude. I'm just saying he's all about living that life without hitting that life. It's not like we made it. We're big on the small scale in the city, sure, but the world abounds." ("That wasn't a disagreement.") "Don't get me wrong. Dude's got talent. Over the top talent. But that's it. No drive. No long term. Just content to work his menial day job and bang fanboys, off himself by twenty-seven into infamy." He washed down the remarks with beer. "But the crazy thing is, the real fucked of the fucked, is this is what I want to do, all I want to do, and yet somehow no matter how I excel, no matter if I can keep the beat better than time itself, I'm the one who's in the background, replaceable. I know this. He knows this." ("Stop it.") "But that's the world we live in. At the end of the day, he'll still be him, and I'll still be no one."

"Why don't you do something about it?" Dave asked with the naive intrusiveness of an old friend. ("See," echoed Maya.)

"Oh, I do. Or, at least I think I am. A no one never knows in the now. To wane philosophically, Dupox said something like the present being 'an amalgamation of hiccups and chances' while the future 'digress[es] in a semblance of both everything and nothing.' So I play, I play every day. For an audience. For myself. The thought of stopping, hell, of even going a day without sticks on skins feels dreadful. And yet there's still a bleakness to the whole damn thing. But 'persistence is the pepper,' right?" He dropped the butt end into the bottle, which hissed to silence, and replaced the empty in the cooler for a full.

The weight in Zeek's own mouth was noticeably heavier. His tongue, neglected between the walking and the pizza and the falling and the waiting, now an arid landscape. Zeek consumed most things in high quantities, however beer was not generally one of those things. And even if this qualified as one of those rare times, a Pale-ale-ican was neither his first nor last choice. Even the flat, artificial Cola at the bar seemed like the ultimate thirst quencher by comparison. Yet he decided against asking if there was anything other in the cooler. When it doesn't rain it doesn't pour. His lips deserted of words.

"Still thirsty?" the guy asked with the breezy nonchalance of his monologue not only over but as if never taking place.

"No. No, thank you." Dave swallowed whatever little remained and handed the bottle back. "We best get going. But, again, thanks anyway."

Zeek nodded in agreement.

"Spot on then. And I'll let Matt know you were looking for him if I even see him."

"Don't even worry about it."

Zeek found the seventeenth to twenty-eighth piece of eggshell in an egg carton. The night was in full force, the moon large overhead like a distant opening from the bottom of a well. While Dave and Zeek cut through the thinning crowd, Zeek mouthed silently to himself, "It's all in his head," the five words Maya whispered in his ear.

Wait, what?

Let's not get ahead of ourselves.

While Dave was making their goodbyes, Maya leapt off the rock she sat perched on and skimmed over the patches of grass to Zeek, seemingly under the guise of night to never once touch the ground. She held Zeek's face as tender as innocence, her pinky fingers brushing the edges of his mustache, her breath a warm wisp around each word delicately placed in his ear, before leaving her genteel spirit on his cheek with a kiss, which still lingered after its brevity. Zeek, characteristically prone to blushing, continued feeling the radiance in his ears, simmering on the embers left behind, kindled by this most recent memory. He wouldn't tell another soul willingly, this his and his to keep, but if pried hard enough he'd swear and promise till the end he had seen a transparent luminescence trail behind her like smoke, glittering her glide to and from him. He would then blame this on the tricks the moon plays on shadows, but it would only be a rationalization he wouldn't believe.

They found Shellie and Don Bronco sitting on the ground conveniently where they left them.

"Did you find everything you were looking for?" Shellie asked.

"Stranger things have happened," said Dave.

"To who?" asked Zeek.

"To anybody," Don Bronco said. "A life is based upon others' lives."

"Poetic," said Shellie.

"Hardly." (Don Bronco)

"More philosophical waning?" Dave helped Shellie to her feet.

"Aren't most conversations? Inherently. Buried within." (Shellie)

"Anything to drink around here?" Zeek asked, each word as thick as paste, looking about as if he didn't already know the answer.

"There's an idea, Buddy Boy! There might be a bar nearby." (Dave)

"No. Not another. It's too late for that." (Zeek)

"It can't be that late yet." (Don Bronco, having gotten up)

"Hasn't this turned out to be an evening for the books," Dave said more to Shellie than the group.

The foursome began their meandering towards the entrance, not necessarily trying to leave but drifting on the aimless progression of ending events as natural as the night air swirling up and down the city block. Zeek led the pack like the z in zephyr.

"What's the rush, Buddy Boy?"

"I'm not rushing."

Dave scrunched his brow and lips in disagreement, paralleling his index over his thumb.

"It's just well beyond time to head home. Are you not tired? I'm tired," Zeek lied, in a way. Truth: he believed it was well beyond time to head home. Truth: he was tired. However, these truths implied a desire for bed that wasn't wholeheartedly the case. What he wanted more than anything, other than obviously a drink, was to plop his roundness into his Plushback and relax under the flickering glow of his giant 77" Kyoshiri, torn between catching up on recordings of *The Show*, *Cop Drama*, or *Family Situations* and the aimless flipping of channels with no set program in mind to watch where the night takes him.

"You're not tired," Dave countered, Zeek unsure if he was antagonizing his truths or just being antagonistic, both possibilities equally plausible, both filed under classic Dave. "You're alive."

"You should tell him," Shellie said.

"Should tell who what?" Dave asked, his voice still tinged with exuberance.

"Not you, darling."

"Which way to The Family Mansion?" Zeek looked up and down the street sparsely populated with stragglers abandoning the abandoned masonry. The electric lights blocks away gave no hint to the lighted path. Both ways seemingly the same under the moon's blue-gray shadow.

"Where?" (Again, Dave)

"It's what he calls his apartment," Don Bronco answered across a single tone.

A click disrupted Zeek's mind with the realization of not only what he said, for the first time aloud into the world, but that he and only he called it that, likening it to whatever relevant reason reeling around his mind at the time.

"You shouldn't know that."

"No, you're right. Yet I do."

"C'mon, Buddy Boy. Let's round out the night."

"The night's already round," Zeek said, not taking his eyes off Don Bronco, a glare more observational than malicious.

Don Bronco's returned gaze burrowed through Zeek and beyond to the street behind him. "This way," taking the first step.

They backtracked around the block, weaving over and down then up and across streets, Don Bronco leading the pack, resigned in his silence. Shellie rambled like a stream to Don Bronco, low, her words further snuffed by Dave's airy and up-tempo tongue clicks, the beat keeping pace. Zeek, unheroicly quiet, walked with no real significance closest to the streetlight poles planted on every corner, head down, mentally shuffling through the contents of his fridge, or what little he remembered being packed in there. He would drink at least two liters of Cola, actual Cola, if he had any. That was a given. It was a shame he finished off those wings. Cold chicken was certainly better in the after hours, a complement to both late night comedies and keen fit infomercials.

The wanderers hit a brick wall and continued along it, until reaching its end where they turned in front of the marketplace department store.

If the building was asleep it was dreaming. The lights inside were dimmed to a nocturnal yellow while the neon Mercatos sign decorated delicate overhead in its red and blue fused ethereal glory. A few night stockers could be seen shifting around the darkened aisles, cutters in hand, displaying and organizing the wants and needs of others. The store, cleared of shoppers but full of goods, bared a hushed awareness of desertion into the quiet. Zeek considered rapping on the glass on the off chance of picking up a few items, necessities, things he regretted not picking up earlier. But he knew that was absurd. With the hours clearly marked and set, now was not the time. There would be no more intrusions this evening.

He was almost home.

He could take it from

"Here we are," Zeek said about the obviousness of standing in front of The Family Mansion (which Zeek and only Zeek no longer wished to call it likening it to no longer feeling like his own, like a small film stumbled upon, a hidden gem held dearly for years that suddenly boasts cult status, becoming nostalgically vogue to pastiche people, the perceived bond once felt now waning with so many others at his doorstep) realizing how sore he'd be in the morning.

"We should do this again, make this a thing." Dave punctuated his contentedness with a cigarette. Don Bronco took one when offered.

"Right," said Zeek.

"You stay around here?" Dave asked, handing over his lighter.

"Relatively."

"Good. Good." Dave took it back.

Zeek covered a faint rumbling from the depth of his stomach with "I'm going to let you finish. Have a good rest of your night," while inching himself closer to the sanctuary of food, drink, and high quality cushioning all in HD.

"Night, Buddy Boy."

"You're going to find more eggshells inside."

Zeek didn't stop. "That's fine."

"I can tell you what they are now."

"Are you about to try and monologue we're all in some sort of egg together waiting for the big cosmic hatching, and I happen to be the little chicken watching the sky fall, because if you are..."

Don Bronco choked a bit over the smoke. "We didn't come all this way for you to be so trite. Even old Walt D. couldn't pull that off. They're previous drafts."

"Of what?"

"My story."

"Did you guys get something from Shellie?"

Shellie backhanded Dave's shoulder with the playful force that contradicted the seriousness of his tone.

"Wouldn't it be my story?"

"It's as much about you as it is me."

"No, seriously. What's he on about?" Dave asked Shellie.

"I'm a writer," Don Bronco answered point blank, "this is a story, and we're all characters. Or something. Or whatever. Do what you want with the revelation."

"You're a what and what now?"

"A writer, as in an unknown author, as in I don't even know myself therefore only have a vague idea as to what might happen. Like where were you two or three days ago?"

"It wasn't work."

"I do know that. But where specifically?"

"With Shellie, like *with* Shellie."

"Exactly. But that's just a conjecture. Give me details."

"Watch it, buddy," Dave said with a puzzled look of missing pieces he couldn't put together despite the cautionary, pointed tone.

"See. There aren't any. And for the sake of my story there doesn't need to be. None of us were really anywhere three days ago in accordance with how we understand things or time or chapters or whatever. But we've existed before and will henceforth continuously, doing the same but always elsewhere. That strange, perpetual repetitiousness of the day to day: we're being written or rewritten or read. It's like how people read the same words but no one reads the same book. Forever a cycle that's both the same yet ever-changing. So understand, like yourself, I know what has happened but it's on top of this sort of vague, created memory we share of what happened before that. But that's writing. I can't say with any authenticity what will happen before, during, or next until it's happening. So it's my job to figure it out. It's the thankless driving force, generally unnoticed. Except Zeek's particular story here happens to involve compounding drafts that slip through. So here I am."

"You're saying I'm not real?" Even Zeek heard the quiver of cliché in Dave's question.

"I'm absolutely not saying that. You're very real, just no more or less than I am."

Dave lit his third cigarette.

"Have a good night." No one noticed Zeek had made his way up the stairs to the foyer door. "Shellie, nice meeting you. Dave, see you Monday." And with a curt wave he was inside the building then inside his apartment. Finally.

He breathed in the smell of conditioned air, that sweet home-sweet-home smell, a seasoned blend of his essence and serenity.

The fridge was as empty as he hoped it wouldn't be but expected. Amidst the condiment packets was a carton of eggs because of course, what else? And although they certainly weren't what he had in mind, given the circumstances of the day they would have to do, representing some sort of metaphor his rumbling tummy didn't care about.

But inside, and again to no surprise, there were no eggs. In each oval divot was a single jagged shell. He dumped them on the counter, and using the light from the open fridge, arranged the dozen pieces with a single finger, lining the cracks and letters to read: Zeek realized he would need to go to the store.

So he settled for half a glass of water and went to bed.

Chapter 3

Everyone rested Sunday.

Chapter 4

Stff,

Pls s ttchmnt dtlng nw cmpny plcy cncrnng ml crrspndnc (https://www...).

Smmry dtld s fllws:
ll mls mst b rd r nt rd.
ll mls mst thr b
Sbst 1) Rpld
Sbst 2) Frwrdd
Sbst 3) Dltd
ll mls cnsdrd "lst" nw mntn vldty.

Flr r flr crrspndnc s nw cnsdrd cmmnctn nd mscmmnctn n rdr t prvd th hghst qlty n prdct srvcs. Ths nw gdlns nsr nfrmty vrll (frm tp dwn) nd strmln ll cmmnctn.

ls, pls rvw ttchmnt fr vrs lvl's schdld mtng tms.
Thnk y fry r tm nd ptnc drng ths trnstnl phs.

Ezekiel Douglas Macrae
Technical Task Point Managing Specialist
Multi-Unit Cross Personnel Overseer Technician
Level 6

Chapter 5

Zeek found more eggshells again in his keyboard, having lost count by now. He was two bites away from polishing off his second Sal's Counter (which Zeek and only Zeek called it, or at least he once assumed he was the only one who called it that, but obviously that wasn't the case, no fault of his own, which was just as well seeing as he'd given up justifications) High Country omelette, while listening to Sally's gracious reiterations for the umpteenth time to tell his friend thank you. "Another tip like that and it'd be Whykiki and rainbows for us." There was conviction in her chuckle as she topped off his coffee. Even after all the glorification he'd seen on screens, he still never understood the appeal of sand.

Personally, he was grateful that wasn't something he had to concern himself with. As in did that that refer to the friend or the sand? Didn't matter. And why should it while he was debating if there was time for a third omelette. Screw it. He'd make time, covering the binge by complimenting the chef.

"Glad to see you're feeling better."

"Me, too," he agreed, unaware he had previously not been feeling better.

The sun began its climb up the multicolored rungs into the sky. It was the perfect sort of morning cinematographers would capture to wax poetic in their cameras knowing full well the justice outlining heaven could not be properly served. Zeek kept his attention inside the diner, mainly on his plate and fork. He no longer tasted the food he packed into his face, but he ate anyway. Chock full and never better.

He paid at the counter, waved goodbye to Sal through the window, and with his brown leather briefcase headed off to the bus stop, leaving behind all the money he knew he had and even some he didn't.

An antemeridian haze absorbed the morning's song into its mist, where Zeek sat in silence on the corner of Alabaster and MacDade. A poster advertising Sweet Relief Organic Candies and Charitable Contributions "for those who need something sweet and something sweet for those in need" was on his right. To his left, an animated pelican's smashed face, flat and wide-eyed, onto the furthest reaches of its computer-generated world, which in this case was the poster. The titular BIRDS, bold and blocky, marked the edge, "Flocking This Summer!" The studio name scribbled over the R anticipated the neo-vaudevillian, family-sized romp as a strong contender in award season, which if true, would teeter Zeek's curiosity because there was no way it could be that good. Across the street, police tape was strung around the brick store, encompassing the car parked at an angle, and x-ed over the double glass doors. Zeek accidentally kicked over his briefcase.

The Grey Line Number 12 sauntered to the stop and opened its doors with a whimper. Zeek was positive the driver, hunched over the wheel, was asleep for sure, the route conditioned by repetition, the driver symbiotically one and the same with the bus and the line.

Zeek boarded up the steps, turned into the aisle, and inadvertently made eye contact with Don *Bronco in the back of the bus wearing the same plaid button down and gym shorts. Zeek broke it immediately, looking at the grated, rubber track at his feet, at the seats, out the window, anywhere and everywhere but. He settled into his seat in the middle of the bus and kept his attention forward. If Don Bronco wanted to ride the bus, Zeek had no authority to stop him. The transportation was public. So even if Zeek could feel Don Bronco's glare tousling the black hairs over his balding crown, he wasn't there to reaffirm the acknowledgement. They would never be strangers passing as friends. Strangers commute. Friends reminisce.*

He watched out the window and waited for The Bolster to come into view and couldn't help but imagine the lowbrow motel with the manual lock-n-key doors on the outside had holed up inside two jacket-less, suspender-clad detectives with their empty, inter-folded Chinese takeout boxes, one listening in to the tap, the other peeking through the sheer curtain at a plain woman in a one-piece at the pool, reminding him of his wife and remembering the strain of failures this job put on their marriage.

The bus slowed and jerked to a stop.

The doors opened with a whimper.

The morning habitual.

When the throat cleared behind him, Zeek didn't divert his attention from the window, and hinged his legs under his seat. The oversized bag dragged across his belly.

"What was that?" Ms. D tucked herself into the seat, wiggling and writhing, unnecessarily over-adjusting underneath the bag pulled up to her chin.

"I didn't say anything."

"Exactly. You always greet a lady with nothing less than a 'good morning.'"

"Even in the afternoon?"

"Or sometime there before."

The sun during its climb pulled with it a sky surprisingly blue for the hour. Outside the motel a neon pink followed a neon yellow highlighting a trajectory into the pool with two exceptionally horizontal splashes. Lo and behold, family fun. A mother yelling towards the water now that her magazine and bathing suit were dampened. A father fiddling with the plastic-strapped chair, fully dressed, and early-morning cigar wedged in his mouth. A cameraman strapped and rigged, steady and one with the camera, flowing invisible like a breeze around the family four pack. A lighting guy adjusting a stretched white tarp, softening the artificial light into the natural. A director in a ragged ball cap and under an umbrella pointing, pointing, pointing, pointing, a conductor for a symphony of action. Seeing first hand this idea of sun, this idea of fun, was better than Zeek imagined via the TV.

"That's the one true test to knowing what's real in this flipped sided world."

Zeek snapped back into the bus, saying "What's that?" like inhaling out of a dream. He had heard every word, but cognitively wasn't paying enough mind to delineate the pieces apart from the string of sound.

The bus jerked to a stop. Can't fault consistency.

"Precisely."

The narrowness of her astute eyes widened like a child's draining innocence, causing Zeek to question the precision of what he said.

"Hello, Dorothy."

The man in the burgundy jacket hunched over Zeek in the seat, smaller in the light, a tie dangling between the zipper, his untrimmed hair combed and set, his face freshly shaven, polished with aftershave, accentuating the loose lines hanging from his cheeks.

A small "You," cold like cracking ice, escaped with a breath from the otherwise silent Ms. D.

"May I?" He indicated Zeek's seat.

"You certainly may not," Ms. D said, also indicating Zeek's seat.

"But my stop?" Zeek forewarned its pending arrival.

"Never stop."

"Still must get to work."

"You don't need work. Living is work. Breathing is work. Keeping your ass planted to this seat is work."

Zeek pushed his weight up before the tension crushed him. He wanted to say sorry but didn't. The man in the burgundy jacket dammed him to the back of the bus and away from Ms. D's ladylike "coward."

With his stop looming but not loomed, he shuffled to the last row, the row with Don Bronco, and watched the pair reunite from a distance like the movies. His body overlapped comfortably where armrests should be. If not for Don Bronco, he'd consider making this spot his routine.

"What do you think they're saying?"

The man in the burgundy jacket's grayed head hung low, nodding, resilient to the pendulum of barraged words and physical silences.

"He's apologizing. She's not having it. They're both still madly in love. Emotions before actions."

"Typical," Zeek said before quietly finishing out his commute.

In the lobby of George Gilliam, that towering infrastructure where man's mind reached towards the heavens, an embodiment of bureaucratic greatness, effectually progressing efficiency as the epicenter for thoughts funneled into a single advancing transmitter, two men in paint-splattered jumpsuits were touching up the wall behind the lobby's main desk with beige rollers while a third, on a hinged ladder, pulled calligraphic letters with a steady hand. Storytelling is the salt of life. Persistence is the pep was as far as the scribbler had smoothly stroked.

And Zeek stood there, reading the line over and over as the man painted the second p.

"Excuse me." Zeek startled himself, unsure as to why he deemed it necessary to interrupt the man's work. But "It's hard work," corrected nevertheless.

"What's that, bub?" the man on the ladder asked although all three men stopped and looked at Zeek.

"It's hard work."

"Nah. This gig ain't too bad." The man on the ladder admired his handy work. "I've definitely had worse jobs, by and far. This one's all poise. And it's inside with the AC."

"I mean the quote. Hard work is the salt of life."

"Did Ryan send you? That asshole's always changing shit and not telling no one," he said like an accusation laced with an undertone of second-guessing himself as he snapped his fingers and pointed to a scrap of paper on the tarp-laid floor near their supplies. One of the roller men, splattered in a pollack of paint, picked it up and handed it to Zeek. "You can tell him it says what it says now and ain't going back."

With the same italicized calligraphy as emulated by the painter was the phrase on the wall followed by per – Donald Bronco *in blue ink.*

"My apologies." He handed the paper back and took the elevator six floors away from the lobby.

Zeek went to say "Good morning" to Matte (Dave and Zeek still adding the e because of his hungover flatline shine) but followed the good with a pause, not finishing the salutation as he headed into his office.

He tossed his brown briefcase under his desk and plopped into his Office Lounger 2970. He swiveled to his computer but looked around the room. The windows glided on the virtual stream across Dave's computer. Dave's picture perfect family smiled behind their frame. Zeek wasn't expecting Dave in today. Maybe tomorrow, but unlikely. It was not like he quit or anything. He existed somewhere out there in the world. He just wasn't ever showing up here.

But that was the way the story goes.

Zeek woke his computer to a record 254 emails and rested his fingers on the keys. However, the day's work was impaired at every other letter, the e, the a, the o, the i, and the u, when used, jammed like small stones across the board, refusing leeway in transferring the symbols to the screen. From his desk drawer, he pulled out his trusty scissors, the ones with the plastic pink loops too narrow for his fingers, and popped off the vowels to look for what he knew he'd find. Sure enough, five dime-sized, white flakes sat in the hollows of the keyboard, each with a tiny typed letter, in the same electronic typewriter font seen in the daily electronic messages, of the vowels it replaced.

He carefully placed the scissors back into the right-hand corner of the drawer and closed it with arched-back fingers, slow like quicksand into his desk. He leaned into the recline of his Office Lounger 2970, stretched his arms over his head, and checked the time. He had a meeting to attend no time soon with time to kill. So he forged ahead, with or without the letters, to make a dent in his workload routine.

Zeek found another eggshell during the inconsequential thus deleted meeting on the eighteenth floor, a conference with the board of cardboard cutouts, "talking" over one another, literally and figuratively, through a speaker in the ceiling but saying nothing but a static white-noise cacophony of blahs. Unencumbered by the use of vowels, the barrage of emails were answered faster than received. This stuffed Zeek like breakfast with an exhilarating freedom he'd never experienced. The letters, or the lack thereof, improved his own work's conformation within the demands of whatever the authoritarianism rote. Satisfaction was on the screen in front of him, the proof was on the page. He broke away from his computer and strolled giddy to the blank beige wall where a window would be, or should be, an illusion behind blinds draped from a fluorescent bulb. If there was anyone out there who would ever care to ask 1) why he'd never opened the blinds before? and 2) what compelled him to open them at this moment? Zeek would not have an answer. But he was compelled, so he pulled the cord. And as sure as it was day he saw the window newly installed. Like a screen showing the city in the highest of definitions. His eyes followed the street that lined his route, the cars flowing due north towards the heart of the city, and cars being pumped south. People zigged and zagged along sidewalks and across streets, some dressed as fit as the morning, jackets now off in the leisure of the afternoon, some dressed as plain as their neighbor, casually never leaving the city. And then there were the little packs of outsiders, those of the past ogling every ounce, every brick, every rundown wonderment and revitalization sprinkled with modernity and those of the future ignoring it all completely. He could see an old brick house renovated as a bakery. The delights of Maillard reacting and Joe brewing coaxed his view from his window to theirs. A visual wafting come hither he couldn't smell, of course, physically so far removed. But looking in, behind the arched nom de shoppe painted on the glass, sat Ms. D and the man in the burgundy jacket over two cups of coffee and a chocolate muffin, she looking pointed towards him, his eyes pointed towards the table, their toes pointing towards each other. Zeek's view from his sixth-story window then craned away over the buildings, sweeping the blocks and landing on the gray. The bus driver puttered and jerked from stop to stop, further hunched into sleep as the weariness of early-rising tires into the weariness of work. The bus passed the diner. Sal and Sally packed a suitcase into the trunk of their junker before slamming the door. Sal behind the wheel wasted no time peeling rubber onto Alabaster, the car's body rocking on the frame being slung from the parking lot, his hand on Sally's knee. The closed convenience store barricaded in yellow tape drew further into the distance and out of view as the window tracked with the car, maintaining pace until passing Zeek's apartment, where it panned to the shingled roof and through the round window into the lit loft. Dave and Shellie rolled off the floored mattress, their nude bodies taking the bed sheets and smears of paint with them on top a canvas. They bumped into the easel. Zeek's window exited through the skylight and continued westward past the

Marcatos until finding the unlit sign for Fellows where it looped again and craned towards the shambled apartments in a refurbished mill. Peeking through its oversized panel window into the shell of concrete walls and bare pipes, Maya adjusted the blue and gold marching hat on her brother's head, while he tugged at the strap under his chin, both laughing at something only funny between them and the moment. The window didn't stop, lifting the view up and over the ex-granary, over the overgrown lot of the ex-masonry, and around the steeple holding hands with Heaven, ending its defenestrated tour full circle as the view flowed into the towering high rise infrastructuring ideals for the world of the future today, and onto the sixth story where the secretary's muted brilliance was spinning a pen on his thumb at his desk with Zeek in deep focus through his office door, staring at the wall.

"Matte, can you come in here?"

"I haven't seen Dave," he called out without getting up.

Zeek didn't see Don Bronco.

Nor the motel.

"That's because he isn't here. But just, for a minute. I have a question."

He got up but stopped in the doorway. "The meeting's at 1:30."

"Also insignificant."

"Okay, then."

There was, in fact, a question Zeek wanted to ask, whether about his secretary's weekend extracurricular extravaganzas and what it was like to be someone real when not forced to be someone's other, to be an explosion, a now, an afterparty, to be that place he'd never climb because he was too afraid to fall off its high standard, or about philosophies on existence, the balance between what one has to do to survive versus what one has to do to live and finding out it might all be for naught, a figment within a loop, an idea outside and inside one's self simultaneously rearranging being and begin, or why he would want someone in the room with him just to be left alone as a means of challenging the comforts he so desired. However, Zeek didn't know how to question himself, so he didn't trouble with it. Instead, in no particular order, he: asked for the current time, replaced the blinds over the wall, relieved his secretary, and overhead a muttered "pretend us plastered."

Chapter 5

Zeek found another eggshell in the convenience store. This was after he found the note taped inside the glass door of Sal's Counter, that beloved diner setting not succumbing to a complete modern overhaul unintentionally laced with nostalgia where characters pass through, meeting to exchange information and inflate the plot:

"Closed until" (the until left blank) "Sorry for the inconvenience."

Management

Zeek cupped his face in his hands and peered past the sign. He eyed the counter where he should have been hunched over an omelette or quiche or other egg centric dish, his stomach rumbling with desire.

The morning was too early, if there was such a thing, the purple deepening and peeking into pink. So Zeek, also early, picked up his little brown briefcase and moseyed to the bus stop at the expense of his dissatisfied pangs.

Unnecessarily coinciding with the shift in routine, Zeek crossed Alabaster and MacDade, putting him on the corner in front of the convenience store bandaged in yellow tape. The small lot, a strip of asphalt between a brick wall and the sidewalk, now vacant, the compact that had sat angled gone, making the dusk a shade quieter. The lights through the glass mimicked the morning, a soft string along the far horizon produced by the upright beverage coolers in an otherwise lifeless darkness. The sign hung on the door read "Come in, we're OPEN." Zeek cupped his face in his hands and peered past the sign. The mise-en-

scene of the store looked less like a crime scene than assumed in reference to Cop Drama's hard-boiled realistic approach. In fact, it was more depressing and almost boring. He scanned the counter cluttered with candy, gum, scratch offs, and other uppers on the right, the end cap of muffins and other packaged baked goods on the left, and a scattered collage of items flung in between. Closest to the bathrooms marked "for customers only" was a small, plastic tent, a rushed 506.A scrawled across its yellow bracing face and centered on a brown stain. And as foreshadowed or predicted or anticipated, a piece of shell, more egg-sized than most, leaned against the peaked marker. He pressed into the glass door as if by doing so the words "ry I'm sorry" would enhance into legibility. They did not. But the door creaked open under pressure, slow and slight in its unpleasant moan. Zeek stepped back, looking around for witnesses to his crime. He left the door creaked. He knew enough not to leave prints. And instead, crossed the sleeping street slowly not to wake it, where he'd wait on the bench for the bus as if he was where he belonged the whole time.

Zeek pulled his already-stretched suit jacket taught over his frame trying to fend off the last bite of cold on the still morning. An unseen songbird cooed the sun, delighting in the chill. On his right hung a poster for Buy LoCal, a new mega-chain retail mart of local art and craft foods: "names we trust from a Name you trust, by locals Buy LoCal." The overly enthusiastic couple in the aisle of out-of-focus bottles, embracing, chic, modernity at its white teeth finest, were impervious to the marked-up prices of status. Zeek's mind, emaciated from hunger, swelled at the thought of artisanal cheeses, an item he was by no means a connoisseur of but rather a dilettantish admirer, as he was with the specifics of most foods. To his left, block letters demanding, "Don Bronco's (Working Title) Shell / a film(?) by Donald Ryan" were stacked all neat above the tagline, "The unfilmable page on screen," that was below three average-looking eggs, the most prominent, forefront one of which had a tauntingly small crack. Zeek rationally ignored this the best he could. If he didn't see it then it wouldn't exist. No matter whose name was attached. He'd never heard of Donald Ryan, despite his cinematic repertoire. And he didn't care to. The name didn't appeal to him. Neither did the film(?). He liked his stories straightforward. None of this utterly complete nonsense of slapping fragments together and calling it art. But whether old fashioned or neo traditional, right now he aligned with his appetite.

Which reminded him. Candy Bars. That's what he forgot. No going back now.

Cars began passing along Alabaster with more frequency. In the distance a faint tick-tick-ticking could be heard spliced between the sporadic hum of traffic. The bus would be arriving any minute.

And it did. Creeping from the vanishing point of the street's narrow horizon, The Grey Line Number 12 behind a muffled sludge of blue and gold, tat-tap-clink-clanking closer at a 4:4 rate. Zeek could feel the beat. The cymbals and snares ricocheted shockwaves in sizzles and bursts in every wayward direction through the air. The belting of bass drums and street/can/sign tappings reverberated vibrations from underfoot. The sonic "Inner Mid-Land Recreational All Drum Marching Band, Chapter 2AA, 'Can You Feel The Beats'" train rattled down the Alabaster track in a frenzy of step-stomp-shuffle-step underscoring the tick-tap-clash in a marched rhythm all its own.

Crammed between the sun and the sounds, the morning was no longer an abstract awaking. It was alive.

Zeek's stomach rumbled in measure.

Mixed into the penultimate players before The Grey Line caboose, Zeek recognized a single face peering from the mass of blue and gold hats whose blue and gold arms clapped together cymbals on every fourth step. Zeek broke eye contact immediately.

"Hey!" (two, three, four) "Yo!" (two, three, four)

Zeek studied the handle to his empty brown briefcase. A small crack in the leather was jagged and branched like lightning from the seam.

"Hey, man!" (two, three, four)

A pair of bulky, loose-laced skate shoes skimmed by the gold hem of blue pants stepped into his peripheral as he analyzed the shock he could grasp. Cymbals clashed, and Zeek's attention startled and shook with the reverb.

"Hi," Zeek yelled over the drums.

"I thought that was you." The drummer, the one from the band the other night, was beaming down at

him behind the two gold metal disks. He continued marching in place.

The bus rolled to a stop behind him. Undoubtedly, the driver was somehow asleep through the noise.

"This is my bus." Zeek pointed as if there was another.

"Right on," the drummer said like he was riding one of the sound waves exploding across the morning. He slammed the disks together in punctuation and regrouped, leaving Zeek to board.

Zeek chose the first in the row of bench seats flanked against the wall closest to the door.

The bus, without rush, caught up to the band march-march-marching onward, down Henry and up Jones.

Zeek found the last, in terms of this narrative, piece of eggshell under the water. He watched the drummer through the large, unobstructed windshield dance in step with his pack, playing his instrument with a delighted fervor, his entire body producing the resonating clash. As the bus came to a crawled stop, the drummer spun into the grooved step. Zeek's eyes met his spirited gaze through the glass. Now, at this nanosecond of retinal convergence Zeek could have potentially witnessed a miracle in the exuberance radiating from the drummer, the essential self-exploding essence, and the tangible aura, the literal denotation, of what it means to be actualized and those fleeting moments to savor. However, Zeek was too hungry to notice.

Who, honestly, would have known if he'd snuck into that convenience store?

The door next to him folded open with a whimper.

"Get off the bus," resounded in a soft echo from the back. But other than the driver, no one else was on board. His pangs sounded like Don Bronco, and Zeek was in no mood for that discomfort. So that was that. He stood up and brushed his hands down the belly of his tucked-in shirt as if wiping off nonexistent crumbs.

But.

But.

But.

But.

But.

Dammit, but now what?

The exit down the steps was blocked by Ms. D's struggled climb aided by the director like they were connected tin toy mountaineers relevant in their day.

She braced herself upward on the final rung and stood before Zeek no higher than his tie. "I've got a bone to pick with you." She wagged her finger into his shirt buttons, playful like controlling an unruly yo-yo, but her clear eyes clearly dominating.

"That's alright." He sucked in his stomach, with more gusto than ever before, and in some gut-busting miracle of the physics of not breaking fast he managed to squeeze down the stairs without crumpling the wrinkled woman. But for every newton there's an equally opposite newton, for getting off the bus couldn't be that easy, so Zeek stepped out and into burgundy-coated arms. He froze. The director

squeezed. So, like any other law in the natural world named after man, Zeek broke free and followed the band. Forward progression in motion.

The parade marched up Indiana Ave. in what could be considered the worst recorded cavalcade, the banner followed by the drummers followed by Zeek followed by the bus, in the long-running history of promenades. And if that wasn't awful enough, there was the noise. The noise. This couldn't be the only way to work? In all the noise. Cluttered and clanked. But this was it, the only route to go. The drummer slowed, forcing Zeek's trudge to catch up. He clashed into the din (two, three, four) leaving more ringing through Zeek's ears than the city. He attempted to drain the shrill, shaking out the hum like swimmer's ear, but to no avail. The pitch was already resounding from lobe to lobe in a pendulum that must slow its own inertia. The director waved from the front of the bus. Visual clamor. Inundated clash-a-lashing.

"I've never" (¡TsHh! two, three, four) "felt" (¡TsHh! two, three, four) "more" (¡TsHh! two, three, four) "alive," (¡TsHh! two, three, four) the drummer yelled skyward, an eruption of graciousness spouting from his cheek bursting smile. He spun again in step.

Zeek palmed one ear, but the other had to be pressed against his briefcase resting on his shoulder. This, however, didn't block the sound he was drowning in, but muffled it like through water.

The Bolster, the last true slice of a dying Americana, was ahead, the destination the lead marchers veered towards. A feeling of exhilaration and *hesitation washed over Zeek. The banner holders opened and held the gate creating their blue and gold walled dam. Zeek saw the fun-in-the-sun mother and children watching, huddled on the second-story balcony. The crew huddled with their equipment on the first.*

"Roll camera," propelled a voice through a cone, annunciating the words like it was 1939. "Someone get the family on set. Now."

Zeek, currently, stayed with the flow onto the sidewalk.

The Grey Line Number 12 lumbered on its path behind him.

Ahead he could see drummers splashing into the pool, one by one, instruments and all, into the chlorinated water.

"What's the point of all this?" Zeek either asked himself or the drummer, caught in the undertow.

The father showed up behind his family eating an early-morning hot dog.

"Chaos in cadence," ¡TsHh! two, three, splash.

Zeek toed the stucco edge of the pool.

Snares and bassists splashed their sticks and mallets on the water's surface. Cymbalist paddled below.

"Keep rolling," propelled like it was 1940.

Don Bronco opened a door on the bottom floor.

"Cut, cut, Cut, cut, Cut," like 1941.

Zeek stopped.

"Who does this guy think he is?"

"Zeek!?"

"Get him out of here. Now."

"Ezekiel," he said low and to the water. Beneath the waves of sloshing percussionists Zeek saw an eggshell vacuumed by the drain but saved by the grate. He placed his brown briefcase at his feet, slightly over the pocked, non-slip edge.

Chapter 5

Zeek found the remote control in the crook of his Plushback. He had forgone going for breakfast at the dip and jive sort of dive, hip in its pastiche of then, that fond bygone era of hanging in diners, slipping quarters in the juke, falling in love, the jingle-jangle of the door only open in the fondness of zeitgeists, reruns, and the way things should be remembered. This automatically by deduction meant foregoing putting on pants, taking the bus, and going to work. But Zeek didn't seem to mind and didn't know anyone who would. His UXHD microplasma cored 77" Kyoshiri enjoyed the company.

But he'd be lying if he didn't admit he really wanted an omelette.

Zeek clicked from channel to channel in careless wander, navigating the seated exploration of linear time travel. Laze-eyed and feet propped in an upright and locked position, the channel roulette eventually flipped onto a little girl's laughter accentuated by bright streaks of pink and yellow and a blonde mother in her blue, white-dotted one-piece bathing suit in the sun next to the splash-happy bodies. "Why settle for this?" the voiceover asked cued by the cut to the family disappointed, children deflating into their neon floaties, the mother not removing her face-sized sunglasses, the father open-mouth chewing a third of his hot dog. Zeek watched their displeasure from the camera tucked into the far corner, the one the family wasn't quite facing, the shot hovering over ruffled sheets and around a box TV's antiquated jagged rainbow static. Zeek paused the commercial. He sat up in his seat, compressing the ottoman into the fold under the Plushback, and leaned towards the 77" screen while squinting as if it would enhance the image. He replayed the previous five seconds. "Why settle for this?" The children deflated into their floaties, the mother wore her sunglasses, the father masticated the mouthful of hot dog. The Plushback tilted forward under the weight of Zeek's examination. "Why settle for this?" The box television replayed its multicolored jazz. He split his focus, first out the still open door, across the open walkway, through the railing posts, and into the pool crowded with blues and golds. "Why settle for this?" Second through the sheer curtain and between the posts, to the mustached face and balding head, dropping below the screen, out of view from the window, and presumably into the water. "Why settle for this?" He watched it again. "Why settle for this?" And again.

He leaned his chair back into self-satisfaction. "Why settle for this?" He watched it once more for good measure. He'd never been on television before. Even considering his harmonious bond with the screen, the idea of appearing on it never crossed his mind. But now, seeing it to believe it, he was briefly keen to the idea.

The moment passed with the commercial break over and The Show coming back on.

JESSICA

No, Kenneth, it's no longer about the show. It's about us.

KENNETH
Baby. It's always been about The Show.

Zeek had seen every episode, considering how it was one of the nation's top-rated series in both basic and premium demographics, and knew Kenneth, the strong-jawed shortstop from Chicago transported to the south via the Biloxi Wildcards, who became entangled, amongst other plots, with Jessica and her Casino and Resort rich father, Barron "Bulldog" Stampede, was about to slam the door as he leaves Jessica's beachfront high-rise.

KENNETH slams the door, leaving JESSICA alone in her luxurious suite apartment overlooking the ocean.

CUT TO:

Match on action. ALEX enters into BURROWS' apartment. Nothing snazzy. Bachelor pad. ALEX is dressed to the nines. BURROWS is at the stove, cooking in the nude, buttocks exposed.

ALEX
This. This is why I shouldn't have accepted the key.

BURROWS
You don't like?

BURROWS turns and playfully dangles his penis towards ALEX offscreen.

This being the syndicated, basic-cable rerun, the scene panned-and-scanned out Burrows swinging his bat.

ALEX

Not at the moment. Aren't you the least bit worried about burning your dick? What if it pops?

[Over-exaggerated expression.]

He hears a POP, faint like in the distance.

BURROWS

That's what makes this the last truly great American extreme sport. Omelette?

BURROWS turns back to the range.

"Can't. Running late," Zeek voiced over.

ALEX

Can't. Running late. I just came by to drop these off.

Zeek would have taken one, he had time, but instead stuck to the way it had to be, the previously pre-viewed, ever unchanging script, "Sausage, then?"

ALEX tosses a manila envelope on the counter.

BURROWS
(Coy)
Sausage, then?

ALEX
I'm not one for breakfast when there's eggshell on the platter.

Oh, look. Another eggshell.

ALEX
(Con'd)
Four o'clock.

ALEX spins out the door, flipping her hair, amping the sex. Lascivious. The door shuts.

BURROWS
(To himself, alone)
Four o'clock.

BURROWS looks down and brushes something off himself offscreen.

This time as originally shown, edits unnecessary.

Zeek shifted in his seat behind a smile, feet propped and spirits lifted. This was the episode where Barron "Bulldog" Stampede finds a drunk Kenneth knuckle-deep before noon in the dayshift hostess of one of his multiple dining establishments, who moonlights as an aspiring showgirl at one of ex-league CEO and

Stampede's forever rival, Foster Malone's, legal-only-on-paper business ventures, while across town Alex discovers she accidentally dropped off the wrong envelope, the one with sonogram photos, and her attempt at getting them back before Burrows finds them. She wanted to tell him, personally, not like that, not until the season finale. It wasn't the best episode in the series, more filler/less substance, but it did manage to seamlessly blend staunch melodrama with situational comedy to fill the order.

So he decided to stay awhile, slipping the remote back into the crook of his Plushback.

Where he then found twenty dollars. Then he caught on fire.

Notes

D.B.

N 20__

Found a piece of eggshell in the omelet Matt made. He was for sure bored or stoned, usually never cooking food he didn't have to unless he was one or the other or both. But he made two. Either way, got one.

--> When your work friend is the KM.

I was tasked with grinding meat, bulking up for the weekend. Instead, I was dogging his carelessness, chomping around the bit.

#

Side Note: Grinding meat is undoubtedly my favorite paid activity in a I find it fascinating and chill to stuff meat into a tube and watch it come out in a playdough kind of way, that is until some silver wraps around the blade and ruins your day, hindering the flow and wasting your time in the disassembly and reassembly of the headway being made.

#

"You losing your culinary boner, top chef?"

"A little shell never hurt nobody."

#

The General Rules: Don't start a story with the character waking up. Write what you know.

But what if you can't sleep so instead of just laying there staring at the ceiling fan and missing her you remove the stained sheet to have your apocalypse now and rise at some absurd anti-sun hour? Is that too early for in media res?

I don't think it would honestly make much of a difference.

Because I came here to write but got stuck in media nowhere.

--> Upending everything to no new beginning.

Plus there's not and never will be a ceiling fan in a motel room.

--> No matter how cheap the rate.

#

I decide to get breakfast at that little joint across town she likes so much. The place is pretty much empty at the hour so obviously she's not there. Then again, why would she be? (See: what was I expecting?)

The diner has that sitcom set vibe, where it feels the same as any other diner yet unique unto itself. Homely like decades before, everything polished and in place: waitress in an apron over her light blue dress, dishes stacked and rowed behind the counter, a tile floor so white reflecting the fluorescents and confusing the hour. The only thing missing would be the jukebox.

--> For sights, not sounds.

When the waitress comes over to refill my coffee, I put down my copy of *C.o.D.* for cordialities. She smiles, shining that type of pretty that won't fade, and asks if I was sure I didn't want to order anything else. I have a weak definition of breakfast.

Before she puts the pot away she takes it to the other lone customer. The jackpot. Slovenly. Concentric balding. Suit hugging him so tight while he hung off the stool. I watch him shovel food into his mustache.

Folks, I think we have our winner.

#

I asked the waitress about him. Nothing worth noting. Just some guy who's been showing up most mornings lately but still gets her name wrong. She "stopped correcting" him because "with the way he tips I'll answer to anything."

#

I split my time between early cups of coffee at the diner and staring, staring, staring, staring at the pages before me, watching for the screen to fill itself.

This pattern persists without the fruit of thy labor.

Nothing, said the story so far.

"He pays at the counter like always and picks up his brown leather briefcase." Enthralling.

He leaves so I leave and tail him to the unlucky corner of Alabaster and MacDade. No better place to be for worse. When he crosses to the bus stop I continue straight along the convenience store. A. Tony hasn't opened for the day. Which is just as well. I won't enter. I've been there, done that, know better.

#

Side Note: This stop's on what line?

#

Donald Ryan (I know, what are the chances of two guys with the same embarrassing, what could possibly make it worse?, anatidae name, who claim to be writers, working in the same restaurant, who would still be strangers if I hadn't come across a story he'd written about chickens, "I thought that name seemed familiar," when I was reading through a lit mag looking for a right fit.

--> True story

At least he has the right idea bartending. That's where the money is. But I'm sure as a shot not a people person) asked if I'd read his story.

I lied.

Why?

Because it's better than what I do.

And I'm mostly not ready to verbalize my own failure.

I apologized the normal bullshit, sorry man, been busy, time snuck out from under me, lie lie lie. He wanted someone (see: me, specifically) to give it a look-see before sending it out into the world. "These days it's not every day you cross paths with a fellow writer. Or at least a real one." But he's got nothing to worry about. See: he's published.

#

He also says short stories are "what's up," his words, not mine. You're in. You're out. "On point and on to the next one."

#

The bus, otherwise officially City Transit Commuter Grey Line Number 12's, route according to the posted transit authority map and current first-hand experience:

(Starting with his stop)
Alabaster
Henry
Jones
Indiana Ave.
Farmers Ave.
Farmers Blvd.
Barnard
Sanfran

#

The bus stops in front of the convenience store.
--> Which means I've been on one rotation.

--> Which means I've had enough time to finish *C.o.D.* under the faint lights the color of smoke stain.

--> Which means I'm feeling employed with the tooles to get the job done (see: inspiration).

I skipped the diner this morning and headed straight to his bus stop while I knew he wasn't there.

Turns out, the bus passes behind my low-rate, one-room home between homes.

I devise the plan for the next go-round. To be asleep when he gets on. But don't snore. Nothing's more inconspicuous than someone quietly sleeping. Might even aesthetically stick my hand down the front of my shorts. For veracity: can't count how many times I've seen that trip on public transport. It should really punch the ticket.

#

A retrospect.

Maybe a Kennedy, ahead of his time, isn't the best inspiration for making it?

#

The bus rocked me like a cradle.

I wake to see him getting off at a nondescript highly fenestrated high rise.

Of course he does, I yawn.

-->Content to finish my nap.

#

"A writer is a world
trapped in a person"
—V. Hugo,
not a laughing man,
by order of the king.

#

Side Note: Things I've learned thus far this week include our mustached protagonist doesn't work weekends like some of us, so that's now good to know, I think I'm now considered a regular at the diner and still have yet to order anything more than coffee, which is mediocre at best, and Michelle will only talk to me at work, and even then, if our shifts just so happen to miraculously coincide, which like other miracles is a rarity.

#

The Pelican House (lovingly: The P. Hole) takes pride in their fancypants plates in a casual atmosphere. "Mi casa es our guests' casa, so let's make them feel at casa." Dave. Dipshit. All-American G.M. who dresses like a mafia lackey out of his element at a beach resort, gold chain on his bear as in hairy chest, F.O.H.-approved Hawaiian shirt wide open at the collar and tucked tight into his khakis to really accentuate that belly.

Wonder: Does he know he's his own caricature?

"Is this how you'd treat a guest at your casa?"

Well, seeing how I'm staying in a motel, hip-hip-hooray for day shifts with Dave.

Bartender Donald, Ryan, made an offhand comment about quitting his job to focus on "the writing thing."

--> Take luck, dying breed.

--> Try grinding meat.

#

Matt no called no showed. He's the only person I've ever known that can pull this off every couple of months, showing up the next shift like nothing. He never gives an excuse, just an "oh damn, my bad."

So I got volunteered for the night shift.

Another fine day at The P Hole.

#

A list of things I should do, it being my only day off:

1. Not be awake at the pitch black buttcrack of dawn.
2. Since I am already up, wake and bake, minor technicality: no flower.
3. Watch what I can of a film on the jacked-up TV.
4. Meditate (see: think I'll take a nap but end up just laying there).

5. However, that might take a turn to her: don't think about her.
6. Read.
7. Even God took a day off.

#

But I'm not God, so I'm headed to the diner.

#

"Honestly I swear
glasses,"
said Honest Lee.

#

I'm here before him or seemingly anyone else.

The place smells like the coffee brewing.

Before I even settle into the booth, the waitress brings me a cup. She's also holding a plate.

"These were made by accident, and they aren't going to sell. There's nothing wrong with them. They're just cold and yours if you want them."

She slides French toast in front of me.

Lucky day to treat myself.

"Let me go get you the syrup."

#

Ultracrepidate, because what better way to slip on the day than beyond the sandal?

#

He arrived as I finished the toast (compliments to the chef), looking beautifully disheveled this morning.

--> Is his hair gelled or sweaty?

I watch him cram wideload bites of omelet into his gullet. Each bite stretching that mustache further around. It's almost an art form the way he packs it in. Makes me look like an apprentice in a craft I'll never master.

And then it happens.

He finds an eggshell in his food.

It's subtle, the first piece in place. The incubated breakthrough.

Using his fork he moves it to the edge of his plate. Doesn't say a word.

Pays. Leaves.

I slam whatever odd bill and loose change on the table. Don't count. Just slam.

I must book it like a backstory away from where he's heading. See, I know where he'll be, and trust me, that's where I'll find him.

I am the background.

#

I barely make it, but I make it. Catch your breath.

I'm sprawled across the back seat. Catch your breath.

The bus crosses over MacDade. Catch your breath.

So I shove my hand under the band of my shorts. Caught.

He steps into the bus.

#

He gets off at The Fenestrated, which looks about as optimistic as 1984 meets Brazil, after a completely mundane bus ride.

--> To expect so much more or to expect so much more?

Admittedly, not the best start but it's where I'm at now. Stuck circling the excitement of new vs. the incitement of new. So get comfy. Cozy up. Because this back seat is my new office for the day. Ride this thing out to the end.

--> Of the day, at least.

#

Basic Italian Loaf Buns in Grams

La Spagna:
2250 Flour
2250 Water
23 Yeast

L'Impasto:
4500 Flour
2970 Water
45 Yeast

180 Salt
180 Sugar
Tutta la spagna
Mix, Fold, Proof, Fold, Proof, Fold, Proof, Cut, Proof,
Bake

YLD: about 56 ciabattas
(or focaccia, depending on technique.
The ol' P Hole chooses
ciabattas for their burgers.
So a big shout out thumbs up
to whoever thought rolling out 200+ buns a day
was the most efficient use of time.
For flavor, they say,
quality and quantity.)

#

Side Note: I dozed off, for real, on the bus, but woke to the sound of a woman either laughing or crying, which sounds completely synonymous when muffled.

#

Now I'm awake I'm as unproductive as ever, losing count of the times my little spot off Indiana has passed.
--> There it goes again.

#

Character Development:

Is not stalking.

Is discovering an unsuspecting friend.

Is learning said friend gets off work at 5, which isn't out of the ordinary for ordinary folk.

Is happening to get off at the same stop you decided to get off in order to inconspicuously follow him to his historic house turned apartment, conveniently by the Mercato's not far from Michelle's.

Is casually passing his apartment as if heading for the supermarket department store, where you run in and, out of all the everyday low price options, choose a Candy Bar for dinner because it suits your bank balanced lifestyle.

Is making that trek across town to the room and calling it a day in front of that busted box television.

#

Terebi is the Anglicized Japanese word for "television," which oddly enough isn't a play on words considering the terrible quality of the box, as in both physical construction of the set and the on-screen clarity. Terebi was based out of Plankford, Idaho. Terebi's founder and only company president, Thom Davis, thought a foreign name would draw more customers. Terebi filed bankruptcy in the mid 90s, less than two years after startup. Terebis, even when in pristine condition unlike the scrambled and fried one I'm in front of, still look like an uncalibrated VCR playing an unwound VHS. Because remember those?

Well so did the competition. So if kyo is Japanese for "big" and shiri is Japanese for "bottom" then effectively together a 70+" screen of optimal picture clarity as if eavesdropping through a window of space and time is a bigass TV. But that little fun fact isn't useful at the moment. Our (see: my) Kyoshiri knows a home on Michelle's wall. So I'm stuck with the prorated terrible.

#

D 20__

#

I can't f-ing stand dream sequences.

Unless you're an 80-year-old Kurosawa or it's absolutely integral to the plot, get off Elm Street.

--> More oft than not they're just thrown in to turn something short and awful into something long and worse.

--> Sleep is a waste of time for those who can't (see: those that can do).

#

That being said, I must have fell asleep in front of the TV because somewhere between what I remember and waking up in a panic I was standing on a farm. It was beautiful. Picturesque really, like I was standing in a screen painting. There were pointed snowcaps in the background. Cherry blossoms in the mid. The sun was shining while it rained, yet dream logically I stayed dry.

It was that type of place I'd never been, but I thought I'd be alright if I never left.

"Why settle for this?" a voice boomed from the heavens, in a language like lightning I didn't speak but somehow understood.

The rain fell at a consistent rate, but the sound picked up-pa-pup-pa-pup. Puddles accumulated in the roving grassy plain. Splashing and rat-ta-ta-tattles...

#

"I can't."

#

I wake propped against the wall, sitting erect, pillow in my lap. My neck is cricked. Tiny beads of sweat line my hairline.

Splashing and rat-ta-ta-tattles pour out from the Terebi.

"Picturesque Farms insurance."

What time is it? Half past still K.O'd.

I've slept through the most important meal of the day.

-->Procrasthole.

"If life was this perfect, you wouldn't need us. Why settle?" overlaid a drum line jingle.

I slam the door, the final note.

#

I make it to the bus stop in time to see the bus turning onto Farmers Ave.

In theory, if I cut down the alleys and book it down Jones, I'll hopefully hit the stop on Barnard.

But right now I'm not so concerned about the map. The map will get me wherever I need to be. Being out of shape and in sandals won't.

I need a diversion, a merciful act of creative freedom.

Pant, clop, pant.

It's either a flat or failure.

Clop, pant, clop.

But breaking down now means we'll all be getting nowhere.

Pant, clop, pant, pant, clop.

Find your rhythm.

Pant, pant, clop, pant, clop-a-top-top.

Slow it down.

--> Don't stop.

#

"Out of all the ideas
in all the minds in the world,
this one marches into mine,
like Williams' infatuation with springtime."

#

The embodiment of lassitude is sprawled across the back seat, drenched like warm soup, gulping too many breaths, now stuck listening to an all drum marching band. Can you feel the beats? Genius in the air. So fresh the whole bus can literally smell it.

--> A treat for the senses.

#

Briefcase in hand he gets on the bus. Same middle, aisle seat.

I pretend I'm asleep, but fool me once no matter how exhausted I am.

The prattling and the rattling and the tattling won't cease.

Most men lead quiet desperation. But my cacophonic 4:4 measures are about to beat me to death.

Pounding. Pounding. Pounding.

He seems unperturbed.

The motel is coming up full circle.

I could get off, sure. Waste more of the day. At least that would be consistent.

Or:

I could drown out the noise.

Option or.

The band veers off the road towards the motel. One by one, one after the other, they march themselves, hats, coats, skins, and all into the pool. If I could see it it would be a sight. Wonderfully muted and fascinatingly dramatic in its simplicity.

He rubbernecks but nothing more. An iota of the purest curiosity.

The bus drives away, keeping this show on the road.

#

Side Note: Don't do that again.

#

Back to reality, our regularly scheduled events, the featured presentation.

Her name is Dolores Fry. She's old enough to be a grandmother, although as far as I know she isn't. Under the wrinkles and age you can tell she was once quite pretty before her time, back then more aligned with the current standards of beauty. She sounds like Katherine Hepburn in cadence but Bette Davis in tone. Her eyes cut like Lauren Bacall.

She's a collage of idols in their golden years.

But what does this have to do with anything?

She's about to strike up a conversation.

--> Welcome aboard.

#

Ezekiel.

Isn't that just a bit overtly literary? Biblical? Like the name itself carries more weight than the character?

No pressure.

#

And their conversation! Thrilling to the max! A true mark of literature and craft!

--> No wonder I feign sleep.

#

"Any more legit
and I'd have to quit."

#

A Brief History of Theodor Dupox
(As recalled from last night's scrambled
rerun of E&ME's Lost Inventors.)
Born in 1923 in Branebridge, Ohio
to T. Matthews Dupox (a bank clerk)
and Shelby Madison Fortswaller Dupox.
Around 1935, Dupox family moved to
Biloxi, Mississippi.
T. Matthews worked as mate on a shrimp boat
(developing a secret passion for the sea).
T. Jr. peeled shrimp on shore, penny a pound
(this his first contact with a hydraulic foot pump,
a prototype for motorized conveyor belts).
As a boy he would steal salt and pepper shakers
for his mother.
His mother was a handsome woman, strong and tough
and loving, raised right by her father,
raising her son right.
Except for the seasonings.
She never asked.

He never answered.
After his father passed at sea
(a heart attack while shrimping,
it was T. Jr.'s 16th birthday),
he worked his way up from the factory
to Pelicano's Italiano Ristorante del Mare,
starting work for "Mr. Pelicano" (a 6'6"
Irishman with a yank accent that
bit through the region's southern drawl),
first as the fastest shrimp shucker in town,
to entremetier over pasta,
to poissonnier over proteins,
to an unofficial chef de cuisine and chief of the kitchen.
Mr. P took a liking to T. Jr. citing his hard work and persistence,
traits T. Jr. credited to his mother for instilling.
Mr. Pelicanos died in 1955
(on T. Jr.'s 32nd birthday).
In his will he was left the restaurant.
By 1962, Pelicano's was renowned,
greatly in part by the boom of tourism,
and its Swordfish Sicilliani,
a cracked black pepper and orange crusted fish over risotto,
a loose interpretation inspired by his mother's love of strong seasonings and Florida oranges.
She died on his 39th birthday of that year.
To meet the high demand for a labor-intensive dish,
T. Jr. came up with a mechanical mill and zester,
powered by a pump charging an internal circuit,
an idea based around his habitual foot-tapping from

his days on the docks.
Revolutionizing technical speed and quality of freshness,
it became an industry standard until 1971
when Jon D. Russel patented a true, cordless, battery-powered mill,
and the Kennedy Kitchen Tool Co. did the same with the zester
in 1973.
However, Theodor Matthews Dupox, Jr. is still regarded as the father
of the handheld electric appliance.
He died in 1988 on the 65th anniversary of moving to Biloxi, Mississippi.

#

There are two types of people: those who think there's such a thing as too early and those who realize it's never too late [for pizza].

--> Pelican Pizza's first and longest running slogan, as opposed to their new "Pizza, consistently the best idea."

#

Book today as a bust of time and effort.
I'll start anew tomorrow.
For the night shift is nigh.

#

The Basic P. Hole Patty
Grind beef
10 lbs lean trim
2 lbs fatty trim

¼ C garlic, minced & sweated
½ C shallot, minced & sweated
10 eggs, binder
¾ C Worcestershire, if nothing else definitely add this
1 T pepper
2 T salt

Ring mold 7.5 ounces,
and old industry technicality:
once on the bun with accouterments
can still be marketed as ½ lb burger.

YLD: 25 patties or so
(depending on the accuracy of measurements)

#

I'm getting careless in my two-handed cracking skills.

Found a decent-sized shell while pattying patties.

Better me than the guest.

--> Not for the guest's sake.

I don't want to have to hear Dave drone on and on about "the customer is not your enemy," or "we put the pel-I-can in perfection," or some other attempt at wit followed by the oh-so-motivational chop-chop handclap.

--> Some people find their calling.

#

The shift was a rare sort.

Ryan mentioned in passing something he's working on.

-->Generally, he's quite tight-lipped when it comes to his projects.

Said something about creativity being its own implicit narrative. Said it's part of the process. Give him time "to polish shit into gold." A true alchemist.

Things he says aren't always practical, but sometimes you pick up tids and bits.

--> But as long as it makes sense to him, at the end of the day, we'll see...

#

"If mine is the jam
then yours is the jelly."

#

2:

Ryan claimed *Pnin* was Nobokov's greatest novel, which is fine and all except he's wrong. The obvious victor is *Pale Fire*.

He cited structure, how the character doesn't change, instead the settings change "the reader's perceptions and shit" of Pnin in environments. He's "the same dude reacting true to form based on where he's at in the world around him. One causes the other. It's the sincerest representation of the human element, holding true to anyone wherever they are."

I countered with but if you want structure then a narrative weaved through an academic text, a novel without novel elements, composed of an introduction, a poem, and commentary is the sincerest representation of pure storytelling. The structure is and of itself inherent to the human element.

Pnin has a solid foundation, true, but *Pale Fire* is the impenetrable fortress.

The friendly discourse went unmediated,

Like arguing in your own head, outside insight couldn't be sought. No one at The P. Hole had the vaguest notion of what we were going on about.

"Fucking nerds, lol. Southwest chicken walking in."

#

3:

Michelle said she wanted to meet for lunch tomorrow. Citing something about closure.

--> I was in no open position to say no.

#

The room is dark except for the flickers of the screen. The volume is turned to zero. The conditioning unit hums a one-note melody.

Near dark. Near quiet.

--> Symbols, rituals and preferences.

I go over chapter one.

The first line I can handle.

It's everything after that needs revision. A fine tune of focus.

--> There's actions but no reactions.

The bed is a mess. I took the Do Not Disturb from the door, but I guess I've been pulled from the rotation.

Reminder: Get towels from front desk.

If that's where towels are from.

Is that where towels are from?

I hack away at my missed inspiration, go over my notes, rearrange words then arrange them back the way I found them.

Am I more surprised by the recurrence of eggshells than he is?

Answer: Questions with questions.

If this is the process then what is the problem?

If this isn't problematic then who is the character?

If I don't know the whys then does what happens lack reason?

There's a watercolor bolted to the wall above the desk, simple and kitsch, an element ideal in the environment. Stupidly soothing. There's a tiny red rowboat empty on a sandy cove, high grasses in the foreground, maybe a lighthouse in the back, behind two layers of matte boarding before the frame.

Still, something is obviously missing which keeps it locked away in a motel room away from the mystical realms of greatness (transcendentally, symbolically, unfathomably).

Speaking of Matt, he posed the question: What if it's not five times fast as in phrase, phrase, phrase, phrase, phrase, but five Xs fast as in phrase multiplied by a speed of five?

I'm not sure if high or not.

He also went on about some movie I should write: Throwback to when late night comedies had a budget and effort, clichés and tropes and plotless nudity smothered in quick-witted dialogue, spoof without the gimmicks, keeping the word movie out of the title. "Every generation suffers, man. All the classics seem to come out before you're born."

"And what's this grand pitch?"

"I haven't got that far."

"That's not very fleshed out."

"That's why you're the writer. I'm just the idea guy."

"We're all just the idea guy."

"Then write what you know, man. Do it about us. It's not like we take ourselves seriously. We work here."

#

The jagged lines of color remind me of an old screensaver.

#

J 20__

#

It's early.

--> When else would it be?

Someone on the television is scrambling eggs. A simple enough cooking segment for those antemeridian hours not sleeping.

Everything cooked on this TV is scrambled.

Did I remind myself to get towels?

I go over the changes made. Reread what's been rewritten.

(Don't quote me:) "Nobody's ever had to change anything they've got up in the middle of the night to write – S. Bellow."

This needs not apply to things read written the night before.

Back to the diner, then the illusion of truth.

#

I'm as lost as the morning hidden within the haze.

I keep my nose buried.

If there's structure on paper then what's on these pages?

I read somewhere the color blue calms the brain and opens channels of creativity.

The waitress comes over. I order two cups of coffee (heavy sugar, no cream, bittersweet) to flood the gates.

I explain to her I'm a detective of sorts doing research of sorts for a venture of sorts.

She says don't you mean case.

I say *Cop Drama* doesn't set the bar for law school television.

She says do I have a badge.

I say, again, it's not that line of detecting.

She says this would explain the sudden frequency of visits.

I lay an extra fifty on top of the tab and tip to hide me behind the counter.

She says she's sure that's illegal.

I say at best it's ill-advised but not illegal.

She says if the health department walks in I better start cleaning. "They are due any day."

#

I'm curled under a hand sink, braced on the piping.

This one needed some refinement before follow through, sure.

--> Remember: all ideas aren't worthy ideas.

But he's already at the counter, ordered, and eating. Does something that requires old world advice and baking soda passed down through the generations.

--> Another unmoving richter on the emotional scale.

"Sally." (Sally he says?) "Have you guys had any problems with eggshells?"

But even the dumbest ideas might pan out a nugget.

"You find some in your toast? I'm always telling Sal, 'You've got to be more careful,' but he can be so blasé, always saying things like, 'A little shell never hurt nobody.' But you're loyal and Sal's lazy, so breakfast is on us."

"No, no. I mean..."

Keep meaning.

"No, no. I insist."

Desist.

"I mean shells in general. Like in Candy Bars or in napkins."

"I'm not following you."

But do follow.

"I don't either."

"How about I get you some more coffee?"

Aaaaand scene. I wait for them to banter this out.

(See: I'm done.)

#

"Even realism is manipulated."
—DiSica

#

He leaves.

I keep my end of the bargain.

(I'm a man of my words, for they're all I've got.)

I throw in a bit extra for his meal.

(In a way I feel responsible.)

I race up the street.

At some undesignated point in time and space between the run's accelerated heart pump blood flow oxygen to the brain and the just barely catching the bus it hits me.

Martin Hearty.

The cook at the diner, with the salt and pepper sideburns clipped tight above the manly, better-with-age jawline underscoring the unmistakable black mustache.

He looks like Martin Hearty.

(Or Martin Hearty looks like him.)

(Or Martin Hearty is researching a role as a short order cook.)

(But let's not get hopes up ahead of ourselves.)

#

Things I know about Martin Hearty:

(Based majorly in part on a good morning talk show's segment celebrating his 60-aught birthday and introducing his appearance on the show to promote the network's returning season of *Cop Drama*.

--> Possibly a repeat airing.)

• Got his "start" as a "child actor" in a popular and Oscar-winning Naval war drama from the early 60s. However, to his dismay, his scenes were cut. He didn't know until watching the film at the premiere.

• His big break into showbiz came 20 years later, landing the titular character, "P. Wade, P.I.," a totally rad dude who moves from the surfs up beaches of Maui to the streets of Detroit and sets up shop as a private investigator to aid his ailing mother. A wildly popular fish-out-of-water story surfacing 9 seasons.

• A running gag on the show (as most people know) is the "P." is never revealed. Hearty jokingly claims it stands for Pieixoto.

• He is credited with popularizing both the mustache and the soul patch, however not at the same time (the exception being the film *Quincy Stands Tall* and its made-for-TV sequel *Quincy Stands Tall*er).

• His newest series, *Cop Drama*, returns right here tonight, Tuesdays at 9.

• Ladies and gentlemen, please give a hearty welcome to two-time Emmy-nominated actor

• Martin Hearty

• Applause

#

"They had to explain it to me.
Slowly.
A couple is literally a. couple. 2.
And a few has three letters so 3."

#

He sits on the bus like a corpse, blank stare off kilter, jaw dropped in a lack of cognitive function rather than overloaded inspiring awe. It couldn't get more exciting.

Except he's holding a muffin.

From the outside looking in, it does seem like a moot point worth notation. The minor technicality is he may have received it from a guy who moments before committed a Capote-cold double homicide.

As long as it's not a double double chocolate.

But I already know it is.

So like an usher's admission of stealing popcorn or having an affair, this is my confession:

A couple years back I wrote this one-shot experiment to explore the thoughts and commentaries of inanimate objects, in this case ones in a convenience store. But sometimes, no matter the intention, a story will force itself in its own direction. And this one took a dark turn quick.

Maybe too dark? Maybe that's why I haven't tried doing much with it?

--> Because no matter what road the kit takes me down, I'm ultimately the one associated with the wheel.

In the end, the murderer takes a muffin and leaves. But apparently this character now meets a certain overweight man with a mustache waiting at a bus stop.

What are the chances, amiright?

Higher than you'd think. I knew the moment I walked past the store not opened for the day that I didn't want to be around when it closed for good.

[Paste copy of story here:]

The Con of Muffins

Ron Way, 28, walks into the convenience store on the corner of Alabaster and MacDade. His expression is focused, meaningless. There's a fine line between narcotics and insanity, or at least that's what the muffins associate with truth. The man with patches of cratered skin on his cheeks watches behind thick glasses. Ron Way snags a bottle drink, wondering if nutty muffins are saner than bran.

Truthfully, what Ron Way comes in for is cigarettes. He's decided to quit, just not quite yet. The man at the counter turns to the left when reaching behind for a pack. Ron Way jingles most of the total in change. The rest in paper money.

"Stop back by and see us," says A. Tony, dropping the change into his palm. His thick glasses accentuate his magnified blinking. Ron Way twitches a nod.

The front door dings, "Customer." Tanasha holds the door for Ron Way. Tanasha enters. A. Tony scratches behind his ear. His glasses bounce on the bridge of his nose. Light stretches around the store like a lighthouse guiding snacks to safe harbor. The mysteries of what lies across The Great Beyond plague the muffins daily. The potato chips are not concerned with such trifles. Indifference is the candy bars' take. Except for the Nero bars, which are scared shitless. However, no one pays them any heed.

Tanasha uses the restroom marked for customers only. If she's in the store then she must be a customer.

Tony taps his fingers on the counter. 1234. 4321. 1234. 4321.

The front door dings, "Customer." Ron Way reenters.

"I. Uh, forgot—" points to the back corner aimlessly—"yeah," tweaks Ron Way and, with the fluid motion of a sprinkler, jerks a pistol from underneath the back of his jacket. The pistol is only an accomplice, or at least that's what its understanding was. Is. It's not even sure anymore itself.

"Not a fucking movement." Ron Way does a terrible job of steadying the business end in A. Tony's face. "Not. A. One."

"No—A. Tony." A. Tony chuckles and points to his name tag.

A. Tony is no longer with us. His cratered cheek rests on the tiled floor, and his memories accent the cigarettes.

Tanasha screams. "Oh. No. No. God. No." Her freshly emptied bladder makes a failed attempt at expelling urine. Her knees make a proactive attempt at buckling to the tiled floor.

"Don't. No moving either." Ron Way spasms. The gun jumps, startled, but remains together under pressure.

There's nothing that can be done, realize the muffins. It's the con of being a pastry.

"Please. No. I have. I have money." Tanasha motions towards her purse.

"No movement." The gun is relieved it does not fire. As are the muffins. And the chips. The candy bars remain indifferent, except for the Nero bars which are scared shitless.

"What do you want? Please. Anything."

Ron Way wants a cigarette. He again convinces himself now is not a good time for quitting. Ron Way reaches into his jacket's pocket. His thumb slides up the cellophane. The pack hasn't been opened. "Fuck," his rattled nerves eject as he begins packing the pack on the counter. Ron Way rips the tab with his teeth and spits the plastic off his lips. He pops the box with his thumb and uses his tongue to slide out a stick. The lighter remains in his pocket.

"Please. God. Sir—"

Ron Way's hand moves towards his pocket when the gun reacts. I'm sorry, I'm sorry, I'm sorry. Tanasha reluctantly accepts the apology.

Ron Way loosens his arm, the gun hangs at his side in shame. He catches vomit in his mouth, which causes the cigarette to fall to the tiled floor. Ron Way follows suit. He gasps for air that cannot be found.

The gun smokes, trying to calm itself.

The muffins are speechless. Such needless destruction. The insanity affects the nutty ones the most. The bran muffins find the atrocities irrational. Why, oh why, oh why?

Ron Way pulls himself up, assisted by the counter.

Stay down, you bastard.

Penis enhancers and other uppers fly across the store as a result of Ron Way's sickeningly shocked frustration. Two steps are taken forward and retraced. He skips over to Tanasha and nudges her elbow with his foot. Limp. "Oh. Oh. Oh." He hops back. "This isn't. This isn't."

The gun goes back into hiding. So much shame.

Ron Way kicks over the rack of candy bars. The Nero bars surprisingly display unalarmed poise. The rest protest to nothing that's listening.

However, it's the muffins that feel genuine woe. While the candy bars complain and the chips feign compassion, the muffins realize tragedy. Ron Way takes a muffin, a single double double chocolate, leaving behind all else. The door dings, "Customer," as the muffins cry out for the stolen.

#

And now here we are, an overlapping of circumstance.

See: These events become the narrative when they intersect seamlessly.

One's plot into another's, where one ending becomes a new beginning no longer accounted for.

The crime is committed. The killer is at large. So the muffin that remains binds the events. Get rid of the pastry, untether the overlap. The circumstances become circumstantial.

--> There's a right way and a Ron Way.

--> Remove the logistical path of reintroduction.

Action is as imminent as the peeled-back plastic wrap.

I tap, tap, tap on his shoulder because I lack a better plan.

His response is nil. Nothing registers with him. Ron Way could show up and want his muffin back and he wouldn't even know.

I poke the bear, the metaphorical sleeping giant, like I want the adventure.

He checks back into where we are, getting back on the bus from whatever train of thought he was riding, his eyes still lagged from the trip.

And I, the passing hitchhiker, need to be lean and concise, stripped down, thumb out, the hemming way:

"You're not going to eat that." Point blank. A trajectory as flat as his character.

--> Ron Way isn't the only one to make a mess of things at close range.

Brief hesitation but no questions.

He hands it over, and I'm taken aback. I would assume he'd naturally be the slightest bit peeved or annoyed or any other word connoting a negative reaction across his brow or stache. In all fairness, I am taking the man's muffin. Instead, I'm the fool with the furrowed consternation now with pastry. My brain stutters like a scratched disc of exit strategies. It lands on "obliged."

What am I doing?

#

I'm already on the bus so I keep going (see: literally nowhere) from my unintrusive position sprawled across the back seat.

I hear the old lady start her morning barrage of old ladyness, making out her lyrical cadence ripped from and rippled like 1950s cinema.

If anyone can get a rise out of him it'll be this beautiful woman.

She begins like the calm before the storm, simple enough, with advice on mornings and a non-threatening gust calling out the generational woe-is-me boo-hooery with that edged sassiness dying out with the decade. And by the time she picks up her flow, there's no time to evacuate the gauntlet of questioning truth and questions as truth.

His silence stares into the eye, ignoring the sands and locusts.

--> Still: there's nothing stoic about this.

Her cold affront drops into personal terrain. Who he is vs. who is he.

And what does he do, this captain of his soul?

"Those are some very surprising insights to muse over" as cordially as possible and bends at the knees to pick up his brown briefcase.

I cover my face, palming my nose, fingers over my eyes, the unofficial yet universal rosebud of defeat.

--> The muffin falls like a snow globe in Xanadu.

#

The bus creeps to a halt but not at the stop.

Traffic rubbernecks in both lanes in front of the convenience store.

Blues and reds flicker flash a vulgar blurring mimic of the sun's rise into day.

Uniforms and suits, dressed for success, hustle to their tailored roles.

Worse than going nowhere are circles.

The driver opens the doors before crossing MacDade.

Across from his stop, this is where she gets off.

I follow her, leaving the loop open.

#

She cares about the going-ons at the store about as much as the journals I submitted that story to.

I maintain a safe distance, as in she's pretending she doesn't notice me behind her. But it's instinctual to know you're being followed. No matter the distance removed, presence can't be helped. The art demands it. Form meets function.

I typify my blatant inconspicuousness by kicking around the small rocks and dried leaves on my path of nonchalance as we weave further up blocks towards the side of town I'm not particularly familiar with. I've just rekicked a bottle cap (see: plastic soda not metallic beer because sandals) I've become particularly fond of over the last block or so when she stops under a lamppost unlit on its off hours after the night's shift.

Now:

Here's what I should do:

I should assume my walk, although purposely misconstrued as leisurely, has a destination.

I should continue onward towards said assumed destination.

And I should say good morning or anything else to literally call attention to my having an assumed destination.

But instead, I also stop.

--> The bottle cap skips onwards without me.

--> Amateur -our.

I realize where we wandered.

Tangential paragraph break digression, out in the open for all to see: When a story appeals to your literary sensibilities, you take a piece of it with you. Whether you realize it or not, it knows. A character's action, a description, a phrase waiting for the moment in your day to day to creep up and say "oh, yeah" or "that reminds me." We're so inundated, you may not remember the author's name, but you remember that time "I read somewhere..." clear as day. Well, daylight has arrived to that place across the street. And this time, I even know who wrote it (see: personally). When he last invited me the neon Fellow's sign was pronounced against the backdrop of night. Now, the current glow is dulled. I get this uncomfortable feeling I'm being watched.

I start walking, on edge. The line is drawn at the street. My sidewalk is still my side of town. Tread lightly in nearly bare feet.

I go for the bottle cap, pick up where I left off, consistently for the show of it. My pretend pretenses rigid with overthought.

An assumed destination made up in my mind, this should be my exit, where this rough act should end.

In strolls out a denouement.

To say the man in the burgundy jacket walks out is too simplistic, and ultimately doesn't stay true to the character the author intended. A view from another angle is in no way a fallacy on my part when he stumbled out and me merely upon.

He's crutched like an old friend to the bartender locking the door.

"Openfffbuisness," he calls out like a songbird off key.

"Heresshome."

"Isleepere."

I slow to an observational pace.

"Bigfuknlites."

"Bigfuknscreen."

She watches from the post.

"Immthe trademarked cfuks."

Outsiders looking in not welcomed into like an observer without admission at a window.

I hit the block and turn away from the fourth wall the city street implies.

#

I don't look back to know she's behind me.

With every unplanned turn I make and directionless street I cross.

--> It's like she's inside my head.

#

Her path deviated when she turned towards her destination: a side gate in a fence to the low-standing building, rippled in blue metallic siding.

I followed the waves. The Hearty Morning Animal Shelter, "Having A Heart Every New Day."

Sure, why not?

--> Even destiny ends with a why.

An old, copper cat bell dangling from a collar clanks its dented welcome against the glass part of the door it hangs on. Behind the counter a blond guy with that type of ridiculously stylish haircut I could never pull off greets me with a "Hearty morning," then offers a list of what's "here to adopt a dog? Cat? A pelican?"

"Pelican?"

"It's around here somewhere. Damn buzzard won't leave. Swoops in, steals the dog food. So if you can find it in your heart..."

"No. No, thank you."

I look around for a reason to have come in in the first place. I don't see the old woman while I pretend to scan the corkboard of lost pets like I'm looking for the biggest payout.

No whammies. No whammies.

No-wham-freaking-way.

I yank the golden ticket from the tack. Staring back at me with his bulging photocopied eyes is "Don Bronco the Dachshuahua. Gray Fur. Blue Eyes. 7-8 Lbs. Also answers to Big D."

The lack of creativity here cuts deeper than the paper. The name is the essence. Literally, a person or place or thing cannot exist until it's called. There is no existence without a name. That's why we spend so much time creating terms for literally every thing. The words make the intangible graspable. Case in point the story unfolding. At this point it's not a novel, but that doesn't stop me from giving it the working title *Shell.* Forcing me to own its fruition into a tangible reality.

So what are you trying to say here?

Someone gave this little son of a bitch my name and then had the utmost audacity to lose it. I call bullshit.

I wave the yellow paper like good news to answer the question the guy hasn't quite yet put into words.

"The little guy is safe at home now. But let me tell you, the poor little fellow had a hell of a time getting there. When you're lost like that it can feel like an incredible journey, especially out there in the wilder..."

"Can I get you to put your name here?" Thank God he cuts me off, tossing a clipboard on the counter. "The computer's down. Or, the computer's fine. The keyboards fucked up. But it's just for our records that no one reads."

Before I take the step to the counter he's back to doodling a rebus for a 50¢ sale on a long paper bag stippled with the remnant evidence of a once-greased-up sandwich.

"Subtle," I say as I write the first name that comes to mind, close enough to mine to play off a quote-unquote mishap if needs be while maintaining the verisimilitude of someone who'd actually name a dog Don Bronco.

"What, this?" He hovers the tip of the sharpie over the bag.

"Your arm." I indicate with my line of sight the part of his sleeve wrapped around the back of his forearm. A man in an overcoat, a wide-brimmed hat and red scarf masking his face, forever posed with an American Bulldog and Himalayan house cat in front of a waterfall.

"It's my sister's favorite movie. We watch it annually at Christmas."

"Which one?"

"The one in December."

Signed, Donald Ryan.

#

Side Note: The keyboard was missing an E, which he wouldn't have used no matter what name I gave him.

#

Michelle's actually there waiting when I make it to the pizza joint.

I'm out of breath and only a fraction late.

She looks like she just rolled out of bed.

--> Sitting there gorgeous in a t-shirt too big for her, hair pulled back above yesterday's makeup.

She says she's started seeing someone new. Who's older. It's what she wanted to tell me, out of courtesy, in person, so I wouldn't have to find out some other way. But that's all she'll say about him.

This doesn't stop us from going back to her place to find aggressive comfort in the familiar.

She sparks up afterwards. I, for once, decline to go read in the park.

We both work tonight.

How's that for personal growth?

#

F 20__

#

Fresh Herb Aioli

1 C chopped herbs :: 1 Qt Mayonnaise
Parsley
Yolks (room temperature) x 2
Rosemary
Salt (Kosher) x ½ t
Thyme
Dijon (emulsifier) x ½ t
Sage
Vinegar (dw, ww, cider) x 1 T
Oil (blender) x 1 C

Repeat (forever) x 4

#

"Thoughts on quiche. Go."

"What are you on about?"

Matt dunked a wing into the ranch packet that came with the Wing It platter Dave brought in.

This only meant one thing: We were going to have to do something shitty.

We always got stuck doing something shitty when Dave brought in a bribe. "C'mon, man. I brought you wings/pizza/a big sandwich/an ounce of kush/an 8-ball of coke."

Okay. Not the last two. Wouldn't want to motivate us too much around here.

Matt pulled the bone from between his teeth, cleaning it in a single bite. "Quiche," he said, covering his full mouth.

"Honestly never put much thought into them."

"Me either."

I scraped the last of the mayo off the sides of the one quart ("Don't think of it as food cost, think of it as a Christmas bonus") and jammed the rubber spat in the mixing bowl like a sword in stone.

"I mean, till last night."

"Do tell."

I swept herbs into the mix. But I didn't fold them in.

"I got kite high, right, and ended up watching some French Canadian Bug Movie 2, where they, the French

Canadian filmmakers, went around some city and filmed flies, ants, roaches, spiders, gnats, but like super up close. No talking. Just full screen bugs. But so up close they, the bugs, not the French Canadian filmmakers, looked real fake. Like live action animation. Felt like Dr. Grant standing in a jeep, and was so enthralled I ended up eating almost a full quiche which I can't remember if I even enjoyed. The quiche, not the French Canadian Bug Movie 2."

"Who made this mayonnaise?"

"Don't know. Why?"

I scoop a quarter-sized piece of shell sprinkled with herbs onto my finger.

"And where did you get a quiche from?"

"I'd never made a quiche so I made a quiche."

"Can't deny the logic." I flick the shell into the trash. "Like a little eggshell being no harm no fowl?"

"Don't sound like Dave."

#

"Nowadays in the world
you've gots to be
the sheep in wolf's clothing."

#

Since Dave brought wings he spontaneously found it high time to surprise surprise gather the staff for a meeting.

To the front of the house (and everyone else since they were conveniently mandatorily present) he wanted to show the stickers of the new-school-esque pelican he had made up. "They're to be handed out to the children of our guests, not each other."

--> Michelle would manage to pilfer me one anyway.

And to the back of the house he wanted us to "really dig deep and detail the equipment tonight. Show some love to those lowboys. Take down and spray the hoods. Pull stuff out, really get behind it. We're inspecting an expection any day now." He smiled at his spoonerism as if surprised nobody cared.

#

Side Note: Ryan wasn't at the "meeting."

#

I don't remember the last time I worked a shift without Ryan around. Our schedules, for whatever reason, seem to coincide.

I assume it was his day off, but that didn't negate the possibility that he found out about the shelter (maybe they called to check up on me, how should I know?).

Or the off chance he found out I got dangerously close to breaching like copyright the vicinity of the bar he tended to.

My offense, grounded, as in I never technically crossed into the property.

My defense, without grounds, as in passivity to the consistent inundated and inoculated overexposure.

I'd like the courts to consider my ignorance by submitting to your honors exhibit A: this morning's notes concerning the old lady, and the following question: How was I to know where we were going until I'd arrived?

#

I unsuccessfully force upon myself an extra hour of sleep.

I feel the type of hungover even coffee can't cure. The type where a for real hangover would be a treat by comparison.

I still feel dirty from "showing love to those lowboys" all night.

But fuckall if I don't make my way to the desk like a champ, cup of instant coffee, less black than outside before daybreak, in hand.

A word after a word after a word is struggle.

#

Mostly I spend the better part of the morning staring at this stupid watercolor rather than in the chapters where I should be.

But after sitting here engaging and analyzing the shit out of this for how long now, I feel I've degreed into a sort of expert critic and contributing interpreter for this fine gallery solo exhibit.

Shall I criticize?

The colors are dull but not sloppy.

Like Shlllll, the artist deduced from the signature, renders autumn in the midst of summer.

The sky clear yet overcast.

The tufts of dried grass succumb to the stifled breeze.

The rowboat, buoyant on the sand.

The lighthouse protecting ships not at sea.

The elements exist in the lack, in this in between outside the canvas,

The brush tangent, the painter parallel,

Shlllll the observer, parting with but not a part of,

To be hung on the motel wall,

Nonintrusive, between perusal and glance,

In each room, for each passerby,

Always moving but never moved,

Like boasting ersatz is not a real word.

The frame is bolted to the wall for the thieves, so I place the sticker Michelle procured for me on the glass as if it was made to stand eloquent on the sand, its feet angled in a way to arch with the dune in direct proportion between the rowboat and the lighthouse like a cartoon on vacation, yet severely out of place in style and palate, with its flat-brimmed snapback and buttoned-up button down, the bright blue fish in its electric gold beak ignorant of being consumed, and take a break.

#

MAN HIDDEN BEHIND THE TELEVISION'S KALEIDOSCOPE
I'm not submitting to a drug test.

(The voice is a miasma of smooth, comforting in familiarity.)

THE WOMAN HE'S PRESUMABLY NOT SUBMITTING TO
How else will you prove to me and the board you didn't sell the painting for drug money?

(Chintzy and overdramatic.)

[The scramble cuts a jagged green streak from corner to corner revealing an older version of 80s heartthrob, George Gilliam.]

GEORGE GILLIAM
Prove? That's where you're wrong. You have no choice but to believe me.

[There wasn't a housewife not enthralled in his heyday.]

ENUNCIATING ACTRESS
I'll put my faiTH in a DRug test.

[Roles solidifying his syndicated charm: *Behead of State* where he played an early version of the now trope dimwitted boyfriend of a high-ranking official in a police state's daughter, whose antics generally prove favorable for the people resulting in the said high-ranking official's weekly execution. It lasted one season.]

(Sounds of props being shuffled on the set.)

[But it was enough to launch him into the long-running reimagining to *The Monstores Next Door*, making him a household name.]

OLD GEORGE

How do I know you didn't take the painting, my dear?

[He played the dimwitted boyfriend.]

NOT GEORGE

I. Would. Never. It's been in the family mansion for GENerations.

[I'm glad to hear he's still getting work. But I opt to read something I can actually see.]

#

Side Note: George Gilliam isn't his real name, and while I'm not sure what it is, truth be told, I'm sure it's not as strong or eloquent or symbolic as Cary Grant or John Wayne.

#

Also remember to stop forgetting towels.

#

A line in this novel about if on a winter's night a traveler stumbled on some not-yet-revealed plot somewhere in Europe

("The private, young and handsome, spilled the coffee on his commanding officer, steaming hot into his crotch, splashing droplets on our traveler." pg 38, though the translation is questionable.)

reminds you of a George Gilliam, but a classic George, a bumbling, loveable George which triggers a tangent (as thoughts do) to a time you read somewhere that he dated the *Monstores* actress who played Mary during the length of the show's run, only to break up at the series' cancellation. "Life mimics art, art life, the only truth is found in the work."

This requires further contemplation and concentration, but being as you're now removed from the novel it's a good place to exit. You tell yourself, "Speaking of, you should get back to work."

Which you do.

You sit at the desk. There's no reason for "why desk." You could sit anywhere. But the desk fits the task at hand.

Take a moment to appreciate the painting and how you improved upon it. The pelican is one of the better ideas you've had in a while.

Ok. Time to get down to business. Try picking up where you left off. Just another word or phrase or sentence or paragraph from the previous period. Anything that makes sense without hindering the flow. That's the only real requirement, the only burden. The word or phrase or sentence or paragraph must suspend disbelief without an overt awareness. But nothing makes sense. Nothing is happening. Your story is blocked, dammed from the onset.

You check the time. It's later than you thought, but still early afternoon. There's time before the scheduled other job. So you decide on taking a walk. Clear, recharge, replenish your mind. Go out and make something happen.

Let the Reader make sense of things.

#

"This poem by Richard Brautigan
was found written on a bathroom wall
in the coffee shop on Sanfran.
The artist is unknown."

#

I amble across town, just going with the flow, until I'm standing in front of a coffee shop Michelle and I used to frequent. They're not expensive, as coffees go nowadays, and they use the same locally roasted beans like all the other city establishments cornered locally, which even if it didn't perk the best cup in town, beats the cheap, watered-down ersatz from earlier.

#

The guy from the shelter with his hair slicked back in fine, equidistant rows sits at a square table between two generously tattooed people (one male, one female, both shoulder length hair) and across from a guy with no visible tattoos and no hair.

--> A mix-n-match algorithm of themselves.

I keep my back turned the best I can without standing in line completely ass backwards.

--> Like I'm trying to appreciate the one wall without the local artwork.

--> Like I'm the only one admiring the installation.

I wouldn't say I'm embarrassed, even in the same clothes as yesterday. So don't misconstrue my actions. I'm avoiding that awkward I've-seen-you-but-don't-know-you eye contact thing, which leads to that inessential nod of acknowledgment and should be avoided.

"What can I get you?" There's froth to the words, airy sweet and designed, like a lace veil on a cappuccino.

I take that for-show pause people take when they know exactly what they want in order to convey nonchalance over eagerness. I even pretend to read the menu. That little extra for good measure. "Just a coffee.

Black. The one above the smallest size, whatever you guys call that here," I say still perusing the menu. Not looking directly into the eyes of the person taking an order feels less demanding.

"Medium?"

"That's the one. Togo please." Especially when the dark brown eyes I just made the mistake of tripping into are polished pearls.

I watch her in casual glimpses of infatuation as she makes conversation while filling the cup from the urn.

"Your look," she says, "like the way you look. It reminds me of someone. I'm sure you get that."

"Not usually, no."

"Like a younger Martin Hearty." She slides the coffee to me.

"You don't say." I try sounding indifferent and amused, unsure if this is flattery while making sure to avoid her eyes either way.

She smiles and dictates the price.

I pay.

"Have a good day, Martin."

"You too," I read her name tag, "Maya."

#

If I was heading in the direction of the motel I'd be taking what might be considered the long way round.

Nothing of any consequence has been worth noting.

My direction without point.

If there had been inspiration it's gone insipid.

At least the coffee's good, chocolate-black with a nutty backend, like caramelized peanut butter.

--> "Locally roasted has its perks."

But even that was my last sip.

So with nowhere in mind in front of me, and having seen a trash can a block or so back, I retrace my steps in time to see who else but him walk out of the Wing It.

The amused muse smiles upon me on a cloudy day (or as written, from my backlogged perceptions from dead English writers), and being the jovial minx she is, stoned in New Hollywood, she provides for me a broken payphone, the cord cut and rusted, the receiver hung at the nape, detached into loneliness.

--> Archaic and useless timely in use.

I pick up the phone, literally as it once was done, and hold the time-dusted handle between my ear and shoulder to blend myself into the open background, camouflaged in plain sight.

I hear an idea whisper like an echo through the line.

The chances of a bird laying an egg while flying is zero::never.

--> So why miss out on the goose who laid this golden opportunity?

An egg falls from the sky, lands at his feet.

The timing precise.

He leans over to inspect it, gulping down the final, icy quaff of beverage.

He rattles the cup to investigate, the empty drink liquidating the intrigue.

The shell has no value to him. No value means no interest. So in order to be in business here, I charge ahead with small odds for a huge payout.

"I'm glad to have been of service." I hook the phone to its cradle. The bell inside quivers, its little heart racing with mine.

"How's it going, man?" What am I doing? I don't talk like this. Not really.

But it registers his attention: "I don't have any change."

"What. No. I know." Don't push it: button, button.

He neither scurries nor backs down, which is promising. Except he's trying to hide his sagging bag of food.

--> Which reminds me when did I last eat?

"I think you dropped something." No sudden moves. Politely indicate the vicinity of his feet without frightening him. Friend him.

He feigns surprise, and superbly done, I might add: Subtle and nuanced across the brows, a sweeping flick of his toes, grimacing the not in "No. It's not mine."

"You sure," chum, buddy, pal?

Of course he is.

I shrug a physically exaggerated "Anyway." If nothing is going to happen, I need to push it along, keep it moving, send him out to bury a plot, give him something to dig for (see: don't let him find you unsure and insecure): "Then find me when you're not."

And trill.

As if on command.

The payphone resuscitates its shrill heart cry to life.

This couldn't have been more acutely planned if I tried.

I answer with a quickness, not giving it the chance to ring again ("I'm so sorry, I have to take this"), and string together the first convolutedly vague, herring dyed carmine words I can manage without missing a beat between my tongue and cheeks:

"Thank you for calling Pelican Informational, this is Don, how may I be of service?"

--> Let the hungry boy chew on that.

#

Side Note: Obviously the line's cut so I don't hear a thing but dirty plastic pressed against my ear.

#

I hang up the receiver with a ding, its last little life's echo, and wipe the dust to dust from my hand and ear onto my gym shorts and shirt sleeve.

--> My palms feel like ash to my fingertips.

Up ahead, he turns the corner. Out of sight, still in mind. Shuffling his heavy steps unknowingly into my self-doubt. My confidence a con gone with the scene.

What does it all mean if it means nothing to him?

Let's backtrack further: Am I following the right character? Noting the right reactions? Does he have significance, let alone a plot?

--> Like asking yourself "is cake without sugar just bread?" only to end up making a shit cake or shit bread, both equivalently boring and bland.

I retrace my second guessing back to the coffee shop, back towards coincidence if there even is such a thing, to wash out the acidic reflux of why why whys and what what whats I've caught in my mouth.

What if he isn't a story?

What if he's a discursive backstory?

What if he's a wasted poem?

or

Why not the coffee shop girl or the tattooed guy from the animal shelter?

Why can't they end up somewhere worth following?

Why in the midst of my crisis did I leave my empty cup on top of the payphone, doing the world yet another disservice?

#

The coffee shop is empty.

--> Wrong.

--> Exaggerated misinformation.

--> Loose and unnecessary.

--> "Keep it tight" — Matt

My head's out the game worse than a group of preteen athletes singing and dancing their encouragements rather than banking 3-pointers and layups. In fact, so out of it my reference is a tangent more out of place than a musical number.

Let's come back in the second half:

The coffee shop is sparsely populated (not better, but we'll roll with it). An elderly man whose ponytail connects to a poofed mop of curls scans a novel (physical, tangible) like an English barrister in the corner, silently mouthing the words to the court. A group huddled in a booth on the opposite wall prattle on about something I'm assuming has to do with writing ("characterization," "across like poetry," "child murder.")

Another wrong turn. The dead end furthest from the missed chance.

Now what? Externally busted.

Now why? Internally busting.

#

The painting draws me in like a clairvoyant self-portrait.

The tattooed guy is gone, chairs tucked tidy under the table.

Maya isn't behind the counter, replaced by a pompadour combed back from thick-rimmed glasses.

Still got a buzz from the cup and no change for another.

So why stay?

Pulled in.

Set before the canvas.

It's a simple egg. A fat-bottomed oval highlighted by an implied light source on a canvas rippling from black to blue, the strokes heavy like waves at dusk, the egg, soft and unblemished, sinking in. Techniques traditional in style but novel in texture. Even the subject, overt and recognizable, takes on a unique rehash of all the still lifes and character studies painted before. The deception of time and talent seemingly effortless. An artistic sincerity of space. I resist the temptation to touch it. But my eyes won't let go. They scan to the name etched in gray on the lower, blue corner: Shlllll. Out of place, hidden in plain view. A replica of the same looped signature as the print in the room. But by comparison it's almost illogical. Shlllll searching beyond whatever he was searching for on the beach. I try to imagine them as separate people, like the different entities performing under one name. A Shlllll of confidence and a Shlllll of doubt. Of breaking the surface, breaking free. If this painting's the egg then the other is chicken.

"It's all in your head."

But it's not. One came first.

"I'm kidding; but seriously."

A female voice cuts in, bringing into focus the diegetic soundtrack of the coffee shop.

I cage a smile. "Oh, right. Hey."

"Am I interrupting?"

"What? No—" but my eyes taper like a question, "no."

"Came over because it wasn't Martin Hearty. Earlier. I got my names mixed up. You're without question a young George Gilliam."

"Is that better or worse?"

She smiles over a shrug, playfully indifferent. "You like music?"

"I've listened."

"Here," she begins looking around as she pulls the pen from her hair tied back in that sort of messy way where every hair is meant to be perfectly out of place, "you have anything to write on?" She eyes but hesitates peeking into the trash can.

I hand her the wrinkled, folded paper from my pocket.

"Don Bronco ever find his way?"

"Say what now?"

Before I realized Donald Ryan's Don Bronco.

"Oh, right. Not yet. He's still as lost as ever."

"Poor little thing. I'm sure he's out there searching." She flipped over the page, bearing against the wall, and wrote the same insignia the shelter employee doodled on the paper bag. "My brother works down at the shelter, so I'll put in a word. But he'll find his way in the end. You'll see. The incredible journeys always end that way."

"We won't leave bodger to chance."

She finishes with a quick flick of her pen and hands the paper back. "He, my brother, his band, they're putting on a secret show. You can use this as your ticket. I've put the info at the bottom."

"I'll see what I can do."

--> I didn't have the heart to tell her I work the PM.

"Then maybe you'll see me there. Bye, George."

#

I get it in my head to go see Michelle.

--> I meet a girl and feel in the wrong.

--> Round 2 for compelling conflict.

If anything, I'll say I was on my way to the Mercato's and decided to say hi. I won't say anything about the things left ajar.

And it shouldn't seem too far-fetched, logistically in place, seeing how we would walk there from our place all the time. Even used it as a setting for a story once.

--> The only truly great story I've stumbled upon.

--> My unpublished magnum opus.

That one had a plan. A purpose. An end goal: combine a chick mag with a lake monster. Even if it started out as a structural experiment and a narrative joke, all the little pieces fell into place. A whole as it should be. The protagonistic voice, the relationship between characters, the settings all synched into one tight package off the shelf, providing the gift of change for the I.

The narrator's doubt was my self-confidence.

I related on the page. Granted: no wife, no kids. But anxiety is all around.

--> Now all I have is lonely, fat, and flat.

Screwed on or screwed off, I ring the bell to see where it goes.

#

Fucking Dave answers the door.

I know she was seeing someone, but I didn't think she scraped this shirtless buffoon, gut hanging under his unusually large, flat-chested nipples, eating something out of a bowl with a spoon, while saying "Isn't this an excellent treat," in between bites of his lame ass reference to what looks like egg salad, from the shittiest bottom of the shit-heap barrel.

"Hi, Dave. Where's Michelle?"

"Refreshening up. It might be a minute." He's got the same smug look, that one with the pouty eyes where he desperately tries looking like he's your new best friend right before he asks you for "a favor" (the countenance equivalent of bribing with food) as if he wants me to high five him or rub his belly like the bitch he is for being able to refer to my ex as a conquest to his unhappily married brochachos over nostalgic cans of Naddy Lite.

"Then can I come in?"

"I'm sorry," says Dave, "I'm afraid I can't let you do that. It not being my place and all."

"Are you allowed to go and get her?"

"Now that I can do for you."

Fucking Dave, man.

"Leave it to you to show up now," Michelle says in the doorway twenty minutes later, bathrobe thrown over a t-shirt, hair possibly stylistically tussled, make-up gently painted around the eyes. "What do you want, Don?"

"Are you freaking kidding me? Dave? Of all the dicks in the city?"

--> My voice is notably more shrill than the seriousness of tone.

"It's something that happened, not some devised plan," she says into her hand, covering her face like she hadn't seen the sun since Rip Van Winkle.

It's my turn to speak.

Instead, I stand on the step doing this weird pointing with an open hand like I'm waiting to catch whatever words fall from my dropped jaw.

"And it's not like it's any of your business anyway."

"It should be my business."

"What're you on now? It was your decision to ditch me and hole up in that dump."

"I needed an inch of space. I found you—I find you—so distracting."

"You took the whole mile, Don." [She tightens the bathrobe over her chest as she crosses her arms.] "Look, I'm not doing this now."

"Just talk to me. Dave? Really?"

"This isn't about Dave or me or anyone else. This is about you, like always."

"What about you? What about space for your work?"

"I never let it get in the way. In fact, I wanted it to bring us closer. It's what art's supposed to do."

"Then I guess I can give you the ocean but not the ships."

"You act like I don't know what you're doing. You're purposely misquoting Vuong by substituting his name. C'mon, Don. I know you better than you think. I always will." [She looks out over my head, trying to distract the tears. A car passes behind ablaze with vibrations.] "Look, until you get done doing whatever the hell it is you think you need to be doing, I think it's best if you don't show up here anymore. I'll see you at work."

"Shelly."

[She closes the door, soft, for emphasis, her style.]

#

I am furious.

Fuck showing. I'm telling: breathing heavy, trying to keep composure, keep from popping off the page, each step pounding out more vibrations than that car, but right now f a comparative metaphor.

And f going wherever it is the directionless go. That would imply I'm going somewhere, and we've come this far to know that sure as shit ain't happening.

And f that bird perched up ahead that should be punched in its big ass beak. There's symbolism for you.

And mother f the Mercato's and all the wasted work going nowhere. I should storm in there and find that joke in the golf hat and button down and punch his pretentious mustache right off his hip face. Tell him between blows it's all bullshit. The outcome doesn't matter when there's no market for you. Literally beat him over the head with that irony. Then maybe someone would want to read it.

And f me and my useless words. I might as well go out there and search for the killer. Because if I can't be literary I might as well be general. Even these weak ass sentences and jumbled plotting can solve a murder for hire. And once I find one killer I can find another and another and another until I'm buried in my own plot content at six feet and never having to go deeper. How's that for insight?

And f rejection. It's always rejection. It's you're not right for this issue, but can't wait to read more! It's you're good but not quite good enough! It's unfortunately we're going to have to pass because we've chosen Dave! It's thanks for the consideration! It's keep reading!

Life score grade report, overall rating: F.

#

The bird flies off.

--> Shame on you for thinking I'd honestly have the proclivity to cause actual harm.

A guy leaning on a stoop initiates a conversation between drags of a cigarette, some variation of "good afternoon" of which I'm not having.

"Is it though?"

"It's exactly what you make of it, neighbor." He doesn't seem caught off guard, content and confident with his overweight stomach on an otherwise skinny frame, slicked back hair, little gold chain dangling around his bare-chested collar, looking like he stepped out of a struggling mid-aught sitcom tailored for the second-most-profitable boy band member gone solo now desperate for a comeback.

I stop there. "Sorry. That was rude of me."

"No sweat. Don't get it twisted. Legitimacy can't be rude."

He pulls another cigarette from his pack and offers the box of no hard feelings towards me.

I reach for one, poised to snag, yet stop. Don't get me wrong here. I do want. Like the nicotine dream tingle down my spine can taste the spicy cherry on a shit day bad. But I stop. I had quit. Giving up cigarettes is the only thing I've actually accomplished. If I give up giving up I'm finished.

I decline.

He insists.

"You're running low," I say, which he wasn't, but he was kind enough to take the statement at face value, an excuse of conscience.

He says, "Then I'll just run back to the store like it ain't a problem."

"There's a store around here?" I indicate the block like where else would around here be, like I, myself, wasn't once from around here?

--> Like even if I knew where I was going why pretend that I don't?

He points up the way I was heading. "Seeing as you just came from the other way, my friend."

Nevertheless, I display gratitude. "Then that's where I'm heading."

And, for whatever reason, he sticks out his hand. Like we've made a deal. Transaction complete.

I shake his firm grip.

--> Because that's just what you do when there's a hand out.

#

"That Keats fellow wrote
a song about a pot.
Wild what ends up
sticking."

#

Time For A Brief Digression While I Stand Here and As I Walk Away

Always admired this particular house when we'd walk by it on our way to the store.

I had this thing for glancing into open, lit windows.

Michelle hated it.

But I thrived on the glimpses into others' lives.

And this place is covered in windows.

(Windows that usually remained covered.)

I'd make up stories about its residents.

Only this house. Only in passing.

Their eccentricities becoming more tangled and beautiful.

Whole histories and lineages, not one like the other.

But now I stand beyond the house, by myself where the road intersects.

And having met one of its numerous souls, cannot not not cross distressed.

#

But, hey, a five spot.

#

The fluorescents in the Mercato's are surprisingly (see: unnecessarily) bright considering the hours of daylight left to wring out.

Here are my entering plot relevant excuses:

It's possible he followed me (figuratively, with his eyes) down the block, and I needed to keep my facade of reliability.

--> For myself, for others.

--> "Suspend disbelief" or whatever.

I've noted the market so often recently it wouldn't be of justice not to go in.

--> "Like a gun in a drawer."

There's a combination of coffee shop and no way in hell I'm making it back to the room in time to get to The P. Hole when scheduled.

--> I'll order the second-cheapest cup from Big Name Express(o), expressing "from the drip to the sip," located conveniently inside the Mercato's (same menu, no atmosphere) and maybe, finally, set out to get some actual work done.

--> Who cares if the tables are strewn out in the open, in the middle of the market, someone literally thinking this the best idea.

--> I'll sit with something to prove like any good writer hidden in plain view.

#

Deep breath.

Sip coffee slow.

You know they've rehired Matt's many No Call No Shows.

"You're part of the team, sport."

All eyes on you but nobody's watching.

Focus.

There's a hierarchy of importance.

"Writing isn't dicking around.

Dicking around is writing."

(Can I quote that?)

#

"We all need a muse, whoever you are."

There goes that.

A reminder of reasons not to write in public.

An old man, long, gray beard, large, gold glasses, oversized headphones parting into hemispheres his untamed hair from ear to ear, squats into the chair across from me at the date-sized table, situating himself (literally and figuratively) in the aisle.

A child screams in the buggy passing behind him.

--> I feel you, kid.

"That was an early one. One of the first, really. I had just moved to the city and living across town in a little rough n' tumbler. City life was all I wanted, to be a part of something, sync with the bustle. And I had it all figured out. Find myself, find inspiration, find art within. Done deal, albeit a bit naïf. I couldn't find a job, couldn't find hope, couldn't find a single connecting soul in the grand collective. The romanticism of it all began fading away with a quickness. I was fading faster than my dream, my heart hardening like my hopes. But one morning, on the cusp of packing it all in, there was this sharp chirping, so much like a cry for help that when I peeked out the window I thought I'd find an old lady being mugged."

I guess this crazy bastard's got a story to tell, and I look like I'm in the need for one.

"On the side of my rented room, in the middle of the dusty, dirt yard, was the old, wooden pieces of a toppled shed the crackheads had never repaired although tweaked up and raging. From the slope of what was once the roof, a craned neck and bucketed beak peeked over the picketed fence of dry rot siding, arching its largely disproportionate head back and screaming to the sunlight. Now, I'd never seen one in person but I knew a pelican when I saw it. I went outside thinking the poor guy was lost and trapped in the jagged remains, but, as it turns out, I was way off on all accounts. She was right where she needed to be, making the best of that shit heap, turning that pile of junk into a home with every egg she popped out. And she sat there, on the eggs or perched over the eggs, occasionally flying off to come right back."

I can smell the wine-fermented halitosis with every malodorous punctuation. It adds a little, I do not know what.

"I'd leave out bits of bread from time to time, not knowing if pelicans even ate bread, but generously offering what little I could afford so she wouldn't have to leave the nest for too long. Yet, when she did succumb to the urge to scavenge I'd sneak over and look at the eggs nestled in the depression of the broken shed fortified by twigs and moss. They were about the size of my hand, a dingy white with small strokes and smears of brown like a Monet. It was art in nature, nature in art, truly one in one and the same. So I began painting the eggs, being true to nature as nature was to me, trying to capture the details of the overlooked, the earth's impressionism, the creator's subjective expressionism, the magical realism of nature in and of itself. All the while the bird's steadfastness against the crackheads, against their taunts, screams, and cans at all hours inspired my diligence. She stayed with the eggs like I stayed with my paintings, at times frightened but fighting to completion, incubating a small part of me into something new. I'll never know what brought my pelican so far off from the ocean, never know what brought her to my back yard. But I felt she was there for me as much as she was there for her chicklings."

My coffee tastes more bitter with each sip. Like something isn't quite right. Like swallowing anxiety.

"Over time, her eggs hatched, and she nurtured her children until they matured to flight, so I too knew it was time to nudge my paintings from their nest. I began exploring new possibilities for my eggs, personifying them into bar rats, home bodies, office drones, pushing them out into the real world so to speak. Into something alive to fly off with the small, hatched parts of me."

I feel the shift in my stomach. Too much. Not caffeine sick, but rather that nervous drop into a bottomless paranoia kind of queasy which also happens to be amped on caffeine.

I break down his features, look for what I'm not seeing, the not showering for a lengthy period of time, study the forlorn eyes framed in gold, listen to him tap tap tapping the three-tiered jack against the ear-engulfing headphones. I recognize a stranger.

He's the wino.

That Vino fellow from that bar across town.

As in not across town, per se, but "out-of-town." In the city's outer limits. (See: technically, way off limits.)

--> Who Ryan describes as a caricature.

--> Someone "I haven't read yet" so shouldn't know.

"You'll have to excuse me," I say as calm as possible, way more proper than I intend, but stand with a fidgeted nervousness.

"Excuse granted and adieu." He slinks his head between his shoulders in a sort of bow that can no longer drunkenly hold the giant weight of it.

And I make haste.

#

I venture further into the store, which, after a brief period of it's-too-late retrospection, I conclude isn't the greatest choice. It's not like the entrance isn't also the exit.

--> No, escape.

So he's a bit (see: very) drunk and a little (see: very) lost.

How is he relatively different from the other consumers in the market, searching for some meaning before the end?

Because he isn't shopping. He's the consumable.

Get what you need, get out.

Goods and services inspired not stolen.

His ending has nothing to do with what I have in store.

#

I've taken a wrong turn, this time into meandering the aisles.

[Insert something about cereal here: A quip that tries too hard to compare jingles with brightly colored cartoon boxes. Something like: "they're great, {they're} for kids" so hands off parents{!} until, of course, they're handed to you pleading purchase or you're stoned or whatever: but more fleshed and concise.]

[Insert something about that screaming child: yeah, bring him back. But this time sans screams. Instead, he's examining something, rolling it in his palms, lolling his tongue across it. His mother, beautiful at least from behind: yoga pants, jean jacket, blonde rooted hair with the rest a kind of aqua green as if dyed naturally in a pool and straightened to her shoulders, doesn't mind or doesn't notice while comparing jars of peanut butter.]

I intermittently glance over my shoulder to make sure the schizo frantic rambler doesn't trail deeper. What he needs is stability. Structure. Any basic connection for something real to link to. But he's in the wrong place to find it stocked around here.

[The kid giggles at the discovery of physics, at the law of gravity landing the tossed object at my feet.

"Oh my goodness / Donny no." The words come out lyrical but not sung as if a one-hit wonder, often and at nauseam.

I grab a box off the shelf, snagging just to snag, so I don't walk by as if bothered by the spasmodic circumstances of children, so my 'I didn't see it there but still be super chill about it' isn't misinterpreted. And to hide A) she's gorgeous, and not in a cookie cutter *Cosmo* sort of way, but as in she was baked by an artist's poetic sensibilities, the large, retro round glasses and throwback logo from the hyperstylized remake of a vintage, wide-brimmed-hat antihero made decades too late t-shirt the icing on the cake, and B) she said my name.]

Minor technicality if I was inspired by art.

I may have gotten close, but I never crossed the line.

We can even flip back and see how word for word verbatim I wanted away from there.

We can flip back further and see I was asked to read the story in the first place. I didn't search it out.

The circumstances rolled into place found me. No vice. No versa.

["I'm sorry." There's a different jar of peanut butter in each hand.

"It's perfectly alright."

"What'd you go and do that for?" she says to the child more for my benefit. He gives the toothiest grin he can muster with all four teeth his reason knows.

"He's just having fun," I answer on his behalf. "But aren't we all?"

She smiles.

--> Polite towards me, curt towards the little boy.

However, the child has lost interest in smiling. He's moved on to widened eyes and whimpering, using the entire of his fat baby arm to point at the ground.

"No, no. You put it there, so that's where it's gonna stay."]

Plus:

Isn't that what art's all about?

Inspiration. Forging the creative process. Igniting thought and conversations, internally and with others. A source of explanation, like being catfished into a catch-22. It's a point of reference that's as much a part of us as we are it, literally moving us when time stops. It's the bond created when understanding a reference, being able to connect through a quotable when there's nothing left to say.

Therefore, it's not my fault a sweet old lady, as harmless as she is brassy, makes it part of her morning routine to swoon over some old drunk. He, Ryan, resonates that inside her. Not me. She's in love with a man in a role, and Ryan's the one who put him there.

He's the real behind the curtain who reels her from afar, hooked to the character.

Personally, I don't understand the infatuation I merely stumbled upon that was more or less forced upon me, the casual, impartial observer.

What she does, what she feels, is removed from me.

Remember: I followed. I did not lead.

Remember: DJ Boozer sat at my table as a passing stranger. A status, once realized, I upheld. By keeping my end he should have stayed on his. He had no purpose, no connection, let alone the rights.

[He tests the limits of how far he can stretch that chubby arm only to discover that opening and closing his tiny, fat fingers doesn't get him any closer.

"Shouldn't have put it there."

His whimpers turn to grunts in his perseverance.

--> Can't fault the tenacity of the young and ignorant.

His mother leans in, even going as far as to take a step, as she questions the object. "What is that? Is that an egg?"

"Apparently so." I nod affirmation along each syllable. Even going as far as to give it a little nudge with my foot for validity.

"That's odd." She straightens, her hands more on her ass than her hips, as she asks the kid, "Tell Mommy where you found that?"

He starts wailing as if defying an answer.

She looks in her cart. I look in her cart. There isn't a carton of eggs, let alone eleven more.]

And what about all that stuff he said?

That was some beautiful bullshit.

But for real as in literally. Where did that come from?

Follow me: What if it was some sort of inbred offshoot of fan fiction, I'll advocate. Like another existence to an existing character.

--> A hybrid of influence and motivation.

--> What the Jarmusch might call "stealing."

It's only the natural order for stories to intersect, plots to cross, styles to intertwine in a sinuous orgy of finite letters in an infinite language. It's like all the shades of gray. The rooted basis of all art. The creative block. The pieces of what you find inspiring about what inspired others masoned together with such care, such diligence, to last centuries.

But that sure as hell doesn't mean I want him showing up over here.

One must be careful on the path to entertainment.

Love, nature, greed, reality tv.

--> There's the ability for good.

--> But every able has a cane.

--> An unreliable crutch for destruction.

And I was not entertained.

I was not amused.

It's the difference between diligence and dilettante.

Nonsense absolute.

Life is a process. Repeat. Life is a process. Repeat. Your life becomes the body of work.

--> "Everyone's trying to prove they the realest."

And I have no use for his fallacies.

"Anyway, again, I'm sorry." She places the peanut butter with the orange label in the cart. "And I'm sure he's sorry, too, aren't you?"

"Take my word, there's no need for apologies."

The kid's given up on the egg.

His mother combs the little hair he has with her fingers, and he smiles up at her without a care.

They leave. And I periodically glance at the cereal boxes, interrupting the blatancy of me watching her lean against the cart as she walks away.

"Now made with real fruit," quotes a box, unattributed.

--> "Then it must be true."

Why should the cartoon pelican in yellow specs and red kicks, its mouth full of Toasty Froot Smack'yums and milk, care when they're stoopidly delicious?

And! ("But what...")

And it says here with enough box tops you're not only contributing to charity but can enter a code for a chance to win a pair of headphones just like the ones he's wearing...

--> So if that's not a win win steal.

I let the temptation run its course to reason and put the box back into the orderly row I snatched it from, because let's face facts: based on every stoner movie I've ever seen, I'm not high enough for cereal.

#

Side Note: I left my coffee on the table.

--> Don't think of this as an unexpected motif but as a parting gift.

#

"You don't have to be nice
to the gentleman.
You just have to be fancy."
Sunset Red's advice
in the meat department,
dipped in deep-rooted charm.

#

"Why do we, and not us,
but the grand we, purport
to love failure?"
Dr. Justice,
a pulp character
long overdue for
an overblown budget,
in his basket
a mélange of spices:
herbs and powders and dashes and all.

#

"Small world."
Donald Ryan.
"No need to specify. We're not at work."
Smiles.
I didn't know he lived downtown.

"We don't. We just happened to be on this side and been meaning to go to the store, so here we are."

We?

"I'm sorry. My wife and kid. They're around somewhere."

He looks up and down the aisle like where else?

"I broke from the pack. A bad habit of wandering."

Smiles.

Let him do the talking.

"What's that?"

Mentions the obvious.

"So you're having an off night as well?"

Tell him I'm working on something so I took the night off. Be mindful, don't mention who else might be with him.

"That's good to hear. Me, too. The working on something. Not took the night off. I dropped down to part-time, which they interpreted as me needing the busier nights off. But we're getting by. And the work's coming along. Slowly."

Art work or work work?

"Both. Or, at least, hopefully the work will pay off as art. It's like a triptych with two panels shown. The third is implied. Or something. Still trying to get the kinks out. Which I'm sure I will if we ever leave this store."

Smiles.

Dammit, that's an idea I should have stolen. Hell of a lot smarter than just not showing up.

"How about you?"

A novel. Straightforward. Nothing fancy.

"Sounds classic. Maybe we should come together at some point in the process when it's all said and done. Collaborate."

Elaborate.

"You know, read it, critique it, edit it. Combine forces. Whenever you're done. No rush. I'm slow-going. I'll still be awhile, too."

Assure him his input would be beneficial and appreciated. Writers eat that shit up.

"And if you haven't gotten to my story yet, no rush there either."

#

I'm done with Mercato's.

I'm done with Michelle.

I'm done with Dave.

I'm done with pelicans.

I'm done with any person or subplot not ascending Feytag's pyramid.

This is a call to action.

A rising to my own occasions.

The all-inspiring speech at half time three-quarters of the way into the cinematic sporting event: "You're a team player, dammit."

I've nothing to prove and a way to prove nothing.

A plan.

A fool's plan foolproof.

A stage, an impression, a strength: devoted to activity.

I'll go to the diner.

And **work**. And **work**. And **work**. And **work**.

And eventually he'll show. It is his routine. It is his character.

There is no better place to start than back at the beginning.

#

(Con'd)

I'm done with manifestoes.

A final cast off a coat of broken arms.

But as Phillipe "Mo" Tivacional states at the inaugural opening of the first Mercato's, "Declarations force transitions," which has since become something of a slogan for the retailers, where they "declare low prices on brands you love with lower prices for the brands we love."

--> Branding off-brands for the generation of replicas.

--> "A name you can trust."

All that is to say "I'm heading towards the diner."

(See: The minor setback being I haven't quite made it out of the store yet, the homeless tippler within eyeshot, right outside the doors electronically opening for customer convenience, slumped against the bike rack, my(?)/a(?) white cardboard coffee cup in hand.)

#

The Show must be kicking off a new season. Their faces, Kenneth and Jessica, Alex and Burrows, and Bulldog Stampede (more so than the rest) line the register aisles, in character and out.

--> The sleeper hit that became a home run.

--> "The Greatest American Show about the Greatest American Game."

--> Made a celebrity out of What's-His-Name that plays Bulldog "Here Comes The" Stampede, a man with no acting experience goes for it in his sixties, his first role becoming the most well written, smoothly manipulative character ever created, the burgundy leather jacket and white pants with matching cowboy hat starting a trend on the cusp of iconic.

--> From The Great Gambler himself: "Some people have all the luck."

#

The sun's going to set on a so far wasted day.

The diner is a few blocks up. The sooner I get there the sooner I might actually get somewhere. Get this metaphorical show on the road, as the saying goes. (See: let my cockiness continue to screw me.)

Bragging about a novel? There is no novel. I have a character. And not even a good character.

--> Have I already used "roundest flat character?"

--> What about "putting the l in fat?"

I don't think I could make him do less if I tried.

Granted, I might could get a couple of mediocre short stories if I ironed out this stream roller coaster of a character. Definitely some flash prosetry (Ryan's word, not mine) if I zero into a moment like Harrison.

But no matter the length, I'm at a distance without him.

I climb the stairs leading to the glass entryway. There's only three or four steps (depending if you count the platform), but I use the rail like I'm bracing myself for the unattainable, head down carefully monitoring each step.

I place my palm on the frame and look up as I push.

--> I freeze in terror and delight.

--> Like the first screening of *The Great Train Robbery*.

Through opportunity's plate glass door I see him, his broad back turned towards me, squeezing into a booth. "An overblown fortuna."

I set out to write a novel (for whatever reason, the why becoming diluted in the struggle.) I even boasted claims.

So, dammit. That's what I'm going to do.

I'm a man of my words.

#

I have to think fast.

That won't happen inside.

I go around back. An architect always puts another way in.

--> I'll talk to the waitress.

--> Make something up like I do.

--> What did I tell her the other day? An inspector? Or detective?

"Steer clear of them dumpsters, now. Ain't no food in 'm. No food worth eating."

I'll look it up later.

The man the voice belongs to sits on a concrete step, the door propped open a crack behind him. He's bracing his elbows against his hiked knees, balled into the slump of his spine. He smokes, exhaling a peppered potpourri and a double shift.

"Oh, I'm not hungry

--> Except now that I'm thinking about it.

"Or, that isn't my intention. Dumpster diving. I'm looking for the waitress."

"Any business with her can be taken inside. Round front."

This is not the time for banter: "Please, it's urgent."

"Look, bub, whatever it is you've got to say to my wife can be said round front or through me." He snuffs the joint between his fingers as he stands.

And he's flipping huge. As in overall stature, not merely overall mass.

--> Like The Mountain without the definition.

--> Like take a step back.

He's also absolutely right.

I start rattling like a snake: I'm a private eye (see: dick). I was here the other day. My client (see: vague arbitrary legitimacy) hired me to track a man who regularly frequents this establishment. And I would simply ask the waitress, who happens to be your beautiful wife (not flattery, true in her own right), to treat me as if I'm also a long time frequenter of this establishment. As to not raise suspicion to the validity of my presence. And other such jargon for better luck than the viper.

"You don't look like no Marlowe Spade."

"Exactly."

"Got a badge?"

"Got a license. Framed up on the wall back at the office. Could blow my cover carrying it around."

He moves his tongue around the inside of his mouth, bulging his scruff lower lip from side to side, and tucks his hands at his chest behind the blue apron too short for his stature.

"What he do?"

(The perpetual need for justification:) He hasn't done anything, I say. I can't go into much detail (see: I don't have). You understand. But let's imply a very rich and very sincere distant relative is writing out a will and wants to make sure with absolute certainty the relative inside is worthy of the hefty portion of zeros not going to charity, of course.

Why this slapstick ripoff instead of the classic cheater cheating scenario, I don't know. Maybe it's not believable enough. See, that's the trick. Whatever I say doesn't have to be believed thoroughly. It just has to be believed to a point. After which people tend to fill in the inconsistencies on their own. Justify the misinformation or cut scenes and statements. Even the most seasoned Thomas will fumble the ball eventually.

"You might even see some of it, quite frankly. That guy sure seems to enjoy this place."

And when the point isn't caught, appeal. Because with a little finesse, they won't realize the missed connection that soared by.

He eyes me up and down, licks his teeth like closing a high-hat, spits with air whatever he found, the overall act shaking his head into a nod.

Not a yes. Not no. More an affirmation acknowledging words spoken.

And with that he goes back inside.

#

"Can I get a cup of coffee?"

I'm inside. Sitting at the counter. Because like it or not, no matter what ol' Stoic Sal out there digested from the shit I fed him, I have no other choice this far in.

"We can't keep doing this."

I'm off guard but don't stutter. "I've got money today."

I don't care what he said to her or how. Let's be honest: just because I fake a lot of words doesn't mean I think I'll make it work.

"One cup. Maybe two. But you can't stay here all night.

I thought it was too forced.

"I won't."

Too contrived, even for me. But there's no going back once the show starts.

She pours the coffee into the igloo-thick porcelain mug in front of me.

--> The look she's giving me is serious.

--> She's immersed into this role.

--> "I won't."

She winks before turning back to work. A playful break in character. An Easter egg for the fourth wall.

#

Now what?

#

Sip coffee.

#

"It appears
to appeal
to all
demographics."

#

Sip coffee.

#

Fun fact: I read somewhere if a hypothetical we synchronized a couple of watches and then one of us flew around the world the full 360, when we met back up we'd each have different times. Something about gravity causing dissonance.

#

Sip coffee.

#

"Hunky-
dory."

#

I should have thought this through in my struggle to find a way in (as to not raise suspicion. Natural. A flow downstream and believable. I recognize the cigarette guy. He was overly friendly enough earlier. "Hey, buddy, small world. Who's your friend?" might work if we were in Bauchman's Desperation [see: The Theory of Tact]. Secondly, my ego would like to acknowledge the third member of his cast of characters is the type of beautiful you don't want to look stupid in front of) when he pries himself from the booth and hurriedly shuffles to the restroom. I "don't notice."

#

Sip coffee.

#

It's go time now or never to start what I need to finish.

#

M 20__

#

I bust into the bathroom like I own the joint. See badass 80s music television sans the leather jacket or fog machine or laser lights.

--> Because what better place for shits and gigs?

He startles (easily: good. Shows there might be a trait underneath that oversized mansuit) and has the fingers of one hand wiggling in running water. He looks down from the mirror when our eyes meet, but I still manage a nod, upwards, of pleasant recognition. Of "if you own the room it's yours" :: "you're in my world now."

"I need to ask you something." I'm at the stall, using the setting to the fullest. Over the partition, I watch him grab enough paper towels to dry each nubby round finger individually (which he doesn't do, preferring the largely ineffective method of mindless wadding).

"I'm sorry. I don't have any." He reverts.

"I haven't even asked you yet." Or, at least he's consistent.

"Right. Sorry."

"I was just wondering do you now have time for change?" I cast it out there blunt, project into the universe. Face straight, in the zone. If all's a joke to me I'm keeping it serious.

I nudge by to wash my hands.

His face in the mirror is blank. Like a computer stalled mid compute. Like he's traded tennis shoes for new clothes.

So I reel it back just enough to sink it in the current.

"See, I've got just enough to cover the coffee but kind of wanted to leave a tip. There, I said it. Now you can tell me you don't have any."

Lure him with something he understands.

"I don't have any." But his face is dangerously blank. A void channeling through him. Like he's been classically trained for this one performance.

He turns to leave. Grasps the handle. But stands facing the door before opening it.

"Why are you following me?"

He's deadpan serious, like trying to turn the joke on me. But this table don't twist.

"Am I? Are you sure about that?

"You're on the bus every morning."

"So are you."

"And at the payphone."

"Had business that needed attending." Run the control.

"The phone wasn't plugged in."

"Minor technicality." Not the characters running amuck.

"Well what about walking down the street earlier?"

"What street when?"

"Earlier. I saw you."

"Sounds like you're the one keeping tabs on me." I smile to clinch the upper hand. But I'm suddenly unsure of what I'm holding.

What street? When?

An answer he claims knowing that I don't. An awareness. Is this the change I've been seeking?

"Maybe you came in here in the hopes I would follow."

"That's absurd." He scoffs, overacting his turn from the door (there's our actor) in a dramatic-teenage-sitcom-say-it-don't-spray-it sort of way.

But he's not wrong.

"No. You're right. Much too convenient. A bit too deus ex machina."

I step closer to him to drop my wet paper towels in the trash, thinking for an inane reason this action of posting up would emphasize my Nobokov knock-off of throwing stones, but instead the room feels exponentially smaller.

"Too what?"

"Doesn't matter."

Does it? An unanticipated turn in the conversation. It's not rare: these things occur in the process. But where this guy's at? This guy has nothing to turn from, nothing to turn into. Or maybe he has. Maybe it's not some sort of trick and instead a subtle technique, a progression so natural I've yet to notice. It would explain why he's so damn boring.

--> Cross off the ruse.

--> Cross out everything, in fact.

So far, my apologies, it's a giant waste of time, effort, energy on both our parts. Like applying meaning where there is none (see: the door is blue because it's blue). So here's the plan to pan out: I'm also going to act natural and unyielding. Get out before I'm blocked. Regroup myself and rework the situation. He wants to lead, let's see where he takes us. See if we've reached a sort of plot point, because otherwise there's no point.

"Back to it: you 110% don't have any change?"

--> Cause I stay true to my character.

--> Cause I could really use a tip.

"I already told you," he reiterates, flatly.

He stuffs his pudgy knuckles into his pleated khakis and pulls out what the hell?

Pinched between his fingers is: is that an eggshell?

I get it. Eggshells are the overarching link in search of a theme, but it doesn't work when he literally thrusts it at me.

--> The work is me literally dropping them in on him.

"Thanks, man. I really appreciate this." I take it from him with the intensity of a young grasshopper (see: I don't even know how it got there but it's mine now.)

--> Obviously he wants me to have it as it was my idea in the first place.

--> But an idea I didn't put in that place first...

"I'll be seeing you." I'd scene enough for now.

Determination overload.

--> Wax off.

I keep my breathing regulated, a rhythm of cool as I reenter the dining room. But my heart is gasping through my chest.

Will Power over Character. (Primal Rage vs. Clay.)

Regulate my DHEA ("New All Natural Wonder Drug!")

I swing by the counter, pound back the last of the coffee now cold, and slam down the shell like it's a monetary allusion.

The waitress drops off food to the booth as I'm walking out.

In need of fresh air.

Something fresh.

Force the ultimatum: That magical overhyped moment played out for mild amusement before nonintrusive situations, preferring small dream coincidences like food on the table when returning from the restroom (you know it, you love it).

-Or-

Make him find me like the eggshells find him.

A) Take charge of my role in this as writer and/while

B) pester the shit out of him until I coincidently incite the right incident.

Because at this point in the plotting one has to happen, there is no other choice, extenuating the genreless, and roughing this draft.

This business already in too deep like LLCool J.

I post up on a stoop next to the diner. There's no lights on inside the house now offices. It's after 5. And equally convenient, the steps are a straight shot into the diner's window.

--> Balcony seating.

Quiet. The scene's already in progress:

Our hero center stage. He's frantic, out of breath.

He says something to the effect of Where'd he go? And his friend, let's call him Dave, sitting in the booth in the foreground replies real bro-ish like Woah, Buddy Boy, the food is boss or the grub is Michael Scott or some other catchphrase not catching.

The waitress, who the audience doesn't know is the plot's accomplice, Sally was it? Questions our hero to maintain an air of unaccountability, which in turn causes our hero, and dear spectator, to question his psychological state.

The mystery!

The intrigue!

Our hero rambles vague modifiers at best, obviously he too is in the midst of deeply questioning.

Sally toys with him, emulating the femme fatales she sided with years ago when life was still black & white. She implies the stranger is a good guy. No. A great guy, with a casual remark about his gratuity. She catches steam with her smile.

So what does our hero do? He rushes to the exit, of course (of course!). But he stops. His food is on the table. Hot. Ready. And he hasn't settled his account.

Seriously!

Stop dragging!

Right. No excuses. Our hero subconsciously channels his motivation: "You have to unwind before you unravel" — Wm. Wilson, best-selling novelist, crime fiction, and showrunner for the *Cop Drama* spinoff *Cop Drama: Glass City*.

He pushes the door, the hairs curved to his head sway in rows (props to the effects department) in the rush of what's outside. He blurts out something on the verge of unheard of, a line about a tab: a luxury for a protagonist in a pickle.

Sally says it's all taken care of. Pure, old-fashioned class. But he doesn't pay much heed. Instead, he gives one last glance towards the table, feasting his eyes on the food spread where he should be sitting, savoring what might have been but choosing to taste the unknown.

He exits.

The lights dim.

Curtain.

He's outside the diner, and I watch him look for me.

Maybe there's more to him than meets the eye. Something deeper that resonates with strangers. That thing that draws them in. That makes him more naturally compelling than others. An ethereal connection between routines and what ifs hatching a chance encased in emotion. Every move, every thought, every perception a vicarious association in a closed loop.

It's all just a projection.

And it's my job to look for it. Feel for it. Discover and nurture it. Incubate "the little things in life." Up close. In depth. In person.

I was drawn to him, exposed to him by circumstance, a force of nature naturally compelling me. For no other reason than I have to (see: why?).

"Where you off to in such a hurry?" I call from on high.

His legs stop at the sound, but his torso jerks forward not expecting my voice. He turns his head slowly, like well that was easy while questioning too easy, looking at me as if I'm a mirage either to trick or destroy him.

But opportunity had arrived.

"I'm not sure."

"Then by all means, don't let me hold you up." So pious. So unobtrusive.

"No, it's not as you make it seem."

It came to me: come to me.

"It's more I'm not sure why you took it."

Coax him out of his shell (for a lack of a better term, the best term).

"The shell." (I know.) "Back at the bathroom. Why did you take it?"

"You offered it. I distinctly said, 'thank you.'"

His body slumps inward and he looks toward the ground. "Doesn't much answer the question."

"True," I say, nurturing this curiosity. Bringing it to the surface. I'll play the trope of the mysterious stranger. The hitchhiker coming from nowhere and heading just as far, who in turn takes the driver for the ride. The lurking figure who eventually steps from the shadows to reveal his true amity.

--> A saint herring.

"Look. I'm sorry to bother you."

I snap back. (Passively mysterious).

He's turning to leave.

"You're not the main character." (Actively mysterious.)

That gets his attention. (Structurally mysterious.)

"What if I told you you're not the main character?"

The streetlight flickers, struggling into the high key natural light of night. (Technically mysterious.)

"And I'm supposing you are?"

"Not necessarily." Be vague. "I'm more of an imitation." Too vague.

"Right. I have to get back."

Convince him he's lying.

"I don't think your friends mind."

"I need to pay my bill."

"'It's all taken care of.'"

He looks towards the diner to find his next line.

"I thought you didn't have any money."

"You're welcome."

"Well, I need to..."

Cut him off: "Left a hefty tip as well, so you're running out of excuses."

"I'm not."

I hold back the laugh but not the smile.

"I need to say goodbye."

"You don't."

"Excuse me?"

Sure, if you want one: "Fine, here's your excuse. It's obvious you left and they'll catch up later the next time you see them." Is this true? Anything is with enough confidence.

I stand and descend the staircase.

--> Get on his level.

"C'mon. Take a walk with me. No more no."

He won't look at me. "Who do you think you are?"

Bold move, cotton. Don't dodge the question (Isn't it evident who I am by now?).

"Where are my manners?" Let's see if this pays off. I stick my hand out into formality. "The name's Don Bronco."

He lifts his head. "And what's with the small tablet?"

"It's actually a large phone."

"Why are you always on it?"

"Don't focus on it and you won't even notice" how I edit "it" out.

He looks up and down the block. Empty. The only souls on the scene. He lets out an exaggerated contemplation, ended in "Ezekiel."

"I know."

He grabs my hand, unwittingly committing to the pact he doesn't know we've made. As if our hands clasping literally facilitates our personal connection into a physical connection. Creativity ignites in the shake. It hits me. You don't have to see the air about them. But you have to touch it to know it exists. The intangible must be felt, truly felt, to have any change. Inspire the epiphany. What my friend here needs is an emotional connection.

"Now let me introduce you to the man in the burgundy jacket."

I begin up the street, coaxing him with a head nod after a few steps, far enough ahead for a digression:

Let's say there's two Teds. One Ted (Johnson) argues creativity consists of collaborative innovation via gestation. The other Ted (Ferguson) essentially sums this up as a "remix." The only real difference between these twinned definitions is the technicality of permission.

So, the idea is simple.

If Ryan wants me to write him something then I'll write him something. It'll be the best thing he's ever read.

The premise: My pal here is going to play matchmaker.

--> Nothing plots more weight than "love conquers all."

And we just so happen to both know a sweet old lady who happens to be lovelorn.

You experience inspiration. You don't choose it. Without, the story is hopeless.

Plus, for real: If one of his drunks can stumble upon me, we can soberly happen upon one of his.

"Where are we going?"

"To see the man in the burgundy jacket."

"I got that much out of this. But where are we going?"

"Few more blocks." I think.

I don't recognize where we are which means we're getting closer to somewhere.

"Stop. Just stop."

When he touches the street lamp for support it goes out.

--> A sign lighting the way to dark places.

"Can you please tell me what's going on?"

"That I don't know."

He looks at me like a cartoon trapped on a desert island, where he's famished and I'm the big sandwich. Crazed on the verge of ravenous. "What do you mean 'I don't know?'"

"Exactly. I know as much as you do. Not much more, but not a thing less."

--> A smidge of honesty is the best policy.

"But you know about the eggshells."

"Yes."

"And that's why you took it?"

"No."

"Right. And what about this man in the coat?"

"In the burgundy jacket. It's just an idea."

I continue walking, continue pushing onward. It's not structurally the time or place for this.

Overcoming block after block along the way not looking back.

I can hear his laggard breathing behind me.

--> A P.O.V. sound effect in a late night, camp slasher.

--> Coming up on his victim.

--> The unsuspecting bar finally stumbled upon.

--> Always seemingly a step behind until it's too late.

(o_O)

/

/

!(@o@)!

/

/

(x_x) Blood

Arrival Too: The Return

Hitting the corner feels like stepping into the night, the blue dusk now black, the air much colder without wind, the lampposts lining the opposite side of the street accentuating the vacant darkness of the lot we're passing.

There's no fog or damp or expressionist shadows.

These things are replaced by an ineffable uneasiness.

Like the blue and pink moniker's low drone, the type of consistent frequency used in disturbing scenes (see: irreversible), an added level for perceiving the unsettling.

However, we're not walking out of a story.

We're going the deepest in.

I grab the doorknob, an old-fashioned twist lock. It's slick. Slicker than any knob should be. From the years of tarnished fingers polishing the gold tint to bronze.

I'm about to turn it. I am.

--> Defiantly no going back now.

When that cliffhanging moment is decided for me. The once green door opens, pushing me a few steps from the entrance.

And who walks out but unmistakably him.

Even without the headphones and glasses, you couldn't miss that overall mass of head. The wine laced halitosis still undeniably self-fermenting, bubbling hiccups.

"My pardons, good sirs."

I hold the door.

--> A reflex, arm extended when the door came at me.

But now I'm stuck, frozen, am I breathing? studying the light gray rectangle where a mat once laid like I was piecing together a timeline for how long it'd been gone.

My companion's feet step out of the way.

The drunk shuffles by without a quip.

Anticlimactic.

Which is the best type of climactic at the moment. The kind that packs some sort of significance for some outside observer looking in, without calling attention directly to us. Independent new sincerity. The kind I don't have to personally deal with currently.

So we enter the bar.

The air smells like warm vanilla in a junk room. That old mold smell. Like stepping into what the Bunker's house would smell like these days in summer reruns, with all the wood paneling and muted reds and oranges.

The place is sparse on lights as it is on patrons. Spotting who we've come to see, sitting near the corner of the bar cast in shadows like a stock character in his trademarked burgundy jacket was easy enough.

The hard part is where we go next: the stool next to his.

My eyes are unusually dry. The air stagnant, harder than the drinks. My abnormally frequent blinks look as uncomfortable as they feel. I order a soda from the bartender. His upturned brow reaffirms the infrequency of my fraught order.

The word "same" passes over my shoulder.

--> Great minds.

I greet the man in the burgundy jacket. Or, at least that was my intention. He doesn't pay me a heed of attention. To him I'm just another casual observer to get my fill then leave. In and out. A glance around the room. The same as the last and the next.

At the bottom L of the bar, a man with a disheveled collar under a nice suit slams a shot glass on the stained wood. The blast reverberates. He leaves to find his story's ending.

As they say: "Time is a construct, but timing is key." (See: *Right Place, Right Time* by Dr. Hap N. Stance, if that's even his real name.)

The bartender sets a rocks glass in front of me. I fold the stir straw over the rim.

--> Why even put one?

--> That's just how they do things elegant.

I take a sip, the ice clanks a chill against my teeth, the beverage the perfect blend of flat::diluted you'd expect in a place like this. Like drinking in the mood. Stripped down and possibly diet.

With the protagonist gone, I strike up a casual "So, how are things?" then sip my beverage and don't wait for an answer. "Good. That's good to hear."

Minor technicality: I'll be lucky to get any acknowledgement.

--> Didn't seem narratively important to mention earlier.

--> But now we're here there's no flow to hinder.

That's the thing about these extra side characters: sometimes they're just not meant for more than what they are. Their place, inherently, is to stay the same. The story simply moves around them. Not about them. "Consistency is key." (See: The bartender tending bar.) Therefore, this leads to a blatant hesitancy for any interaction outside their zones of established comfort.

However!

However, there are times you can construct a break. The trick is making them think you're part of their world. That they're not part of any other.

Just take the puzzle and build the pieces.

Create the narrative for them.

Paint them real.

Guide them with responses they don't give.

"Who, Zeek?"

"Ezekiel."

And, eventually, if they fall backwards into the part then they'll fall into character (see: the seven minute case of one B. Fett).

"No one, really," I continue. He still hasn't moved. Not even to sip his beer. On pause. Unsure whether he's buffering or too drunk to compute. So I keep feeding him conversation. "Just some guy I've come across. But we've come to have a little chit-chat with you," I poke him. "Buddy Boy here's been having the, you know, *the problem*," I prod.

I briefly digress into what's this italicized "problem?" I've no idea. So this is open for discussion, if I'm being frank here. It just sounds good. Vague yet legitimate. Because (A) my guy hears it and associates it with the shell, thus propagating his internal dialogue with the seeds of change and (B) the other guy takes it any way he knows how. If we're going to get emotional then we need to test those waters.

--> Find a spot to cast off.

He picks up the glass he'd been staring at with all intensity and drinks, tilting back the amber like making up for time lost. For all the sips I've interrupted. And he begins talking to the glass, the place he's been storing his memories for years, so naturally the place he finds them.

List of claims (adjusted):

- He "was once a captain on a warship."
- The Sea Fox is "as big as she was beautiful."
- WWII is "the great war."
- The French have subpar navigational skills described as a "miscalculation petite."
- "A lifeboat of four sailors, one soldier, and a war criminal" cannot withstand a warship's impact.
- Even sailors drown.
- [Pause for remembrance (see: dramatic effect).]
- Words aren't necessary in recognizing an "evil a step down from pure."

--> A body implicit.

- French soldiers can be "surprisingly rugged."

• War creates factions.

• Fractions create war.

• Neither creates what's just.

• Just creates destruction.

• [Pause before outcome (see: swirled memories).]

• Tension mounts. Blood blackens.

• Mob Mentality

• Vs.

• Quiet Condoning.

• "And me?"

• [Pause to finish beer needed to finish story. (See: A. effectively dramatic or B. clichéd.)]

The bartender as if on cue wordlessly swaps the empty, the foam sloshing over the edge in the exchange. Badda bing, badda bang. A regular reflex.

• "Picking the wrong side can be shit, but not picking a side, (see: pause, pause, pause) that is weakness."

• If "that chain weaken[s], there's no soldering it back."

• [End by beginning new beer from the top. (See: cyclical metaphor.)]

• Okay.

• That's it?

• Okay.

• I can work with this.

• Recap the recapitulation:

It matters not if the man in the burgundy jacket's backstory anecdote is historically sound or unsound, and if I'm at best minimally educated on all the victor's rallies fought, then I can learn my way into his worldview. Stay true and connect.

Or, given the plot crunch's more than a mouth full, for the sake of time and effort in a story not about him, I'll just convince him into mine.

--> Knowledge is power.

--> Power is beneficial control.

--> Based on True Events.

--> Flip the script.

Chin up, buck-o.

[Presumably friendly. Old-fashioned, brass tact "bro."]

(Cont'd)

We all know how it ends.

[Sip from the rim of the glass because he's not the only one who knows how to use a drink to influence conversation.]

(Cont'd)

The crew barges in. Scared lil' Joey antagonizes. The soldier gives a soul-drenched morality speech. Blah blah blah. Cold War implication. The audience eats it up. You win Best Director 1962, snag an award for screenplay, yet still snubbed Best Picture.

[Know this isn't true, but make it true by saying it. The words become the facts. What can be convinced as real is real. And real is understood. Understanding alters perceptions. And what are perceptions but reality?

*Clarified: Don't let the characters dictate your actions. Accept what's given to create your own answers, then provide the questions. There must be stuff in the box in order to think outside it. The character's backstory is deeply personal but only to that character. So not knowing what's in the box is fine as long as you can claim what's pulled out. Own it. Vindicate the personal: the art's for others but the creation is yours.

**Tempered: Command such facts as if you know. Not being in World War II is a non-issue. You've seen enough bits and pieces on screens to grasp it. And you know screens, big and small. You understand screens. You understand their characters. So be direct, and action. The characters can only be understood by your perceptions, and therefore, naturally align with your understanding. Take the prize away from that Story on the West Side, from the Splendor in the Grass. Tell him they no longer exist. He's now in the annals of history, no longer just a man in a burgundy jacket. He's The Director. The best one, in fact, in '62. And his film, whose edgy screenplay (also now by him) was lauded at its time of release, can be found from time to time after hours on price-point programming packaged towards nostalgia, "uncut and commercial free."

***Processed: Manipulate his story. Use the gap between the production and the understanding (Broca__/__Wernicke). The change in format doesn't falsify the past stripped down. The conflicts of war and men and men at war rage true. It's the role that adapts. The character he creates is then no more and no less contained by the parameters stated. Facts don't change. Instead, adjust, design, work, and release his truths as true into a readjusted, redesigned, reworked, rereleased, reassimilated remix. Create the interpretation the creation creates.]

I swallow. He digests.

The long and short of full steam ahead is a reckless quickness followed by now what?

In-digesting: The man sits like a glitch, still and unmoved. The silence trapped like a bubble in his glass searching for air.

I sit tight, tense in my fabricated confidence, hoping for once what he's looking for in the glass in front of him is registering an answer at the bottom.

But he doesn't move. Doesn't rush the process. Sitting silently focused, not drinking. The wait of contemplation its own paradox of halves, perpetually cutting itself off at the middle, centered but forever going nowhere.

All the while, I'm the arrow Zeno fired.

My one shot.

Not even necessarily needing to hit the center directly, per se.

"And what of the time I was an Arkansan farmer whose son returns home years after his release from a stint in the federal pen downstate with a lascivious siren on his arm? And me being the hard-drinking, Sunday-going man without convictions like I am, I lust after the bombshell, and she welcomes it, seducing my touch right under my boy's nose, he all the while remains shut off and shut out like he was still locked up, like they never did release the boy that went in."

As long as I hit the target deep enough. Penetrate close to the core.

"What of it?" I dig into him:

"It was critically and commercially a flop."

"Your first, at least in terms of critical disdain."

"Which, let's be honest, generally doesn't account for squat with the general public."

Stillness.

"Don't get me wrong," I pick deeper, jackhammering statements:

"Casting real Arkansan farmers as father and son was a strategic move."

"Their performances were raw and real."

"And against Dolores 'Dorothy' Chip's sublime subtleness was naturally visceral."

--> Find the avenue, take the street.

--> OctothorpeNameDrop

"It's a shame it marked her only big screen appearance."

"A blip on the radar before obscurity."

"So while the screenplay could have benefited from some editing, the direction was precise and the New American way it was pieced together innovative..."

I trail off when he sips his beer. Action means reaction. Motion means emotion.

--> Drive it home.

"The real downfall was the affair."

--> OctothorpePoundItIn

"You leave her out of this," he says into the drink like a man drowning.

I lay into him poetic jabs, flowing word after wordplay, buzzing on a writer's high. His body tenses absorbing the shock, knuckles white around the glass, brow furrowed from the blows. This: this is how you extract emotion from a character. Drawing resonance like drawing blood. Scrape for scrape until open.

The showdown.

The payout.

My protagonist appears intrigued by the current progression of plot. I cannot confirm nor deny this, but for the record from the corner of my eye witness account he's fidgeting with anticipation. Right hooked into the story I'm throwing. An unstoppable force of mayhem where I might not know what I'm doing but I'm doing what I might. Damn the damage. I'm connecting with two different characters in the same building on separate levels. Literally the same floor but separate stories. I can't let it go like a blow to the head. But I push harder, thinking quick in quips and phrases. This is where perception puts the key in king. I see the opening that will bring them together and create something bigger outside myself.

"My friend here knows Ms. Chip, alive and well, living of all places here in this city."

The charge down my spine confirms how good that felt. I conform to the curve. I sink into the chair.

"I don't give a damn, you son of a bitch."

Bask in the gnashing.

"I'm hearing clearance to land a blow that'll take off that shit-eating grin. Does your friend know that, you imperious fool?"

I turn to see if my said friend knew this, but fall out of the bar stool, barely landing upright, saying something stupid like "That's our cue."

This is bad bad. Like badder than bad, who's bad, you know it. Mr. Jackson nasty.

He's holding an eggshell.

Where he found it isn't as important as he shouldn't have it.

--> (I'm sorry, *Mrs. Jackson.)

Not here, not ever here.

--> (I am for real.)

My hand literally shakes a tap, tap, tap, tap to his shoulder.

"Now's about the time we should be leaving." I don't wait. I heed my own advice.

--> A Chuck Jones warning sign tacking together [WRONG WAY] with [NO EXCAPE].

--> "That's all, folks."

"What about the bartender?"

I'm one foot out the door. The false security of one step ahead. We don't have "time" for this. As it is all relative, and our presence isn't familiar. We (see: I) may have gone a bit too abyss into a background character's background, unresolving a slew of unnecessary subplots to the original being, that final draft text, which can be easily and skillfully entertained with filler. However, the mess is made when these flash paced anecdotes now narrating his world don't exist on this side of town. Never did, never will. We're visitors flipping through, infringing on the rights of overstayed welcomes, drafting a plague of isms. Nothing but an echo should resonate when the last sentence is said at the final paragraph's punctuated end.

So what does matter at this time is his being behind me, the synchronicity of not missing a beat, not the "He's been fully compensated" I slip him out of courtesy. There's a loophole (see: cul-de-sac of inspiration). If we can cross the street, and if the man in the burgundy jacket meets us next to our terms, the wards get rewarded. Any interaction within this proximity could be argued as an appreciation of influence. "A work after..." Like an homage without the lengthy passing of time. Fandom as artistry. To be caught arranging what's already arranged is frowned upon. However, rearranging is flattery.

And that line is fine: a shadowed edge cut by the streetlamp. I toe it without standing out. Not hiding, per se. More in plain sight.

"With a minimum of 20 percent?"

Is this his theme?

"That's what you really want to know?"

"It's just anything less isn't industry standard."

"Heard." All this escalating drama and he's conflicted with gratuity? Here's his tip: "Move on."

"I didn't hear anything." Sound connoting thought.

"And you won't with this banter stalling."

"I thought you said we were leaving." Which he doesn't have to completely complete.

"And we left, right?"

"We didn't get very far." Just get close enough to give me something to work with.

"We're far enough, literally. And we'll go further. But that's on you, my friend."

"When?" Give me that precious standard minimum.

"That's relative."

"What?"

"That's more like it."

I don't exclaim, not the punctuation, but my insides are fireworks. Minor technicality if he asks to question the question rather than the situation. Posing the right one vests for an answer, and this investment, at its very least, is where the story lies.

"Rhetorically, what time you think he leaves?"

His lower back slouches as his shoulders rise, head slightly cocked, pointer up, mouth dropped, as if the correct answer relies on the position of his body.

I continue in order to keep my ally to this rhetoric silent, pre-misinterpretation. "Basically never. He's there, in that bar, beer in hand, perpetually. Before, and the during, and the after. In a sense, always. That's why we had to set a trap, lay the bait."

--> The hook.

"No one ever just complies because you show up or ask. So we good cop/bad copped it."

--> The line.

"I know you watch at least one of those detective dramas. They're on every night."

"Was I the good cop or the bad cop?"

--> The titanic.

"Bad cop, obviously. And you played the part with gusto."

--> True lies.

"I'm sorry. I can't. I've exaggerated liberties," I say even though he looks satisfied with the answer, as if it was the only and obvious choice. "You're actually neither cop," because that's not the path we want to travel, "but you're doing fine. Just keep doing," because telling him he's a waste of time is unproductive of the time already wasted.

"So then what exactly am I supposed to be doing with this?"

This? This should be the tipping point. This should be where all the pieces start coming together. This should be where the sparks of magic begin to fly.

"What about it?"

It being the present gifted before you? Taking in your surroundings? Giving attention, like I am, across the street? Following my lead?

"Do you at least know what's going on?"

"Specifically?"

It's the specific interaction between people in relation to their place.

"Specifically."

It's the setting and the temporal state.

"In a way of sorts."

It's the emotional surge and the change of direction.

"And nonspecifically?"

"Nonspecifically? Then, yes, I know."

It's the hollow shell of a story.

"And?"

"And it's nothing specifically, yet." Just an exposition of events from an uninvolved observer, a channel reporting real time occurrences going nowhere.

Footage pleading for something to happen. The neverending backstory. "We're nearly halfway there."

--> I hope.

--> Say his name to: the next chapter.

The man in the burgundy jacket opens the bar door across the street.

Abrupt and subtle that a) even with astute focus it would be missed if it wasn't for the sound of the hinges scraping into the nighttime and b) it isn't opened wide but cracked enough to peek from.

Confession: Honestly, I'm not altogether positive if it's actually the man in the burgundy jacket. But when you don't know you assume what's made up (see: guess and hope for the best).

And then he appears. (see: right all along).

Or, at least his head does.

Close enough and better than nothing. Especially on this stage of the process.

Or did.

--> The door shuts.

Is.

--> The door opens.

Was.

--> "Here kitty kitty kitty" never works. Can't force a character nor coax one that isn't yours.

Is.

--> But you try kitty kitty.

Was.

Past tense like your hopes now you've started this thing.

Now you're literally and figuratively standing in the dark with a stranger and nowhere to go.

Stuck on the outside looking at.

Until he shuffles out.

Is.

--> Good kitty kitty.

The figure sulks forward in the darkness against the pink and blue haze of the neon bar sign. And granted, if I was in a better mood, with characters worth the ink and effort, I'd see the poetry in this, the physical beauty of the contrast, a cinematographer's dream. However, this is not my state of mind in this state of affairs. His lollygagging halting my narrative page slower than his liquor lubed arthritic stroll. He's lucky he's on his side of the street, because at this rate I'm so inclined for a car to come speeding down the lane to spread him like traffic jam on the asphalt. At least that would blur the line between inciting action and instant gratification. What produces more intense emotions in a spectator than shock? Fact: horrified people turn pages. Just ask the reigning King of the genre. But alas thou noble squire, the November knight is upon us...

"Something I can do you for?"

"You have my attention."

"Me? No." I look down at the old man in the burgundy jacket without looking down at him. Even without his brittle hunch he's shorter than I'd imagined. Yet the lines on his face are chiseled to stern and his brown eyes full, not taking any shit. Height is the character trait, while stature creates the man. "Targeting me as having something of yours is close but apologetically misdirected." My eyes cut to the only other person on the street, where the man in the burgundy jacket's attention should be, the man outside the spotlight, "My distracted companion, however..."

looks like a black hole trying to solve the mysteries of the universe, a glitch glitching on itself, literally buffering.

Why carry out the punishment to a punctuated term?

"Well?"

Because now, whether intended or not, the man in the burgundy jacket is as much a part of this narrative as he is his own.

And explanations are deserved for being dragged this far into this mess.

Hard-boiled evidence to prove these sentencings.

All the while being held in contemplation.

And yet there's silence.

Hear that?

Exactly.

I watch the old man watch him. I can't tell if this prolonged hush is encouraging or discouraging the tension. Bait for anticipation.

Then my pal blinks, sparking a look across his face like the flash of a clunky box television being turned on, the sound of static humming behind the screen faint but omnipresent, the soft muscles of his face wobbling a warm up, taking their time like the screen's seizure into view, like what we're about to witness is the precise moment we've been waiting all week to see, live and in color.

And he says! "Well..."

An inconclusive repetition.

A touch of kin to syndication.

A rerun for the first time is new if never before seen.

"Sass like that means you think you're some sort of badass, don't you?" The man in the burgundy jacket juts a pointed finger like 1950. "I'll have you know I've seen things, scrounged things, created things out of my own powerless being. More than I've ever put out which is more than you'll ever understand."

He responds with a soft, "Yes, sir," like pressing the right button.

"Don't get soft on me, sonny."

Thus leaving me the sole determiner to whether Zeek here ("Ezekiel," he says) is a genius or a fluke. "No one's going soft. Or hard. Or side up," I throw in for my own amusement to little things, "or any variation of which. We're merely having a friendly conversation amongst friends."

"All my friends are dead."

Now Captain Debbie Downer in the burgundy jacket could have carried enough weight to sink us. All loot, no gold. But I veer a "Not all your friends," and ahoy! What seemed dead in the water is now plotting the course.

As in: at the helm, waiting on the next wave.

--> The one swelling behind his eyes.

He acts like he doesn't hear me, like by looking behind his shoulder to the bar he won't have to register the line I fed him, deal with the reality of the only person he hopes I'm implying but no way could possibly mean. "I'm tired of you two, and I'm incredibly thirsty. So how about we stop yanking my old shriveled." He's trying to sound tough. He's trying to save face. "Do you know who I am, big man?" But his voice is wavering.

Pause for a brief digression on the interest of curiosity: While clearly addressing the largest of the three, he's looking at me. I can't explain why, and I'm not about to do so. That's the way it happened so that's the way it happened. A note of observation. One that does not affect the scene at hand as he keeps the prattle rowing, "Of course not, you're too young. Let me tell you something about who I am..." diving in about his work, his wife, his daughter, which may not be the sweetest soliloquy to swallow, but I'll be damned if it's not a spoonful helping the medicine go down. Poetic in the poetry of Pratchett kind of way: saccharine sweethearts and British pounds.

--> Bravo, Ryan. Bravo.

And then open up the heavens, he says it:

"Enter Dolores Chip, a plain girl known as Dorothy where she grew up in..."

The spirit of emotion embodying happenstance. Like a ghost writing the words of authorial thoughts and character deeds.

A chill heats the tinge of excitement.

It's haunting. Really. That precise moment you see the framework of letters building with word upon word into the grand structuring of symbols on pages.

--> Déjà vu in a dream.

--> A mandala's outermost line.

--> "...she stumbled into my existence, quite literally, when..."

His face (see: my friend) is draped in the dark just out of the streetlight's reach. I look for some sort of Presque-esque reaction nonetheless. A bell of recognition in his silent countenance. Anything but blank shadow.

Comparative facts:

So what if the madam's sir name altered slightly and her given name stylized a bit (that young, hip demographic)? The words still come from the same root (see: taste similar on the tongue).

--> "...of southern culture, on location, real people. The salt of the earth kind of people..."

Or there's always the possibility he's saving face, situationally, both of us on the same page, keeping the negative out from the k and the w, and not getting all giddy as a schoolgirl at the sound of a name.

Stoic.

--> A suitable for the situation.

--> Representational.

--> "...I remember the nerves. Can you believe..."

The man in the burgundy jacket's voice picks up weight and cadence, like his girl Friday taken for carry granted on a Saturday night: "Oh poor boohoo America's sweetheart," underscored by the anger remembered.

But unlike a broken crystal film, it's a delight to listen to. He was made for this monologue. Like I should be jealous at how smoothly rounded he'd been created if I wasn't so involved in his story by the time "the accident happened."

Damn it's well written.

As in dammit, don't compare.

We lock eyes as he says her name one last time with melancholy, and it's as if I can see in this brief moment of verbalized syllables he understands his purpose of recall has nothing to do with himself. His memory, the accompanying act.

"And for what?" he says, casting his eyes to the ground.

Every note and ounce of his being pausing, long and dramatic.

A minor character digging deep for cored emotions.

From pain or for emphasis? He can't help either, made for both.

Another supporting award for his mantel.

"And now I come here, hidden in plain view. Masked without a mask. A nothing. Spending my days or time or life trying to drown out the black bleakness, speckling the infinite hollowness with the memories of once was. I relive the past. Literally. Without boundary. An albumen of thought around a yolk of remembered bliss. Fickle but unhatched, nevertheless, fluid and soured. Every day the same. So please, if it has come to this, please, if there is any chance" he lets the sentence trail off into a natural fragment.

I welcome the pause. Bask in it, really. 50/50 in awe of not having composed this harsh beauty of character while on the brink of accomplishment. I am here wading in the moment. A literary bathing of anticipation for my pal's response:

"A chance of what, exactly?" flows forth.

And it's a wash.

Before I completely and utterly lose it, the man in the burgundy jacket beats me to it: "A couple of dicks. That's what you two are. Bags of dicks" lumping me in with this nonsense. But I'm just as shocked as he is. I'm with him. How my character said the words bleak as the shadow they came from, invading the man in the burgundy jacket's hopes, dull like a knife that jaggedly tears a wound open.

--> The auteur's one hit wonder.

"Now, sir, I must object." My pal Zeek doesn't move nor does his voice waver from casual. As if this be all end all doesn't require an explanation but he graces us with one anyway. "Understand, I've had a long day, and as it's progressed I've grown increasingly hungry on top of not rightly knowing why we've all been dragged out here."

"For serious?" The words fumble over the sheer irritation on my tongue. "Not a clue? Not even a stab?"

He's serious: "I don't concentrate well when I'm hungry." (Insert second clueless knife metaphor here.)

"The bus lady. You know, the lady on the bus." I can't win.

"Ms. D?"

As in ding-ding-ding "Yes!" tell him what he's won.

--> (A "Small Fry," which I reiterate in case he's still unsure, because if I don't know at this point then who does?)

"More about this bus," the man in the burgundy jacket chimes in.

"I don't know much about her, honestly. Except she's rather intrusive."

"Let's get back on the bus."

Stay on course, "Yeah, Zeek, the bus," because the old man in the burgundy jacket is right: we need to get onto something.

My pal throws something out under his breath.

The man in the burgundy jacket catches it: "Is that the line?"

"Is my name the line?"

--> Oh, sweet Buñuel. This is absurd.

"Where can I find the Ezekiel?"

"I'm Ezekiel."

"So you're the driver."

"Merely a passenger on The Grey."

--> "Seriously?"

--> "This is the trip we're taking?"

--> All this built up tension, more backwards than Costello and Abbot.

"When?"

"Bus 12 is any given weekday. Seven:Twenty sharp-ish."

The man in the burgundy jacket cackles full on delight, his old body quivering with a restrained vigor that hasn't jolted since his heyday. "Ha-ha-hot damn.

I'll be seeing you then, you beautiful dick bag. Bright and early."

And with his closing line he fades out by returning to *Fellcws*, dragging the tread of his worn-out dress shoes across the pavement, each scuff, although slow and deliberate, prances like a jovial jazz pianist in la-la-love.

(Which is more than I can say now stuck again with Mr. Blandy McNocharacter and his lack of reactions other than the clap over a shallow) "Well" (his resonation draws from.)

"That's it?" (Aloud but not to him, a chuckle trembling on pissed.)

(He answers anyway,) "I should probably be going," or at least something that sounds along those lines. I only hear red, lacking comprehension.

"I was expecting so much more." (I sputter before my brain shuts up my lips.) And yet here we are, haha, further away than when we started. Full circle? No, no. Completely flipped right-side-upside-down like the b in pathos and stranger things, returned to the same spot physically in the present, you *are* here, stuck behind the future not going anywhere.

"Have a wonderful evening." (See: rolling ditto.)

"That's all you have to say?"

"Farewell?"

A literal anti climax.

"What horseshit." Ridiculous. Absurd without the tradition.

If this is how it's going to play then let's play.

If he's so dammed hungry, let's rush him some cuisine.

Stuff him to the rafters with mediocre slices of mediocre pizza till there's no more room for excuses.

Pull the worst deus ex machina since the eagle left the mountain to put this mediocre story to its mediocre end.

Because at the end of the day, even mediocre pizza is still pizza.

Even if you don't love it, you'll deal.

Headlights turn from the corner, branded distinct by the Pelican Pizza pelican soaring at the same rate.

--> 30 minutes or it's free*

--> *Within a 3.2 miles radius, terms and conditions may apply, only at participating locations, see store for details.

The tires don't screech, which surprises given the speed v. condition of the multicolored compact, as the car comes to a halt across the oncoming land of would be traffic. The engine takes this moment to rev in exhaustion, catching its breath finally idle.

"One you guys 'Buddy Boy' Zeek Macray?" A voice, sounding oddly familiar in a forced northern accent kind of way, asks through the mostly rolled-down window from the unlit interior.

"Ezekiel."

--> This call and response bit is losing its charm.

--> Just answer the man.

"You're 'Buddy Boy' Macray?"

"Yes."

See: was that so hard?

The door to the pizza-mobile sounds like a cat in a vice, but when the dim lit interior light flicks on and the deliverer steps out, I realize it's actually my testicles releasing that dissonant shrill. Ryan is the driver. Or, at least I'm sure he is. His cadence is spoken at a different beat as noted and his hat's pulled real low but I promise that's him. I've already diverted my eyes as if analyzing the cracks in the sidewalk or the metalwork décor of the streetlamp would somehow shield me from being noticed right here in the open.

Or, in a word: nope, nope, nope, nope.

This wasn't what I had in mind. This unexpected intervention wadding more wrinkles than it's ironing out. The device is broken. The outcome unintentional, because here he is, live and in person. Sorry for the inconvenience.

If I had to go to the bathroom, I'd be changing my pants.

But there's no time for that shit.

Think. Rethink.

Backtrack.

Rewrite.

Deus ex machi-nah.

"I'm sorry. I didn't order this."

--> You and me both, pal.

"It's all taken care of."

--> I'm sure it is.

"Receipt's right here: 'Ate your quiche, thx for the meal. Ordered you a pizza. Hope that compensates. If you get it.'"

I got it: when in doubt, feign ignorance. A blatant disregard of respect is one thing, but ignorance is bliss. I'm sorry I didn't realize how far we've come, I was just so inspired, or better yet inundated with inspiration. Smooth this out with flattery passing through a bull. It's simple, sure, but he might even end up thanking me for putting the dumb in fandom.

"You're welcome."

Plan outlined, I put myself back into the situation created (see: look up from my sandals) to tip my two cents, but the driver was already behind the wheel.

"How did you even?"

--> My companion asks on my behalf.

So maybe I'm wrong. Unusual but not impossible. There's always possibility: I've piled more on my metaphorical plate than I can chew, let alone swallow, now literally compiled with pizza like an after-dinner mint for Mr. Creosote. Shadows and stress don't digest.

"Some guy said an extra fifty if I could find a mustachioed Matt Foley with a guy who looked like he might live in a van down by the river. Thought what the hell, I could make that happen."

In fact, in the grand scheme it's best it's not him. Coming in and screwing around where he doesn't belong. So what if I drafted the subversive like replacing the a in illusion? It's taking the scraps and making a feast.

"But who would've thunk it?"

Me. I thunk it.

Because this side isn't his story to tell.

I'm the only possibility of it being told.

Dammit. "It's possible." A last ditch declaration for naught.

The driver takes off, his engine snuffing me into the background. Everyone's caught up in their own little worlds. And here I am, alone again, being offered a slice of my very own "Pizza."

What an absolutely useless waste of an evening.

"Sure. Why the hell not?"

He opens the box towards me.

Or is it?

Something this horrible needs a false denouement. That little bonus scene that startles the viewer into a fear of reality or fear of continuation, where in this case I, the viewer, am viewing the top tip of an eggshell dead center on the pizza.

I snatch the shell before the stringed instruments have a chance to screech, yet not swift enough for the prestige fingering sleight of hand.

"What was that?"

Besides the painstakingly obvious? Haven't the foggiest. However, what's clear is I didn't put it there, or at least I didn't think I incited any incident that resulted in a forced reorder (see: he's holding the pizza). I grab a slice and stuff as much into my mouth until I literally can't say "nothing," palming the shell behind my back.

--> Violà

"That was definitely something," he says going in for his own piece, thus taking the concern off of my lack of accountability and onto his salivating maw.

But definitely something is right.

(I know this is no time for a digression but while my mouth's full I feel it must be noted, love it or hate it, for what it's worth, Pelican 1 delivers, literally and figuratively, and 2 so happens to fit a motif casually building. So right now does an opinion of quality really matter when 1 and 2 apply? If you answer yes, then for what it's worth the pizza is decent in a good way. Personally, I prefer pan pizza, where the toppings are a layered madness atop a crispy since it's been damn near fried pillow, over this overhyped, hand tossed faux-cardboard. But all in all, either I'm hungry or I'm impressed because bite for bite it's pleasing to the palate. If you answer no then continue below:)

At first glance I thought it was the customary pollacking of grease plus shadows on the top of the box, but the semblance of organized rows (see: very unpollack) struck me between chews and changing the subject.

"What's this?" I peek in, raising the lid unsuspiciously.

He answers, "Delicious," with his one-track mind ramming his hand in the box he'd have dropped if he wasn't holding it.

"What? No." I open the lid to a full 90. All aboard. "This."

And sure as the x in eggs, in black ink, printed thick:

1111 W Ebb

2 4 a $

Free w/ box and a friend

--> That sneaky bastard.

"Never heard of it," he said to the slice point entering his face.

Of course you haven't.

Especially considering I wouldn't have either if it wasn't for the fact the information so happened to be in my pocket like a razor hanging on a wall.

--> On the edge of Ryan's side of town.

--> His controlled hallucination perceptional roundabout.

So I guess we're going to a show.

"It won't be far from here." I don't even try to convince him. Don't even try to convince myself for that matter. I just pick up another slice and start walking. If I find it, great: the show must go on. If not then we no show. Either way, my pal's opted to follow along to see what Ryan wants. (See: chosen to unknowingly be played by Ryan's hand in all this.)

"About that thing in your hand. I'm pretty sure you're not about to tell me yet, are you?"

--> The continuing progression of when you're ahead you're behind.

"It's nothing." Or, at least, no thing you should concern yourself with.

"It's literally something in your hand."

"Then it's literally figuratively nothing" because I don't know what it is. ::Rephrase:: Because I don't know how it got there. The literary answer, simple enough, is Ryan's interference on my side of the street because (let's not point fingers here, but...) well, this idea is present. Yet, the underlying truth remains I didn't plant (see: plan) it. So, as opposed to the assumed won't for development, I can't answer because the fact is I can't.

Therefore, I next best scenario and do what needs to be done: get rid of it and pretend it never happened. If it doesn't push the plot then it's no use to me and definitely no use to the narrative path. So I throw it, as hard and fast and absentmindedly as possible. Out of sight, out of mind, off the record, and back on his side of town where it belongs.

And I push onward, asterisks, page break, skip ahead as quickly as this transition allows. (Which should create time enough for another brief digression of note concerning a point of interest: considering the quiet of the night, the shell never hit the pavement, or to clarify made no audible point of contact, and instead an onomatopoeic wind on an incredibly boring, breezeless night. Maybe I should find this strange. Maybe this should be worth looking into. But with the direction it went it's clearly a "his problem now" as if it wasn't already. See, my pal Zeek is a no problem character, and so far, he's keeping it that way.)

A 20__

***

A writer (who will be left nameless, the ultimate form rejection, due to my general disregard and lack of respect for this individual) once gave one piece of good advice: If the scene needs to go from the couch to the kitchen, you don't describe each step, simply put the character in the kitchen.

So see this walk merely following the purpose of going from nowhere to somewhere with haste.

Solid advice if the silence wasn't so poetic.

But slowed down to detail, one enters the dangerous game of putting the ineffable into words. Which is best to be avoided unless you're Malick Walden. Or if you do happen to become Malick Walden, who you are will still be called into question.

And since the fact remains I am not him nor the countless other poets who've over centuries conveyed the feeling of existing in a particular moment, swept up in their given surroundings, that which cannot be transcribed with absolute accuracy (albeit some closer than others), I weave across town with a quickness to a manifested address which ends inside an old stone masonry reclaimed by nature, trekking through the brush, and up to a kid with a nose ring sitting at an uncovered folding table (still following?).

"Ticket," he greets us with his repetitious lack of enthusiasm, a hip boredom accentuated by the septum knocker.

My pal Zeek doesn't move.

Why must I seriously do everything?

"Hand him the box."

He does so without getting too close to the kid. As if something outside of his comfort zone might be contagious.

The kid scans the box, lifts the lid, verifies the ticket.

"He's the friend," I say, making an inside joke that's so deeply personal I don't even get it anymore. The humor deadpan. (See: the character is a friend, not a foe. Or is that the reader? They're all participants involved with the story.)

The kid doesn't care for the joke either, but why should he? That's who he is: as blasé about finding a slice of pizza in the box as he is making sure it lands in the pile of rubbish tickets he flings it towards.

My pal Zeek, on the other hand, huffs like a deflating balloon at the kid's unappreciated discovery.

--> However, this cannot be confirmed or denied based on the noise level of the crowd, but nevertheless is/could be an accented touch.

And speaking of crowds! There are far more people here than I imagined. I'm not much a fan. That's why I write, or if not writing cook. You need people to be appreciated, but that doesn't mean I want to deal with them personally. I prefer a more behind the scenes interaction with the masses. A few people at a time are fine. Sociable I think is a good word. Cordiality. But a crowd is something that needs to be plowed through without apology. Which is what I do all the way to the other side, to a fence, as far as I can go while remaining in the scene, and watch, arms folded across my chest, unamused, on the lookout for any possible reason to be here.

But from where I'm standing there isn't one.

"Don't you ever ask yourself why?" I scan the packed mass, no more than a hundred, I'd say. A hundred stories with a hundred different whys and still I've managed to further flatten this dull edge, just hack hack hacking away.

"What?" He sounds unwary but not (see: never) surprised. Off guard from a post that doesn't need protecting.

"Don't you ever wonder why you?"

"In what regards?"

"Choose one" like are you doing this or do you do this to yourself.

"Alright. Why'd you bring me here now? Or why don't I know where I am? Or why drag me through all that business with that old man? Or why can't you explain anything about all those eggshells so we can call it an evening?"

"I distinctly said one."

"Buddy Boy!"

They were meant to be rhetorical questions anyway.

--> Hack.

I guess Ryan dispersed tickets all over town.

--> Hack.

Here we go:

--> Hack.

His most generous friend, graciously and favorably referred to as "Dave," spots us from the crowd. He really is that type of guy that's always there when you need him. "We didn't think we'd be seeing you again after you ran out on us. At least now we can say thanks for covering dinner." He places his fist to my pal's shoulder to press in the appreciation.

A truly, truly great bro.

(But let's hit pause on him for a minute to give our undivided attention to the friend his ticket brought. She was at the diner earlier this evening, recognized by her long, thick braids flowing half-way down her back from a half-up bun, and I don't know if it's natural lighting or gazing straight upon natural beauty, but her eyes are casting every clichéd, sparkly star on a moonless night to the rhythm of the fire behind her. She is passion, projected and personified. And I'm trying to stay grounded because after one look at her I'm already in trouble.)

"Thank him for the pizza," I blatantly imply for my pal to reciprocate the gratitude, to feed my curiosity of if Ryan then how, two seconds too late from his overtly honest "That wasn't me."

"What pizza?" He eyes me up and down like a good fellow. "Who's your pal, Buddy Boy?" clearly not remembering either one of my most-important first impressions.

"Him? Who I shared the pizza with."

--> An exact representation of our relationship.

Le femme "awws" a compassionated delight, finishing with "charity," her voice giggling sparkles.

"Might as well be with my writer's budget."

Her lips caress every letter making up the word, "Painter."

Is an angel heart finding respite on common ground? Or it's just the hush taking over the crowd.

--> The quiet space before the beat.

Four guys, presumably 2 4 a $, connoted by their uniform differences take position behind their individual instruments on the makeshift stage jetting from a three-sided utility shed.

The amps crackle and hiss, announcing their presence to the crowd. And then the music comes.

"Well I'll be damned," Dave says, slow. Mesmerized.

As is my pal Zeek and Dave's lady friend.

As is everyone in attendance, in fact.

And I'm seeing the spell performed (see: not falling under the mediocre regurgitation of smoke and mirrors).

Now, hear me out: the melodies are there, recycled sound waves from a decade or two prior on their return tide. Nothing overtly new or special, if you will, yet still catchy in their not quite forgotten simplicity of memory. Enough to sway the crowd.

But whatever dream embers they think they're burning into the reminiscence of future generations are being doused with the most retardant lyrics.

"I'm the best / and you're the rest / hashtag blessed / now get pissed / on to piss you off."

Fire poetry which needs putting out.

"Who would have thunk it," Dave says, engulfed.

That's it. I quit. I can't.

Show's over.

"We are Twenty-Four A Money. Goodnight." The singer places his microphone back on the stand's saddle because even rock'n'roll's on a budget and follows his bandmates offstage.

The crowd cheers. The clapping passed from one person to the other. My pal Zeek smiles (he would). I safely abstain.

--> I don't know which would be worse: being subjected to an encore or the pretentiousness of not giving the audience what they want, living up to a surprise third act.

--> Either way, thank Ryan.

The crowd mulls around in case there's something left to be expected.

"I believe it's getting late. It's probably best if I get going," my pal says, breaking the monotony with monotony.

"What are you talking about, Buddy Boy? The evening may be quelled to rest, but the night is just beginning."

--> This guy should have been writing the lyrics.

"I assure you, I'm alright."

"Are you trying to tell me you didn't just witness what the hell I just witnessed?"

What I witnessed was indeed what the hell.

"You mean Matt?"

"Of course, I mean Matt."

(Everyone knows a Matt.)

"It was such a good show," Dave's beautiful companion offers into whatever conversation she thinks they're having.

"What kind of coworkers would we be if we didn't show our support with a hello?"

(And every Matt needs a welcome.)

My pal Zeek looks at me and shrugs, like after all this time he finally wants my approval.

--> Authorization granted whether taken for or not.

--> Please, don't mind me.

Dave lights a cigarette. "Let's do this."

My pal takes a step then stalls: "What about Shellie?"

Side Note: I anticipated something more like an Epiphany or maybe a Denise, but there's something surprisingly fitting considering the playfulness of her beauty, sprawled out, gazing towards infinity, and having shown up with a dude like Dave. That which I can't begin to fathom what she sees.

"She's a big girl."

And with that they disappear into the crowd.

Now, I do consider leaving, call it for the night, work with what I got as if I have any other viable options (See: pass out in front of the TV). But what would that say about my character if I left a friend of a friend of a pal of mine's all alone? I was brought here for a reason, so there's absolutely no harm in this journey having a scenic route.

"I know who you are," she says, her head tilted skyward, her braids draped towards the earth.

"You what now?"

--> But where's she trying to go is fast and to the point, as is my taken aback and softened response.

"I'm one too."

"You're a Donald?" What do I need three for?

"No," giggled, "not like who you are but *who* you are." (She says the word italicized.)

"Okay," pause wearily, "explain:"

"Like, I know what you're doing." She jolts upright with the quickness and controlled chaos of someone who just remembered a forgotten responsibility but stops with her arms on her knees because it's too late to do anything about it now. "Creating the world around you. Being a part of it but still distant." Our eyes meet, more in conversational happenstance than dramatic sincerity, yet I sink into them. "I do the same thing when I paint. Work yourself into the work. You know? Like own the aspects you love and rationalize those you don't." Her giggle bubbles the air. "I can spot it. The rationality. There's a similar je ne sais quoi between strokes and sentences."

"But you don't know what?"

--> The ol' I don't need to explain myself for the sake of sincerity in dramatic conversation.

"No, but I am on the same thing you're on. The look at me of creativity." She sparks a joint and hands it off. "The staying lost until we find it, then wanting to show off where we've been. But often times we forget to celebrate each moment along the black map."

I inhale to get on her level. "Mark Strand?"

"Marks a spot."

The rolled paper smokes like incense between her fingers in the shadowed grass. She takes her time between hits and pulls slow as if filtering thoughts from the air.

"Did you know Maya translates to illusion?"

I take my turn: "I'll have to remember that."

"It's how a struggling novelist survived 2012."

"I wasn't a novelist then."

"And John Cusack was Edgar Allen Poe."

"I'm not following."

"Of course you are. You have to, even if you're the only one."

"Then I guess we started off on the wrong foot."

She plants the cherry into the ground. "Stranger things have happened."

What's left of the crowd is scattered in tufts like weeds in a field, and the bonfire's smoking itself out.

--> Please hold your applause till the end.

Down the line, seen between the long-haired dude in a bandana and jean jacket and the thin woman, birdlike under her nest of curly hair, her friend Dave and my pal Zeek are conversing with the tattooed drummer who's holding up the stage's port cochère with his foot. He drinks from a glass bottle. Posted up on a boulder is the coffee shop blonde. The one I'd eventually see here.

"What do you think they're going on about?"

"Who can say?"

"Then entertain me, Mr. Writer."

"And how do you imagine I do that?"

"Any way you see fit."

She's lucky I'm inclined to impress her.

"Let's see:" the guy with the bottle tosses something, which given the context clues I presume is the metallic cap, into a cooler. He's clearly still holding the floor, as well. "That girl on the rock is the drummer's sister."

"So he's the drummer then?"

"He has to be since he's explaining to our friends that his sister and his kit are all he has left."

"Intense."

"I'm just kidding. That's way too melodramatic."

--> This splendor in the grass.

"But she does mean a lot to him. She believes in him. Sometimes it takes that ounce of faith to runneth over, you know?"

If she does she doesn't hint at it. Instead, she watches with the passion of looking for details on a blank canvas as the drummer takes a cigarette from her friend Dave and lights it.

"And now they're talking about their mutual friend Matt, or whatever they call him. Or, well, he is at least saying 'He can be a real cocky asshole,' and 'it seems all he wants to do is drink and'" (ton-tone it down, kemosabe) "Let me edit. He's saying, 'He's about living that life without hitting that life. It's not like we made it. We're big on the small scale in the city, sure, but the world abounds.'" (No reaction either way means continue?) "'Don't get me wrong,' he says and takes a drag, 'dude's got talent. Over the top talent. But that's it. No drive. No long term. Just content to work his menial day job and bang fanboys, off himself by twenty-seven into infamy.' Pause for beer. 'But the crazy thing is, the real fucked of the fucked, is this is what I want to do, all I want to do, and yet somehow no matter how I excel, no matter if I can keep the beat better than time itself, I'm the one in the background, replaceable. I know this. He knows this.'" (I'm thirsty too.) "'But that's the world we live in. At the end of the day, he'll still be him and I'll still be no one."

--> An imitation of life.

"Then why doesn't he do something about it?" she says.

"Oh, he does."

She arches back, bracing on her outstretched arms.

The slope my words flow down.

"Or, at least he thinks he does. A no one never knows in the now. To wane philosophically, Dupox said something like the present being a combination of hiccups and chances while the future digresses in a semblance of both everything and nothing. So he plays,

plays every day. For the audience. For himself. The thought of stopping, hell, of even going a day without sticks on skins feels dreadful to him. And yet there's still a bleakness presently to the whole damn thing."

She cocks her head to her shoulder without taking her eyes off them. "Persistence is the pepper," she says like waking a breeze.

"But 'persistence is the pepper,'" I agree, to the point blankly, the viscus remnants of the conversation sticks in my mouth without a drink in sight.

Silences meant to be are never awkward.

I think about tracing my eyes over her again, for art and practice makes perfect, but in doing so I would have missed the coffee shop blonde skirt off the rock and in a single swoop glide to my pal Zeek.

Shellie exhales wisps of aerated giggles. "You saw that too, right?"

"Her going up to him?"

"She didn't just go. She's floating."

"No she's not."

"I'm telling you."

Squinting doesn't enhance (...enhance...enhance) the visual clarity, but I do it anyway. Her petite hands are on his face, and she's craning her body, curved high to mimic his eyelevel on her tipped toes at best.

"What is she doing?"

"Telling him the truth."

"Explains the glow."

Sure. Why not?

"Did you find everything you were looking for?" she asks her friend Dave and my pal Zeek when they return.

"Stranger things have happened."

"To who?" (My pal Zeek.)

"To anybody. A life is based on others' lives." (Yours truly)

"Poetic." (Shellie, like a kiss, soft for me.)

"Hardly." (Not yet.)

"More philosophical waxing?" (Don't forget this guy's back.)

"Aren't more conversations inherently buried within?" (Shellie, now standing.)

"Anything to drink around here?" (My pal Zeek always the nexus of conversation.)

(However, I couldn't agree with him more.)

"There might be a bar nearby." (Her friend Dave.)

"No. Not another. It's too late for that."

"It can't be that late yet."

"Hasn't this turned out to be an evening for the books?" her friend Dave says directly to Shellie across the lines charted for ships.

--> Has it though?

--> Because I don't know what he's been reading but this ain't it.

My pal Zeek leads the way, taking charge, good for him, towards the way out. The literal exit to leave the masonry. Not the metaphorical no way out of this wet paper bag I'm struggling to punch through. The one that's the long journey around with nothing to show for our efforts. The soon to be a shelved so this one time...

"What's the rush, Buddy Boy?" Her friend Dave must think he's swell in a clutch, don't he?

"I'm not rushing." He pauses, not stopping. "It's just well beyond time to head home. Are you not tired? I'm tired."

"You're not tired. You're alive."

No matter how inspired, her friend Dave is only partially right. True: my pal Zeek isn't any more tired than a genuinely lazy, overweight man who's been out all night running all over town when habitually he should be in. But he's not alive. He's bored till death looking for ways to pass the time with the least amount of unremarkable conflict. An uninterested character flattened by reality.

Shellie hung back with me, the last two to make it to the street. "You should tell him soon."

("Should tell who what?"

"Not you, darling.")

For someone so dead set on their destination, my pal Zeek abruptly stops at the street. "Which way to the family mansion?"

--> All directions look the same when you don't know where you're going.

"Where?" her friend chimes in again sidekicking all these conversations into gear.

"It's what he calls his apartment."

"You shouldn't know that."

Spoke too soon.

"No, you're right. Yet I do."

"C'mon, Buddy Boy. Let's round out the night." If I didn't know better, I'd assume her friend was high on something stronger than life.

"The night's already round."

Good thing there aren't streetlights, home field advantage at its finest, because I can feel my pal Zeek's eyes burning into me.

In the dark my presence is obscured in view.

--> Life in dreaming.

"This way."

--> To walk this off like Cobb, incepting or following.

I ball my hands into my short's pockets. The mesh does nothing for it being chillier than I anticipated. I was fine when I started out, before the world was out to get me. Now I don't even get me. But Salinger never took the weather too personally. It's best to leave that to the poets.

I'll just note the cold.

Shellie's brisk beside me, prating at pace, before we weave the first intersection.

"Why didn't you tell him back there? He has a right to know, you know. You interfered directly searching for what you don't understand rather than the indirect search trying to understand yourself. This is all you, my friend. The kit you're playing with. The whole caboodle."

Turn.

"I don't follow."

Turn.

"C'mon, Mr. Writer. What's this about? What's your grand theme watching over your art like a guardian angle and elevating it from all the others?"

Turn.

Her friend casually keeps tempo like an uninterested reporter on beat.

Turn.

"Obtuse or acute?"

Turn.

"I'm being serious."

Turn.

"As am I, to the right degree. It's about a guy who keeps randomly finding eggshells or something."

Turn.

"What do you mean 'or something?' Does he find eggshells or is he stumbling upon the next grandiose metaphor buried in American fiction?"

Turn.

"I'm not sure yet really. I mean, I've got a few ideas but nothing set."

Turn.

"At minimum you need that stone to chisel. If you don't know then how's he going to get a remote idea before it clicks to the next. Take the grocery store, because relevancy is good, right? So you got this grocery store here, it seems deserted, it's late, the lights are dim. But come a few hours and it'll be tickled pink with the hustle and bustle of the average shopper in its district. And when they arrive they might leave with exactly and only what they set out to get or they might splurge and who knows. But neither can happen if there aren't necessities on shelves and temptations in bins. And you don't seriously believe these things wind up in stacks and rows on their own accord? You're not preposterous. You know the late night shelvers are in there right now doing the job no one cares to see. The consumers don't give two shakes how the shelves are filled as long as what they think they want is right there in front of their noses waiting for them and only them. The shelvers make that happen. Out of sight is out of mind. Whatever magic is left in this world is from the legerdemain of stagehands."

"So revealing the sleight of hand is actually the distraction to the trick?"

"Sure, if that's what I said. I'm really high."

"Well, here we are," my pal Zeek says.

Shellie and I stop.

Here we are, indeed.

"We should do this again, make this a thing," her friend Dave offers along with a cigarette, which I feel obligated to take, giving up, giving in, despite my thirst considering the paper thin accuracy of his farewell.

"Right."

Don't worry, pal, you'll be there too.

Her friend keeps the conversation going, "You stay around here?" as he hands over a lighter.

"Relatively."

"Good. Good." He takes the lighter and the question back.

My pal Zeek makes no attempt at subtlety making his move towards his front door.

Maybe Shellie's not all talk, smoke, and mirrors.

"I'm going to let you finish. Have a good rest of your night."

You don't have a choice in that.

Her friend Dave says night.

I throw out a last ditch effort without the plan I never had to begin with: "You're going to find more eggshells inside."

Firing point blank might be messy but generally gets a reaction.

He doesn't stop. "That's fine."

Even this close I miss like an unknown intended to thicken the plot before the star arrives.

And it's my job to make him shine.

"I can tell you what they are now" or never.

He's unsure enough to turn his intention to attention. "Are you about to try and monologue we're all in some sort of egg together waiting for the big cosmic hatching and I happen to be the little chicken watching the sky fall, because if you are..."

The brassiness knocks the wind out of me. "Don't be so trite. Even old Walt D. couldn't pull that off. They're previous drafts." And the cards are on the table.

"Of what?"

"My story."

Her friend Dave chimes in with something neither of us gives note to.

"Wouldn't it be my story?"

"It's as much about you as it is me."

A close up of his eyes would reveal I got him where I want him: tucked in my palm.

"No, seriously. What's he on about?" Again with good guy Dave. Hamming it up in yet another offhand attempt at stealing the scene. You might just make it if you stay in your place.

"I'm a writer," and I'm generous enough to help put him there. "This is a story, and we're all characters. Or something. Or whatever. Do what you want with the revelation."

"You're what and what now?"

Her friend Dave wants to play the part, then let's play: "A writer, as in unknown author, as in I don't know myself therefore only have a vague idea as to what might happen." I flip the script onto him.

--> Use the conversation as the classical allegory of progress for our pal Zeek, who's still listening intently.

--> Suspend if for no other reason than to give in to disbelief.

"Where were you two or three days ago?"

"It wasn't work." He says this with the same comedic smugness as the gold chain hanging across his open collar.

My eyes roll out as "I do know that, but where specifically?"

"With Shellie," he looks around over a purposely suppressed smile, "like with Shellie."

I'll give that the ol' tin for good guy Dave to stop, we read you loud and clear.

"Exactly. But that's a conjecture. Give me details."

--> Because if you want to paint it with your smug brush, then paint.

"Watch it, buddy," he says since she's standing there, the what a gentleman situationally overtaking the virile need to boast accomplishment.

"See: there aren't any. And for the sake of my story there doesn't need to be." And let's all be thankful for that.

He's silent, mouth agape. Nice try, wise guy.

"None of us were really anywhere three days ago in accordance with how we understand things or time or chapters or whatever. But we've existed before and will henceforth continuously, doing the same but always elsewhere. That strange, perpetual repetitiousness of the day-by-day, we're being written or rewritten or read. It's like how people read the same words but no one reads the same book, forever a cycle that's both the same yet ever changing. So, understand, like yourself, I know what has happened but it's on top of this sort of vague, created memory we share of what happened before that. But that's writing. I can't say with any authenticity what will happen before, during, or next until it's happening. So, it's my job to figure it out. It's the thankless driving force, generally unnoticed. Except Zeek's particular story here happens to involve compounding drafts that slip through. So here I am.

I break to give my pal Zeek a moment to swallow that, give it a quick digest, but intercut good guy Dave with an m night shocking "You're saying I'm not real?"

"I'm absolutely not saying that" because that's too easy. "You are very real, just no more or less than I am."

"And it's all a big fucking manipulation."

The challenge lies in how to say it: "You could say something like that, as you just did. Like have you ever found a freckle that you swear you've never seen before, and then sit there trying to place if it's always been a part of you? Or contextually, have you noticed the moon disappearing and reappearing all evening? You see it clear as day but later when you can't find it you only think you remember seeing it. That's very much real, as in actually happening. You just notice as I need you to. Same goes for grand epiphanies and out of the blue memories. I realize something: you realize it. I need you to remember something: it's playing in your head. Metaphorically, I am the blue."

And there it is.

The one-two.

A bitter juice in the corner.

That fight or flight part.

And my pal Zeek's got nowhere to go.

(Good guy Dave lights another, solo without proffer.)

Except up the stoop to the door. "Have a good night. Shellie, nice meeting you. Dave, see you Monday."

And with that plus a curt wave my day's work ends with nothing to show for it. He was gone (see: inside).

("Can you repeat that?")

The late great K. Vonnegut is often associated with the quote emphasizing character desire, even if only for a glass of water.

But I, Donald Bronco, tend to align more with the K. Trout's sham pain.

("No.")

#

M 20__

#

I don't leave the room Sunday.

#

J 20__

#

Words run together.

--> The only vowels here are the promises demanded of myself.

--> The blur of the rush.

--> The rush of the draft.

#

J 20__

#

"What's left but God's right hand."
—Laura Chase

#

What time is it?

A woman's voice swoons over the Waikiki Rainbow Collection of all natural, certified hair care products fortified with the aqua marine waters of Waikiki "and a kiss from the sun" from beneath the scrambled waves.

Is it Monday? Or did we skip it?

(If I order now she'll double my purchase.)

(And throw in these beautiful Hawaiian llima hair clips absolutely free.)

I knock over an empty cardboard cup as my hand searches the nightstand for, here it is...

I sit up in bed and take a pull from the stale coffee, swallowing despite how long it's been sitting there, which has been how long exactly?

It's dark behind the glow of the Terebi.

This hangover headache combo I'm apparently suffering from for no reason benefits.

(Again that's
1-888-55Something-64SomethingWhatever or waikikicollections.com/rainbow for this limited time offer.)

#

I wasn't out long, but the hours felt measured in days.

The last things I remember: It was dark outside, and the room wasn't yet throbbing.

--> It's still dark outside.

The curtains, closed over the screen-sized window, is outlined by a flood of streetlights' artificial amber.

#

"For those who need something sweet,
and something sweet for those in need."

#

I kick my feet over the edge of the bed.

The television washes me in pallid shades of grayed blues and greens. Like drowning oh so close to the surface tension, a deluge of acid colored flickers.

My stomach rumbles, not out of need, but of warning.

I never learn, so against better judgement I swallow the bottom sip of the very old, very instant coffee.

Fighting fire with fire burns passion? Or is it sink or swim?

Hope floats?

Why not?

I take the long way to the desk, the leisure cruise between lassitude and lethargy, to manually quell the volume on the box, the remote lost, tucked away somewhere to be found later.

Right now I recline on the chair's back two legs to find the balance.

Ride the unwritten. Write the unridden.

The pelican in the frame blinks.

I mimic what I see to make sure it's actually what I see.

Its wide eyes wince as it unadheres its head off the shore.

Where do you think you're going?

You're in deep over your head, man. He waddles like traditional stop-motion to the rowboat on the bank. *You're in deep bad.*

When the ship sinks, I'll float like a dream.

There's not much difference between ideas and the lies you tell yourself. It perches itself into the boat.

Then why don't you fly?

Nah, man. The lesson here is why don't you swim?

#

A hot 100 refrain: *Anything can happen.*

#

The chair slips out from under me, luckily for me forward, and I'm up and out of it before the legs thud against the hard carpet.

In a disoriented rush, I wake through a shower with the clogged drain, which at least I take, when I remember the minor technicality of not having towels. I dab myself the best I can with the last dry washcloth before throwing on the first thing I grab (see: the same gym shorts/button-down combo) and head out the door.

The situation is picked up by the breeze. / A final push against the current.

My clothes speckled damp will dry eventually as the day progresses.

#

I chiggity check myself. Either I'm right on time or the gray Number 12 is.

"What's the weather like, Action Jackson?"

"Cold as an ice cube."

The song's stuck in my head, its chorus escaping in fragments of hums and clicks across my tongue.

Supposedly by letting the song play out to the end it will cease the trapped airplay.

Problem is: it's one of those songs everyone knows and gets all hype nostalgic for but no one really listens to these days.

See: I don't know how it ends.

#

"Today shall be a good day." Click, click.

#

As the bus wide-turns onto Alabaster, I'm skimming an article claiming unusual font forces "the brain to increase focus on these texts" or some variant to this effect.

Possibly advantageous.

--> Psychological tomfoolery for one.

But I don't finish the read.

Re-enter my long-lost pal, stage right.

He breaks eye contact before it can properly be established, instead resorting to the neurotic twitch of looking at everything but with intense interest. A well-played classic move. The consistency of character is at least refreshing.

Still my restless heart.

He takes his seat by the aisle, middle of the bus.

He doesn't look around. Not a peek or verification. Still perpetually unmoved.

And again, I'm freshed.

This isn't a second chance sequel reboot series serial next level remix nonsense fan fav OTP real MVP timeline offshoot rebranded storyline spinoff universe canonical continuation. This is it. Where I am is all I got. "Can't claim the unfinished." And I'm at the back of the bus, literally in the open, closed off from acknowledgment.

--> Him along for the ride.

--> But believe you me, I'm driven.

#

Side note: The sun's rearing full tilt to morning, and secondly I need a legitimate cup of coffee, a bottle of headache pills, and sunglasses if they weren't so pretentious out of context.

#

Intermingled between my throbbing hemispheres and the apathy masquerading as the driven persistence of easier said than done, especially when not doing, sneaks in a Mr. Kolchak, true to form.

Remember: the episode where our hero in the ol' straw hat (see: not lollipop) had to match wits with the Hyde scientist killing all those beautiful people standing in the way of her research.

--> Admittedly, it was one of the more less popular episodes, despite certain appeal.

Anyway, it's coming to me in flashes and stabs like the glint sharpened off the window.

First, I think nothing of the thought.

(Carl would be so ashamed.)

But let's double back and redo.

BREAK

The bus rolls to a stop, but the story keeps moving.

How so, you may be inclined to ask having made it this far.

With the help of a little old lady and her oversized bag.

Ms. D, of course. Who else?

BREAK

Edit, cut, action.

Either A) When she pulls herself onto the bus setting, she channels the episode in my memory, the one-off role in the Eve of Terror, so vivid in fact I'm now imdb certain that our sweet Ms. D was the Eve once upon a time.

--> "Every face seen within a dream is a reimagining of a face seen."

Or B, and I'm ^ inclined) It's not a matter of when but a matter of must. Unbeknownst to her, she is an invaluable underlining of narrative, a minor excavating. The support of structures. A force that forces. My hand abounds. She must show up for the show to go on.

--> A full circle is a closed loop.

But the memories and applied connections are just excuses for justification.

An overtly exaggerated appeal to reasoning.

My forced to finish.

^desperately^=

^=despairingly

#

"What was that?"

"I didn't say anything."

"Exactly."

#

Slow progression is a glitch on repeat.

#

A closed universe.

#

Can't you think of something more profound than the unknown?

--> The black hole is the professional?

But wait, there's more...

#

For a limited time.

#

The bus makes another predetermined stop, dotted consistent and efficient, the routine inextricable from its route.

We've arrived again to the motel.

More correctly: They've arrived. I've returned. Minor technical flaw.

The foible: I've circled back (see: loopy) and may have "purposely" missed my stop like a chicken without a head.

--> Why not "missed"?

--> Answer:

The man in the burgundy jacket gets on the bus.

Steps right on up, slowly, the best an old man can, steadily.

Granted, this could have been his grand cinematic moment. His 500 days of summer Roman holiday for his girl, Friday, the lady Eve.

Love, actually, while you were sleeping.

Breakfast at Tiffany's bed of roses.

But his sweeping romantic gesture is visually reduced to a shave, a tie, and his hair set with a part, more Archibald Leech than Cary Grant.

An affair to forget.

The doors shut locking in his Double Douse aftershave making the bus smell like a disciplinary hearing for a detective planting evidence on the wagon.

He makes his way down the aisle at a reasonable albeit shuffled pace to the score conducted by the engine, playing out in real time the governed speed of the bus (24 mph).

"Hello, Dorothy."

They sure don't make them pictures like they used to.

--> The golden age an unpanned shot.

From where I'm sitting I can't make out Ms. D's response, but I can attest the temperature on the bus dropped as ice cold as the man in the burgundy jacket's beers. His attire becomes contextual.

He points to my pal Zeek's seat and my pal obliges without contest, standing up to him.

The man in the burgundy jacket doesn't back down the walkway.

Left without the choice of moving forward, my pal Zeek's forced to come back to me.

#

He joins me on the bench despite all the seats laid out before him (see: reluctantly). I scoot to make room for my unexpected visitor, and once he's acquainted with his new seat we face forward, silently watching the reunion play out before us.

If there was popcorn we'd be sharing a bucket between us.

"What do you think they're saying?" This a breath above a whisper as he leans towards me as if not wanting to disturb the nobodies watching the couple's conversation unfold.

"He's apologizing. She's not having it. They're both still madly in love." I turn and meet his eyes and for the first time notice that one of his pupils is larger than the other. "Emotions before action."

"Typical," he says, tightening his hold of the briefcase between his feet.

#

Eerie and lifeless weren't the right words, but the P. Hole took on similarities to both qualities, with the chairs flipped over the bar, reversed for the gray morning, clinging to the quiet before being driven out by the dim lit bulbs and the shadows people cast.

The taps and bottles erected in rows.

The pints and talls chilled in still anticipation.

A TV was on, accidental company overnight. A false companion for the off hours.

I sat in the booth across from the bar but still considered the bar area, waiting for Dave to finish with whatever it was Dave did on the phone at this hour. "Get 'em before they're awake and sleeping off their headaches." (I'll never comprehend this or what Michelle sees in these words of wisdom.)

The empty establishment wasn't a novel sight. There'd been many a night stuck sticking around after the last of the boozers and good-timers "didn't have to go home but had to get the hell outta here." The difference of that hour was the energy. Nothing buzzed in the air because nothing had begun. The prospect of work < the prospect of being done.

I sprawled out and watched the muted screen (now in UHD!). A painter, conveyed by a hip (see: exceptionally tidy) dude holding a brush and smiling at a canvas, stroked with unseen, nonchalant precision "if you buy what we're selling you'll never be covered in paint and frustrated to the point of literal defeat because we are your dreams coming true" so-to-speak in a branded world.

I was getting hungry (see: bored).

--> There's a joke here somewhere.

--> Where I'm the classically conditioned punchline.

The kitchen doors swung open, both of them, like this was a wild western saloon rather than a middle class fancy bar guised as a family establishment. And lo and behold, who might I have the pleasure of walking into this one horse town but the other Donald, Ryan, standing afront the hinges' bucking neigh.

(Ivan the Interested asks:
"Why the sudden urge for
Double shots of espresso?")

If I could have sunk further into the booth or hid behind a poker game, I would have. This was the last thing I needed this morning. Him hunting me down. Sneaking through the back door. You wanted to find me? Have me cornered at last? Account for these cold, hard facts, to copy and to paste, imprinted in this fine print:

Firstly) I was equally as surprised at the unexpected arrival of the man in the burgundy jacket on the bus this morning. I happened to be minding my own business, focused I might add, when [interjectory word conveying a slower to arrive but still alarming surprise] there he was, pining over a love story my hand was never red in. You'd have a better chance in finding fault in the natural progression of influence over me.

Also) We seem to claim, or blatantly imply, the limitlessness of humanity with story upon story for all of time. When the truth of the matter is there's only so many stories we can tell. Love, life, death, happy endings, it's all finite and we're filled to the brim, close to a cap. So just because I reached for inspiration outside myself, wanting to impose that same inspiration into the emotional range of my character, keeps me well within my limits. Understanding people creates stories as understanding characters creates influence, and vice versa since forever, forever.

Thirdly) If you really want to get technical, and I do, so let's: technically, let's not forget the Vino finding me first so [interjectory word conveying a slower to surprise but still alarming arrival].

I sat up straight, all in, still arranging the proofs to my third point in order to draw a possible fourth when he sat across from me at my table.

"I didn't expect to find you here." He bought in.

"I could say the same."

His expression was hospitable yet all too real (see: impossible to read). "Do you think there's any coffee made?"

"Haven't got that far."

"Right on."

Pleasant pleasantries. Get to the point.

"Dave around?"

"He's back there doing useless Dave things."

"Figured unlocking the back door was his well placed ineptitude."

"So why'd the orange cat drag you here on the day he so blatantly despises?"

"What's that?"

Was he bluffing or stalling?

Either way, I call. "What brings you here this morning?"

And he folds, "I see: Look what the Garfield dragged in. Clever."

"Likewise."

"I'm here to turn this in," he pulled out a folded envelope. "I'm afraid my job here is coming to an end."

That it?

"I don't know when it'll be, but I'm sure it's coming up soon. Could be today, although doubtful, or could be a month from today. But I figured in all fairness I'd get it on paper as soon as possible."

That was it.

He tapped his fingers on the envelope.

"You got something lined up?" I slouched into the booth.

"A few ideas, nothing concrete," he says despite the haircut and stubbled shave. "But you know what they say: Persistence is the pep—" he broke into a "I love this movie" airy chuckle.

The bro'd up morning sports talk show on the television intercut a scene from a dude office comedy about some average bros' lives amongst the cubicles, which I personally couldn't relate to on every level but still found entertaining enough (*Cooking...* on the other hand). It was the part where the office rebel, his tie-less shirt untucked, trap music bumping, smashes a keyboard over the desk of his lame-brained superior because none of the vowels work.

Admittedly, it's a funny scene.

"What do we have here. The Dons of a new day," Dave's voice cut in.

Neither of us wanted to take part in this joke.

So naturally, we ignored him.

"Anyway, I've enjoyed working with you," Ryan said.

He stuck his hand out.

"Likewise."

We shook.

"And don't forget to bring me what you got. I still need to check it out before I go."

"We'll see where I'm at."

"We will see. Tomorrow," Ryan said, as confident as the ace in the hole.

#

As of today, I am still gainfully employed.

Allow me to paint the scene:

You start with some Titanium White.

Dave pulled me into the kitchen like a guidance counselor.

"What's wrong, buddy? I thought we were cool."

"What's this we? I thought it was my job in jeopardy."

"Does this have to do with a mutual, friendly interest of ours?"

Now add a dash of Dark Sienna.

"What's working here have to do with Michelle?"

But not too much now.

"Nothing. I just thought maybe the awkward turtle when I answered her door the other day might of..."

"Why you got to bring that up, Dave? Now that shit's fresh in the air again."

Add a dab of Cadmium Yellow Hue.

"You are correct. I just can't, as your general manager, and hopefully as your pal, let our business lives and our personal lives become a confliction of an interest."

"Dave, that barely even makes sense."

"It doesn't have to make sense when it makes dollars. And that's what we do here, me and you. We make dollars."

And drip in some Van Dyke Brown.

"Let's go ahead and put a pin in that, Dave. I'm here to apologize to keep my job. And there's no excuses if I give you one, and you'll want an excuse if I don't, so let's just agree I had something come up but it is now down, and trust me, this thing is now so far down it'll never come up again."

Now with your 1" brush, use heavy strokes to lay it on thick.

Granted, I was made to sign a few forms and am now on what Dave "[hates] to say this, but the global warmest, thin ice."

And I have to be back before the "if you're on time then you're late" 5-CL shift.

Then give your brush a quick rinse and beat the devil out of it.

So I'm on the bus, headed back to the room.

I've got a lot to do and not a lot of time to do it.

Round out the world before tomorrow.

We'll see.

Hee-hee, I love that part.

#

"The writer begins the book,
but the reader finishes It."
--Sam J.

#

A one shot, single take, happy endings all round.

#

"Words don't matter
if a thing works."
--Steve K.

#

Who are you kidding here?

#

You're a fraud.

All your little references or allusions or Easter eggs. Inspirations, you lie. Misquoted quotables. You're not clever, no matter what Ryan thinks.

Neither in a talented sense, acting like you're Ulysses strutting around the city.

Nor the intelligent.

You looked up most everything anyway.

(Including the word "clever.")

And thinking a string of fumbled up mad gabs makes you sort of literary great (see: pretentious bastard). You can't even get your "favorite thing you've written" published for free.

You literally can't give it away.

There's nothing talented or intelligent about dating tips when the characters are already in a relationship.

"Let's write a story about supermarkets and lake monsters."

"Why?"

"To cover up the fact your characters never come to life seeing as you write like you're watching a screen."

No wonder no one reads anymore.

#

A 20__

#

Needless to say for the record, I got nothing done before my gracious return to the P. Hole.

Still no end in sight.

I hope Ryan doesn't want something finished because at this rate he gets what he gets despite grandiose expectations.

--> Honestly, out of all things, why he wants to waste his time with this, I'll never comprehend.

#

PICKLED ROSEMARY (PICKLES)

Pour
3 Cups Sugar
2 Cups Salt

2 Quart ACV
2 Quart WWV
1 Quart Water
1 Man Hand of RM
That has been boiled and chilled
Over quarter inch cucumber
Strummed across a mandolin
And stocks of rosemary.

YLDS: However many cumbers it covers in a Cambro.

#

Either last night or earlier this evening Matt let me in on a little something that would have been useful prior. He was surprised to hear I talked, "like actually talked private conversation style to Dave," this morning, and after a heartfelt better you than me apology to the bad news, he simply revealed "I usually just stroll in like time didn't hiccup and he just gives me the disappointed grandmother face. But good for you, man, using your words."

#

He also went on to divulge while prepping scallions on a bias that he'd been watching these videos about theories of old shows and asked me if I'd ever heard of one called Kolchak.

He confirmed my yeah with "straw hat not lollipop" to which I replied "Carl Kolchak."

He said he didn't even know the show was a thing before stumbling upon the best theories countdown whatever he was watching, but that it looked interesting enough since it wasn't actually about the titular character but in reality his fat, angry boss. He liked this idea.

"Vincenzo," I helped out with the name.

"Right. Vinchinzo. It all actually takes place in that guy's head."

So basically, the facts according to Matt: Kolchak is a figment, a character created by an unhappy middle aged man in middle management at the dying Independent News Service. He's got a daydream job of doing some actual newsworthy reporting, uncovering truths to the mysteries no matter how absurd and giving it to the man no matter the cost. And if he ended up saving Chicago in the process then he was just doing his civic duty as a true newspaperman.

Proofs cited: Kolchak always wears the same blue suit, black tie, and straw hat. Pick an episode and that's what he'll be wearing despite the varied wardrobe of his castmates. Kolchak is never seen at home. This is extenuated by the episode where he shows up to INS after hours to find Vincenzo sleeping in the office, a blatant lives at work scenario. Further proofs for printing, the episode "Chopper" has Vincenzo saying he's ready to go home to the psych ward. Matt also mentioned something about the love-hate relationship he had with the other coworkers, but I couldn't grasp what he was spouting.

#

Otherwise, service was a dud.
It's great to be back.

#

Side note: Michelle was there but I basically avoided her between the detailing and the "if you look busy, you are busy" (see: waste of time vs. all the things I should be accomplishing).

#

Like what I should be doing right now.
Like what I should have done by now.
Like there's no point in polishing the wrong future to procrastinate the goal.

#

Epis'Ode To A Motel Room
(Home)

The pelican hath floated with the tide,
Pushing down on the oars to guide
Towards the horizon. Within the frame
But out of sight. What time is it outside?
The yellow rectangle hath yet to mark the wall
Behind the curtain. So inside the waves
Of static still drowns. Action cometh from

The other side, but they donth dare take a look.

The room is full of coffee cups,
And yet thy am empty of the wanted burden
Placed on thyself. No stress giveth onto this page.
For this is where thy live now
But the gift shalt never take residence.
Thou art the imitation whilst in the present:
"Beauty is truth, truth beauty /
That's all thy needs to know."

#

2.1 SUMMARY AND ANALYSIS

The speaker of the poem, "Epis'Ode To A Motel Room (Home)," is stuck in a motel room, "Out of sight" and, therefore, lost to the world, asking "What time is it outside," away from the initial hope presented in lines 1-3: "The pelican hath floated with the tide / Pushing down on the oars to guide / Towards the horizon." However, it is important to note the line "Within the frame" juxtaposed with "Towards the horizon." The speaker connotes the limitations such as the constraints surrounding a work of art or the literal walls of the motel room. With these unwavering and strictly defined margins in place, the only journey the speaker can take is deeply inward.

This idea of the frame continues with "The yellow rectangle hath yet to mark the wall." Except here the limitations are not yet in place. The speaker is aware of their onset but still convinces himself art can be found outside of himself as the "Action cometh from / The other side," but in reality knows "But they donth dare take a look" anywhere but within. It is the lies we tell ourselves. The man behind the curtain.

Furthermore, "The room is full of coffee cups," the consumption of false inspiration—a cliché quaffed into the assumption of sentences, "the wanted burden." A prison "Placed on thyself." And although now full on the idea of being a writer, the speaker is still "empty" with a blank page.

He is unable to write. There is "No stress giveth onto this page." He is so full on his surroundings he cannot seem to get a cohesive thought together. It would be easier to look outside of his self, be merely an observer to what is around him. Record the world around him like a collage project. But "this is where thy live now." A project. The lowest end of art does not even begin to show until he fuses these fragments into something original from within. "But this gift shalt never take residence" for the speaker. Oh, no. He is a product. An "art...imitation." This idea is emphasized by concluding with the speaker's misquoting "Ode to a Grecian Urn," signifying a half-hearted attempt at alluding to the poem so overtly the original become unoriginal. (Essay continues...)

#

Side note: Remember to paste a copy of "Con of Muffins."

#

(...) The poem and its summary so far also touches on themes of why even write these days? In reference to the pelican floating past the horizon, the speaker emphasizes "away from the initial hope presented." The pelican becomes a metaphor for the speaker's frustrations. He describes "limitations such as / the constraints surrounding a work of art" and "these unwavering and / strictly defined margins" in terms of the lack of general reading overall. Such a limited number of people will know the book exists, let alone read it, on the slim to none off chance of publication, to the point which the work must be character driven and filmable to increase the chances of both. The "journey the / speaker...take[s] is deeply inward" over the obstacles of discouragement.

However, "this idea of the frame" is briefly countered when "the / limitation are not yet in place. The speaker is aware of / their onset but still convinces himself art can be found." Even The Bard is meant to be performed and Adaptation only won for acting. But the work becoming something bigger than itself for show is one of "the lies we tell / ourselves" like "The man behind the curtain."

"Furthermore," the speaker implies these lies are "the / consumption of false inspiration" going on to describe them as "sentences" in "A / prison." Being a writer is a trap of the mind. The speaker must contend between the desire to write when not and the inability to write when able, even going as far as to blatantly state "He is unable to write." In the quiet of the motel, the room does not contain the barrage of stimuli and ideas "outside of his self," noting the ease in being "merely an / observer to...Record the world / around him" as the inspiration becomes uncharted. To channel "these fragments into / something original from within...is a / product...[of] 'imitation'." Therefore, the only way to create art is to simultaneously allude to and break away from what has come before, barring that the "overtly...original become[s] / unoriginal" when it no longer asserts the speaker as some sort of genius. [1]

#

[1] This article is printed with the permission of the author to be read verbatim for furthering education upon peer review.

#

"What a complete and utter waste of time and energy," says Pragmatism.

"What if I wrongly focused on prose to miss being a poet?" Cynicism replies.

Stoicism couldn't be reached for questioning, visiting a cousin in New England.

Idealism and Objectivism gang up on Vitalism, wishing to remain off the record.

Nihilism sips tea. "Coffee geeks me up all anxious."

#

And just what are you trying to prove?
--> And why do you always think in second person?

#

all the random ideas in between actually getting work done

#

It's a technique mechanism. Of fence or of fault.

#

Like a literary version of a jam band. Simultaneously striving for perfection and scattered all over

#

the map. Because once the entire world is explored the only option left is to steal.

#

Pastiche is parody politely. A take off

#

from where left off. A “you’re excused” because
you’re in on the joke. But what goes up
must land (see: becoming the event in eventually).

#

It simply comes down to wording.
--> Change the name and something’s new.
--> Conquer, liberate, flatter, a product of
influences

#

Filch.

#

“You’re a joke!”

#

“You’re an imitation!”

#

Add one part 2X Oscar winner Best Original
Screenplay cutie with equal parts hugely unknown off
yourself at 40 b.s.

#

Bake.

#

--> Altitudes differ in Colorado.

#

And Don Bronco arises.

#

"And the crowd goes wild." A-RAT-A

#

TAT-TAT. "But keep your head in the game."

#

PRATTA-TAT-TAT.

#

Your heart beating in your brain.

#

It's that rush you get when you're almost done with a novel, so you subconsciously start reading a little faster, no longer scrutinizing over every sentence because you must know how mutual accomplishment comes together.

#

(See: how it ends.)

#

Even Dewey knew to put psychology with philosophy.

#

Somewhere mixed in is ethics.

#

BA-DUM-TSK

#

The sound of a joke coming to its end.

#

WHY-NOT-STOP-HERE

#

Because what are endings but prequels to the next

#

part
chapter
series
spinoff
spoof
reboot
ruse
use
cycle

#

Bring the band back for one more tour. They were proficient in times past. That should mean something. And Ms. D. Sweet, Ms. D. Bring her back into the mix. Depart more wisdom on our dear friend, her old heart wrinkle free thanks in part to the stud in the burgundy jacket and viewers like you. Make rounds like the wheels on the bus.

No.

Get off the bus.

#

Before you go full circle lost without your buddy boy. Turn the faucet on as some cowboys might say (see: there I go again, a life's work reduced to a context). Plan this out like butter on a roll (see: otherwise we're toast).

#

FOCUS

Turn off hot tap
Chug 1 C tepid water
Chew 1 Tbs of sludge
Find him for 1 hour,
Maybe 2. No more than 3.
Watch
Return
Garnish
Print

YLDS: 1 novel punctual in time with work

#

ROLL-CAM-RA

Big steady bump-bum-bumps-bum-bumps keep the rhythm to my racing thoughts.

A cadence to the chaos. Previously, the I've never felt more alive shouted in the midst of a deafening world.

KEEP-ROLL-ING

Outside the room is louder now.

It bangs against the door.

And if it's opportunity?
Open it.
CUT-cut-CUT-cut-CUT

#

The Castigatus of Characters

From left to right: A woman, fit slender, sprawls in a lounge chair next to her two children, the kids suited and anxious to play in the water but cannot because the pool is full of drummers, their instruments eyelevel with their feathered band hats, the director, a short angry man who looks like a cone megaphone in glasses and a sweater vest, a film camera on track with its thoughts on its back, a lighting tarp, a lighting guy, foldout chairs, assorted crew, assorted pastries on a foldout table.

Center: An overweight man, mid to late thirties, thinning hair combed over, thick mustache neatly trimmed, brown suit, white shirt, brown tie, standing at the edge of the pool, briefcase at his hip.

POV: Me, hair bunned and tucked under a backwards ball cap, unshaven, plaid shirt, gym shorts, sandals, standing in a motel room's doorway, hand on the knob, mouth agape, trying to rationalize into words what I'm seeing with my throat dry and tongue stale, forcing my larynx to strike a chord and find my voice, but only managing "Zeek" as if shouting at a picture.

"Ezekiel," the picture shouts back.

#

"Who does this guy think he is? Get him out of here."—Horner Anderson, director of commercials and television, *Cop Drama, The Show.*

#

M 20__

#

I showed up to the P. Hole with time to kill. If you feel like you think you're accomplishing something then you think you're accomplishing something. And since I've got nothing else going for me I thought I'd get something done.

But, of course, Dave was there to judge insult to injury. "If you're early you're on time, if you're on time you're late, and if you're late, well, let's not strike out."

"I was under the impression second prize was a set of steak knives," guilty as charged.

"No, the real prize is working at The Pelican House, and today you're swinging for the bleachers, Donny Boy."

#

The reference	9%
The nickname	20%

Sludging through another shift despite all other factors
71%

#

Reflexive Poll:

What was found to be the most irksome thus far given the aforementioned section?

Is it A) not understanding the reference?

Or B) I'm not your chum, buddy, nickname.

#

I finished the ketchup when Matt arrived.

ROSEMARY KETCHUP MARINARA

Stew together:
#10 Can tomatoes
4 Tbs garlic
4 Tbs shallot
2 tsp chili power
paprika*
1 Tbs all spice
½ Tbs clove
1 Cup rwv
1 Cup sugar
¼ Cup rough chop rosemary
Salt and Pepper (for flavor)

Push it (real good)

through a tambourine or other mesh whatever

On a low burner:
Add tom paste until consistency

Finish with:
Chopped rosemary
Salt

He dipped the tip of his pinky across the top of the condiment while stating the obvious (see: "making catsup?") and segued both wheels into a description of a commercial I said I hadn't seen with this family trying to enjoy their "fun in the sun" but cannot due to a marching band's "parade arrangements chest deep in a swimming pool. And for whatever reason it ends with some fat dude in a suit, like an actual suit too hot for the weather, not of the bathing variety which the situation implied, standing in the background at the edge with a briefcase, stunned and sweaty."

"What's it for?"

"Abstract aesthetics so you don't forget the commercial?"

"I meant, what are they selling?"

"That I don't know. But probably insurance. Insurance commercials these days get me every time.

"And you might want to pinch in more salt."

#

Side note: *Allow me this brief moment to get real about some paprika: there's basically no taste, like air has more flavor, like you hear people say add some more garlic or cumin or salt, case in point, but never "what would really set this shit on fire is some paprika" so just dash some and be done with it.

#

Service.

#

"...don't worry about my story..."

<<REW

~~~si ti evif-ytnewt~~~setunim ytnewt naht erom on ni desolc~~~steop ton er'ew esuaceb~~~yad a ti llac dluoc dna sroolf dna steksag dah I :eeS~~~rehtegot eit evah ll'eh gnihtemos sdne esool eht~~~won kcab eh tot emac nayR~~~

<PLAY>

Ryan came to the back now things were winding down.

"You got something for me?"

The tubular fluorescence, which started its fritz during the rush, flickered bursts of noir to an otherwise relatively innocent, within context, question. I stopped wiping the gasket on the lowboy and handed him a drive of all I had, every bit unpolished nonsense byte that he'll have to refine himself if he's looking for a point, the loose ends something he'll have to tie
~~~

together bridging what he can before it drops off so sudden and vague. I'll claim "interpretations make the story personal and unique to the individual" like they do out East. If he wanted something tangible, he'd have to do that on his own. It's literally in his hands now. I'd done all I was to do.

In a word: finite.

In other words: It's his problem now.

See: I had gaskets and floors and could finally call it a day.

"I'm looking forward to this." He dropped my drive into his pocket.

"And if those high hopes crash out, burn out, and end out in disappointment?"

"That's the chance we take with every story."

The exit of luminescence.

#

"Why do we take artificial lighting as serious as the weather?"

"Because we're not poets."

#

The intellectualism of Dave decided our conversation was privy to his boredom. "What are we discussing so in depth over here? Hopefully it's about finishing up because everything should be done and closed down in no more than twenty minutes."

"Dave, dude. Are you psychic? We were literally discussing how it should take no more than twenty-five minutes tops," Ryan cut in with playful manipulation before I could go off on a harangue to explain to Dave that just because he's standing in range of a conversation doesn't qualify him as a synopsis on the book jacket-esque expert in need of his managerial use of we.

"I have been known for my keen observational skills which are often found, as I've been told, enlightening."

"Believe you me, I can see why. Anyway, we'll have it all wrapped up in thirty."

"You said twenty-five."

"See, you are the observant one. And I the fool. Twenty-five it is."

#

"Oh, by the way, before I forget," Ryan stalled on his way out the kitchen, "don't worry about my story. I tweaked a few bits since giving you a copy, nothing drastically different, but enough to get it picked up."

"You got published?"

"Technically forthcoming. So not officially. Still waiting for it to come out."

"That's exciting."

"Not as exciting as seeing how long it'll take Dave to change the lightbulb."

--> Or for Ryan to revisit an unofficial alternate version of a story I "technically" never read.

#

FRW>>

So was he the driver~~~Don't concern yourself with that~~~Find the remote~~~Did this room even have a remote~~~[Heading Break.]~~~Chillax the rush is over~~~It's all almost over~~~Remember: Even God took a day off (Already used this).~~~at the foot of the bed~~~

||STOP||

<<REW

~deb eht of toof eht ta egde eht ta tis I

<PLAY>

I sit at the edge of the foot of the bed.

The mattress sinks in, meeting me in the V.

I lean forward in the balance and reach for the television dial.

I feel like that's something I should have noticed sooner.

The smallest, lowest knob clicks the screen on.

Do they use dials in Japan?

Woman's voice: No, Kenneth, it's no longer about the show.

It's about us.

Man's voice: Baby, it's always been about the show.

The screen's too scrambled, so they're heard but not seen.

The top control dial is stuck.

New voices enter what must be a new scene.

Woman's voice: This, this is why I shouldn't have accepted the key.

Man's voice: You don't like?

Woman's voice: Not at the moment.

I attempt wiggling the knob from the socket.

Old fashioned fixing.

Woman's voice: Aren't you the least bit worried about burning your dick?

What if it pops?

Man's voice: That's what makes this the last truly great American extreme sport.

The knob pops.

Man's voice: Omelet?

The show must go on.

Woman's voice: Can't, running late.

I just came by to drop these off.

Man's voice: Sausage, then?

The knob slides from the socket.

Woman's voice: I'm not one for breakfast when there's eggshell on the platter.

Oh, look, another eggshell.

I pinch it out, see words printed like the P. Hole's schedule.

4 - V

Woman's voice: Four o'clock.

Man's voice: Four o'clock.

It was that about time.

#

THE ROMA ATE

13.5 ODD

An international twist on a homemade classic.
Our world famous, in-house, from scratch Pelican Patty,
smothered in sautéed mushrooms, caramelized onions, and provolone cheese,
on a baked fresh daily Ciabatta bun
topped with crisp Romaine, Roma tomatoes,
and house Herb Aioli, Rosemary Pickles, and Ketchup Marinara.
Buon Appetito!
Add Prosciutto 2 EVEN
Only at The Pelican House. Only for a limited time.

#

RYAN
Why 'ate?'

DON BRONCO
At the end. As in, at the end of the day it's still just a burger.

RYAN
Clever.

DON BRONCO
I really can't take credit.

RYAN holds out a large manila envelope.

RYAN

Here. Brought you this. I figured it was only fair you have a copy of that novel I've been working on. But as a heads up it's less of a novel and more a literary orthographic projection in a series of novellas and poems and quotes and flash and recipes and scripts and whatever else I could piece together into a semblance of a whole.

DON BRONCO raises an eyebrow.

RYAN

(con't)

It'll make more sense once you read it. Trust me. But everyone says that, don't they? Anyway, I think it'll be right up your alley, and see this as a justification for what you gave me.

DON BRONCO takes the envelope.

RYAN

(con't)

I jotted down a few notes that struck me while I read it. You can do what you want with them.

DON BRONCO peeks inside the envelope and is about to verbally display gratitude when MICHELLE'S uncle, BARRON STAMPEDE, restaurateur and proprietor of The Pelican House, storms past with furious speed, shifting the scene. BARRON STAMPEDE stops abruptly when he hears a muffled MOAN coming from the dry storage closet. His face is in a snarl. He hears another MOAN. He opens the closet door as if he's going to pull it off the hinges and finds DAVE and a HOSTESS mostly clothed in a compromising position on a bin of breadcrumbs. He yanks DAVE by his shirt. The HOSTESS, startled, screams.

In the background, DON BRONCO and RYAN stay to watch the scene play out.

#

• Don't take every piece of advice ever given as given.

• Even if you haven't heard the ones about adverbs.

• The protagonist is too simple to be complex while the writing is too complex to be simple.

• The last page should feel like saying goodbye to a friend, or at the very least, a companion.

• That's not how I initially imagined the characterization of the man in the burgundy jacket.

• And the use of names is a bit blunt, on the brink of too blunt.

• I've seen Twenty Four a Money. They are that good.

• The overall structure plays with the form of an adventure narrative, the protagonist meeting companions along the way, and albeit sloppy at times, I think by the end you found your voice, whether you were looking for it or not.

• But however loud, don't think it's long enough to call it a novel.

• I'm positive there's ways you can extend the word count.

• That being said, it doesn't have an ending. Rather, it stops. It reminds me of a friend of mine growing up. Whenever he told a story that stagnated into rambles he would end it with "Then I found twenty dollars. Then I caught on fire."

#

5 HOT FIRST RATE FIRST DATE DATING TIPS FOR SUMMER SINGLES

1. Flirt. Flirt With Your Man. But Do Not Flirt With Other Men While Out. A Guy Likes To Feel Like He Is The Only One.

She smiled at me as she passed.

I looked down at my shirt, making sure no leftovers dripped their way onto the cotton blend. I made sure my hat was still in place over my receding hairline. I pinched the inner corners of my nostrils, discreetly checking for sneaky hang-downs, before casually smoothing out my mustache. All seemed in order. She had smiled at me. There was no one with her, no cell phone in hand. The cute girl had locked eyes and smiled.

I straightened my spine and sucked in my newly forming gut as I hand-ironed my shirt from chest to waist. Picking just to pick, I pulled a bottle of raspberry vinaigrette off the shelf while allowing my eyes to follow the brown haired girl down the aisle. She strutted like a basketball player strolling down court, giving her basketball shorts a warranted swish and shimmy. The mesh fabric, rolled at the waist, teasingly touched the end of her tie-dyed t-shirt, a tourist trap alligator-crocodile, drinking some sort of spring break '08 cocktail, sunbathing across her back. She wasn't tall, maybe tall enough for point guard. There was just something about cute girls who played basketball, about them being spunky, quick, their thick legs adding a bounce to their step...

"Is that what you want?"

"What? No, I—" I turned to my wife leaning elbow braced on the cart, shopping list in hand.

"What kind is that?"

I showed her the label.

"I didn't think you liked raspberries."

"I—I don't." The girl was no longer in the salad dressing/condiment aisle. I relieved my stomach from its upright and locked position and dropped my shoulders to their droopy norm. "I was just checking out something new. Uh, the label. Ingredients."

"Well, if you want it drop it in the cart. We still need eggs, milk, and ice cream. And I'm talking lots of ice cream."

I placed the vinaigrette back on the shelf, snagged a blue cheese, and followed my wife up the aisle towards the lots of ice cream.

2. Chat. Giggle. Be Engaged And Engaging. But Share The Conversation. If You Don't Let Him Talk To You Now He Will Not Want To Talk To You Later.

My wife put a mint chocolate chip on top of the chocolate chip cookie dough next to the Drumsticks. I put my head in the freezer, breathing in the cold air, staring down Freezy Moo Moo, the cartoon cow peddling Bullitin's Home-Made Home-Churned Silk-Smooth Walnut Vanilla Iced Cream. "Shoot," my wife said.

"What's the matter, you?" I wiped a circle of cold condensation from the door and watched her through the smudged, wet glass rotate her paper list with a flip of her wrist.

"Forgot paper towels."

"Forgot them?" My breath grayed the glass.

"I mean, I forgot to write them down. Now they're all the way across the store."

"We'll just have to backtrack on our great Marcato's Market journey." I let go of the door. The seal thumped a dull boom of arctic air.

"Or, you could run over there and pick up a pack. I mean, I already have ice cream in the cart."

"That you do."

She extended her arms for me to step into her embrace. "Will you be able to handle this quest for your princess, brave knight?"

"I shall face perils, thieves, bandits, and dragons to prove my worth to me lady," I rubbed my palm down her belly beginning to show signs of protruding, "and once-and-future king."

"Or queen." She bumped up the bill of my flat cap with the top of her head as she went in for a quick, we're in public kiss. Pulling away, she squinched her nose and rubbed the tip with open, flat fingers. "I wish you'd shave that silly thing."

I replaced my hat to its proper place over my hairline. "But I'm an old man now."

"You're only thirty-one."

"Like I said." I winked and proceeded up the row of freezers.

"One slight question, though," she called out behind me.

I turned but continued walking backwards.

"Why are you still holding that salad dressing?"

"Salad dressing? Oh, you mean the Sword of Destiny."

She shook her head with a smile. I turned back around.

My wife and I met at a Descendents reunion show, two, three, six years ago. She accidentally punched me in the face during "I'm the One," sucked me off an apology in the parking lot after the gig, and we've been together ever since. When we first got together she claimed she never wanted to get married and completely rejected the idea of kids. Growing up, within a year, she lost her brother in a skydiving accident and her mother to surgical complications. She never wanted to recreate the chance of a grand scale loss like that again. I never did well with the whole being told what I can or cannot do thing, so my aging punk rebellious streak manifested itself as a ring and taking a knee. Though, honestly, I was anticipating a no.

Yet, I'm certain her answer corresponded with the fact she found out she was pregnant on the morning I proposed, answering, "Baby," with a strange, soft look behind her eyes, as if she noticed life was in color for the first time. At first, I thought she was letting me down easy instead of informing me. But my other knee hit the floor with the realization. I grabbed ahold of her legs, and she ran her fingers through my thinning hair. Less than a month later we were in the courthouse—me nervously smiling and sweating anxiety, she in blushing bride, mommy mode. So, standing before the judge, I thought we hit a turning point, a step for the future. Our lives. Forever. Holding my hands, she said, yes, her smile so wide it choked back tears. I said, yes, louder than my second thoughts. Our new lives. A new life. Till death do us part.

I scanned the shelves of rolled paper products. There were at least seventeen types of paper towels. I went for the quicker picker upper, but the price rejected my hand mid reach, so I decided on going for a more generic, averager picker upper. We were already spending a lot of cash on ice cream.

"Frank spent all day on the lake again," said a red-haired woman with a perm like my mom had in the 80s to a shorter, older, blue-haired woman standing in front of the napkins.

"Mmm-hmm, the lake," said Old Blue.

"You know, he can go and drink as much beer while he cuts the grass. But I can't go mentioning a thing. As soon as I do it's bait and tackle."

"Bait and tackle," Old Blue said, nodding in agreement as if they were both married to this Frank guy.

80s Perm gently lifted the back of her hair with a pat. "And, oh, his tall tales. Let me tell you what. Did you know this time he saw a lake monster?"

"Lake monster." Old Blue didn't sound surprised. Apparently, she knew.

"That's why he can't seem to ever catch a fish. They all done been eaten up by lake monsters."

"Mmm-hmm, no fish."

"That's right. And when he stumbled in last night he had his box but no pole. And when I asked him where his pole was, you know what he said?"

"Lake monster."

80s Perms emphatically flailed her hands in annoyed delight. "I said, 'Frank, where is your pole?' and he had the nerve to tell me that he was sitting there on the dock, 'minding my own business,' when he felt a tug on the line. 'Honey, I had a whopper,' he said. 'I reeled hard,' he said. So I said, 'What does this have to do with your pole, Frank?' and he said, 'That's the kicker, out of the water came a lake monster, my line running straight to its mouth.' 'Lake monster?' I said. He told me it had big, scaly skin and sharp teeth, a little head like a hairless lizard-dog, and a neck like an elephant trunk. Oh, and big snake eyes. 'And how did you of all people survive?' I asked him. 'I threw my empty soda can at him and he swam away,' he said. Can you believe it? He tried telling me he was drinking a blessed soda."

"You shouldn't drink too much soda," nodded Old Blue.

"I told him he wasn't allowed to watch that dinosaur movie with the grand-babies no more."

"Mmm-hmm."

"Not even a lizard lives near that lake."

"Not even a lizard."

3. Positivity! Have A Positive Outlook. Do Not Spend Your Time Complaining, Even If You Do Not Enjoy The Activity. Have Fun. Be Adventurous. Take Advantage Of Any And All Situations.

My wife was already in the checkout line.

"What took you so long?" She pulled back her hair, tightening her blond roots to her scalp and corralling a green ponytail with one of those thin, black hairbands she always wore on her wrist.

"Lake monster." I dropped the pack of paper towels and the salad dressing in the cart.

"Don't you mean dragon?"

"Nope. I mean lake monster."

"Good thing you had your sword."

"Good thing."

I looked around at all the last-minute aisle goodies—chocolate bars, sodas, gum. We were trying to quit smoking. Well, she quit. I was trying. She said I didn't have to as long as I didn't do it around her and the baby, but I told her I wanted to, that it would be good for me, good for all of us. Plus, I think she was just trying to be nice. Yet, I kept a green pack of Bower Lites she didn't know about under the seat of the car. What she did know was I went through a lot of gum.

We took a step.

The pack in my pocket was heading towards empty. I didn't see the dark blue pack of Sweet Midnight, so I settled for the light blue pack, Cool Mint Flare or something. I didn't necessarily want to settle, but you never know when tense will morph into stress and you'll need that stick of gum.

We took another step.

I tossed the pack on the checkout belt while my wife fingered through some magazine she pulled from the rack. I began unloading the cart, first the salad dressing, then the paper towels. Then I saw it. I was surprised I didn't see it before.

"What is this?"

She looked up from her flipping, a loose page acting as a thin blanket, tucking her finger in. It's a binky, silly. You better get used to it, cause you're gonna be seeing a lot of them." She said this with such a casual ease, like she'd said this a million times over.

"I mean, why's it in the cart? It's still going to be awhile, I think. I hope. He needs to finish baking. You know, at least have a face to stick the binky in."

"Oh, I know. But it's just so cute," her voice climbed an octave into mommy territory. "And it's best to be prepared, anyway, right? They teach you that in Boy Scouts."

I placed the binky on the belt. "I think they more mean Swiss Army Knives and pieces of flint."

She shrugged and tilted her attention back down to her magazine.

Boy Scouts? I was never in Boy Scouts. It wasn't my thing, building canoes or sewing badges or whatever it was they did. But maybe I should have been. Then maybe I'd be prepared for all this.

I placed the Drumsticks on the belt.

A wife. A kid. I was certifiably unprepared even if I thought otherwise. This was what you do. You grow up. You quit smoking. You go grocery shopping with your wife. These things. You're supposed to do these things.

I placed the mint chocolate chip on the belt.

This was what I wanted, right?

I placed the chocolate chip cookie dough on the belt.

"How are you today, sir?"

"Scared shitless." The words flew out of my mouth before I could stop my lips. I looked to see where they crashed and watched a short cashier's face morph from braces gleaming, forced customer service smile, into pimpled confusion.

"If you forgot your Marcato's Merry Customer Val-U Card, I got one you can use."

"Oh, no—no. Sorry." I handed over my keys so she could scan the keychain Val-U card while looking over my shoulder at my wife. I had to admit, she was beautiful, standing there with the magazine at her side, eyeing the candy bars, glowing.

"Did you find everything okay?" She beeped the keys over the laser and handed them back in a single motion.

The binky raced its way towards the finish line of plastic bags. "Uh—yeah. Sure. I guess I'd say we did."

"How old's your baby?"

The beep cheered the binky across.

"The baby? Oh, the baby. There is no baby." I was sure my expression inadvertently screamed rude confusion. I loathed checkout small talk. "That is to say, not yet at least. But he's on his way. We, uh, only stuck him up in there a few months back." In a last-ditch effort at appeasing the awkwardness, I forced a smile, which stretched my mustache across my face. I was one wink away from looking like I should be on posters warning children about getting into vans with strangers. I tried reading the name tag pinned to the girl's yellow and red Marcato's Market polo, yet the felt tip marker had smeared, leaving all but the first letter illegible: B-Smudge. Now, in my defense, I was merely lingering, focusing, leering, whatever, trying to make out the letters when B-Smudge began blushing, her acne on the verge of molten explosions. Even I could feel her embarrassment in between the frantic beeps as she breathed loudly through her nose, her braces peeking from out from behind her lips.

I pushed the cart down the lane, out of the way of whatever thoughts were penetrating that girl's brain.

"These too, sir?" B-Smudge's voice cracked like candy as she held up two chocolate bars and the magazine.

"Yes, those too," my wife said, stepping up to the counter.

B-Smudge looked at me for confirmation, like I was in charge.

I glanced at the magazine, a *Cosmo* with the breaking cover story, 5 Hot First Rate First Date Dating Tips For Summer Singles, plastered underneath Celia Wood's bulging right tit's cleavage. It was highly uncharacteristic of my wife to want a *Cosmo*, especially one with Celia Woods on the cover. But, hey, I guess she did.

"Yeah, those too."

4. If Things Went Well, Do Not Be Afraid To Call Him. However, If He No Longer Seems Interested After The First Date Do Not Chase Him. You Will Run The Risk Of Running Him Off For Good.

I shut the door and slipped the key into the ignition. "What's with the magazine?" I waited till we were in the car just in case the question backfired.

"Oh, I dunno. Fashion tips." I was unsure if she was asking or telling.

"You of all people do not need fashion tips." That may sound like I was just saying what a good husband should, but I genuinely believed it. She always had her own style. Chic, yet simple. Flashy, but not gaudy. Naturally, it did take her a bit longer to get ready, but the end result was worth it. She pulled the *Cosmo* from her personal bag she took to the front seat with her.

I gently let the car roll from the parking spot.

"And dating tips. What if that dragon would have eaten you? I wouldn't know what to do in today's social scene."

"I'm sure you'd be fine. You could always just stick with your method of giving blowies in parking lots. It's foolproof, really."

She playfully slapped my arm.

"And it was a lake monster, not a dragon."

"Same difference."

"Huge difference." I pushed in the brake at the stop sign in front of the crosswalk. "One breathes fire, the other lives in water. Each requires their own, separate battle strategy."

The girl with the basketball shorts walked out of the store holding a single plastic bag. I figured she'd be long gone by then, but there she was, stepping in front of my car. She didn't smile at me this time. She probably just saw the car not knowing I was behind the wheel. But what if she knew? Would that even matter? Everything I'm supposed to have was in the car with me, right? A pregnant wife. Groceries. I shouldn't have even looked at her with mild infatuation.

But she had smiled at me.

"So, we staying here awhile or you wanna head home?" My wife looked up from the magazine.

"I—I'm not ready."

"For?"

I shuffled my hand under the seatbelt and into my pocket. "Just—just needed some gum." I pulled out a piece and reopened it in my wife's direction as I watched the girl through the passenger window bounce down the lane of cars, stopping at a silver compact.

"Don't mind if I do."

Dropping the pack into the center cup holder, I regrouped, changing the conversation. "Learning anything profoundly insightful?"

"Only Katie Garner's recent breakup from Martin Hearty will end world hunger."

"About time we feed the world."

"See, now aren't you glad I got it?"

"I still don't understand your sudden interest in that prefabricated nonsense."

There were many things I didn't understand.

"Don't be snarky. This is pertinent life information. I'm not sure how I've made it this far without it."

"Oh, really?"

"Yes, really."

I wish I had a handbook of pertinent life information. Walk into the store for snacks, walk out with the guide to life. A play-by-play. My life nearing halftime. Offense was set. Now, if I could just get my defense in order. Team Tie-Dyed Alligator-Crocodile traveling up and down the court without penalty. Three pointers at every pivot. Thick, strong legs boxing out, setting up fouls. Personal fouls. I needed the ball back in my court.

I could hear myself ferociously chewing my gum like I needed a fix.

"Like these five hot dating tips—" she read each one aloud. "See, they don't mention a thing about blowjobs. I'd be screwed if a lake monster ever ate you. Pertinent life information."

"We should go to the lake."

"When?"

"I dunno. Now?"

"We can't. We have ice cream."

"That we do."

5. Be Honest, While Out And After. If You Think Of A Compliment, Tell Him. If You Are Interested, Tell Him. If You Don't Think There Is A Spark, Do Not Keep Him Hanging On, And Tell Him.

I park the car on the gravel drive and, after stepping out, reach under the seat for my cigarette stash, but instead of a box my finger grazes some sort of tube. Unable to pull it out from the front, I open the back door and dig under the seat. Picturesque Farm's Peppercorn Bleu Cheese. It must have slipped out and slid under on our way home. Breaking the paper seal, I twist off the cap and dab a drop on my finger. I didn't realize I didn't get plain ole blue cheese, but honestly, it's not half bad.

I tighten the lid back into place, toss the dressing onto the passenger seat, and remove my cigarettes from their secured spot jammed against the little seat motor. The car honks as I lock it while walking towards the specified trail.

After helping my wife unload and put away the groceries, I told her I needed to step out for a bit. I did ask if she wanted to come but she was busy scooping two types of ice cream into the same bowl. It's just as well—I didn't really want her to anyway.

The trail opens up to the sandy bank of the lake. Veering a left, I make my way towards the public dock. The sun is on the brink of setting, bleeding orange and red onto the water gently rippled by the breeze. Two geese call out, flying overhead. Three others peck at the shore's wet sand.

I nod a hello to an elderly gentleman sitting on a cooler surrounded by crushed beer cans, fishing off the end of the dock. I stop half way, not to disturb him.

"Want a cold one?" he calls out, casting his line like a whip.

"Sure, why not?" I walk the other half of the way. He gets up, digs around in the cooler, cracks one open, and hands it to me with the graceful ease of doing this a thousand times over.

"It's hell'a pretty, ain't it. I'd be out here ever' damn day if I could." He licks the foam off his fingers before shaking off the excess.

"I know what you mean," I lie. I take a sip, soaking in my surroundings. The beer washes out the lingering taste of peppercorn.

"You mind if I—?" the fisherman asks as I pull out my cigarettes.

"Not at all." I open the pack in his direction then pull one out for myself. Flicking my lighter, I burn a cherry before offering it to my newfound company.

"It's alright, got one." He removes a Zippo from his tackle box. "Always be prepared." He lights up and chuckles like a smokehouse. "Cause life comes at you like a shitstorm, lemme tell you what."

"I know what you mean." This time, honestly.

"Always have somethin' you can fall back on. Like sunsets and cold beer."

I take a drag, but it doesn't feel right.

"Sunsets and cold beer," he repeats.

I flick off the cherry, and it sizzles on the water. I don't need it—I have gum. "Trying to quit. Baby on the way," I offer, putting the burnt end back into the pack.

"Hot damn, good for you. There ain't nothin' better than becomin' a father." His words, coated in smoke, wisp around the stick dangling from his lips as he recasts his line. "As long as you don't go muckin' it up, ain't nothin' better."

"Yeah?"

He laughs from the corner of his mouth, shaking ash onto his lap. "You got fear in your voice."

"Just—just don't know if I'm ready."

"Shit, ain't nobody ready, lemme tell you what. But you stick with it, no matter what. Ain't nothin' better."

I slip off my shoes and roll up my jeans so I can sit with my feet in the fiery water that looks as warm and inviting as the feeling washing over me.

"Just gotta be careful, now," he snuffs the butt on the sole of his boot and tilts his eyes towards my submerged feet, "and watch out for lake monsters."

Acknowledgements:

Thank you to Colby Webb, Mel Paisley, Taylor Walton—(the cameo of coffee shop writers)—and Viktor Amaechi for putting early eyes on early drafts. Then Vik again for doing the insane thing of putting eyes on it again (and again). Thank you to Dan Eastman, Emily Costa, and Wallace Barker for the kind words. And most importantly, this book you're holding wouldn't be possible without Alan Good and Malarkey Books. Thank you for seeing something worth a chance, and your willingness (see: patience) to deal with all these fonts, colors, and formats. I can only imagine the words muttered in italics as you regretted this decision.

This also wouldn't be possible without for accepting the story Spark of Magic:

A flash of light streaked towards the curve of the earth like a scratch on the nighttime. King paused at the sight, half expecting a mushroom cloud to rise over the city's horizon. He waited for some sort of extraterrestrial hovercraft. Yet, it was merely a shooting star, a close one, but a star nonetheless. King continued his laggard pace atop the cracked, jagged concrete blocks of sidewalk, still wishing skyward, when he bumped into the unkempt flesh of grime and poverty. "I'm sorry, sir," King blindly apologized without turning from the sky.

"It's Sir Vino, I'll have you know."

"Yes sir, Vino."

No other stars were out after the fallen, which raised concern in King's anxiety. Only clouds, misty, sleepy clouds drifting, hiding the stars that never sparkled. Windows from late nights and lights too lazy to be shut off took their place, speckling the skyline. A traffic light winked from green to yellow, shifting the aura around the evening strollers.

"That's more like it, young lad. Now run along."

King pulled his focus away from the night, giving attention to his sidewalk companion. Standing before him was a ragged gentleman of unique proportions akin to 19th century caricature: a peppered beard of arm's length hanging from an oversized head, whose wrinkled face held, under an extra flap of eyebrow skin, eyes of hatred—not full of hate, per se, but callous from years of hatred against.

"Scurry. Scoot, now." Vino showed his disapproval of King's stillness on the sidewalk by waving his downward hand, palm in, like palsy permeated his brain. Like he couldn't wait to get that hand on the next drink. King looked past Vino's tremor towards the pink and blue glow of Fellows. He moved aside, and Sir Vino stumbled a wobble forward. "Now that's a fine chap."

Politeness scintillates its poetic glint even at dark moments, foraging in the shadows, finding dim lights of hope to cling to, like the light from the signal above glowing red, which was just enough to spark the offering. "I'm headed for a beer. How about you?" King assumed his compassion had something to do with the night. People seemed more hopeful around falling stars. And maybe a side effect of hopefulness was generosity.

"My poor dear. I do not touch the wretched stuff."

King shrugged off the offer. He preferred not drinking alone, but the night did not dictate preferences. At times—rare times—but times nonetheless, there was an atmospheric alignment that created a force outside the laws of preference. Yet man, being so close to the ground, could only guess the nights falling into place.

"However, if you could splurge for a chardonnay?"

And King could.

The neon blue didn't get brighter as they walked closer. It remained the same buzzing hue, drawing thirsty moths to its well lit well. The only shadows from the sign emerged from the flickering o, and not in a symbolic, holistic blink, but a decreasing volt's strobe against an influx of gas. The front door, chipped with bits of dark green paint, creaked downheartedly. This gave the regulars a moment to look up from the dark stained paneled wood and see who was worse off than they were. This gave the bartender a moment to regroup and remember he didn't care about the patrons' problems. A whiskey for their misfortunes added towards his missed fortune.

"A Makers. Double. Neat." King sat at the bar's curve near the sinks.

The bartender, drying a pint glass, took the order. "Is he with you?" King nodded, so the bartender didn't raise debate to Vino's ordering a chardonnay.

King, not sure what he was looking for and even more unsure if he would find it, scoured the bar populated by poor night rats coming up for their nip and nibble. A graying man in a burgundy coat nursed a glass sweating out the fever in front of him. He seemed like he'd been there, that spot, claimed by him, all day. All month. For years. King envied his get up and sit lifestyle. No suit. No tie. No accounting job at a firm that didn't even know his name. At least in a bar, everyone knew your name.

King could, however, sympathize with the graying man if he too didn't have a woman keeping the nights warm and the bed worn. King was jealous of how the graying man found the womanly touch on the curve of a pint. He was glad he followed his heart, ordering a whiskey over the intended beer, wanting to feel the burn of its kiss on his lips.

"We ain't got wine."

"Then how about a dry merlot."

"How about liquor or beer?"

"Any bottle, any year," King's companion concluded.

The bartender didn't care, didn't argue, and didn't care to argue, placing two smooth, stout glasses in front of the gentlemen. He filled a double, neat, for King, and without changing bottles spilled a single, out of spite, into the other. King picked up his glass, but setting the dry rim to his lips caused Sir Vino to clear his throat.

Vino held up his glass by the base, angling the single whiskey. "To God and country." King nodded a simple acknowledgement, dinked glasses, and sipped while Vino swirled the brown liquid, eyeing its clarity in the amber light, before taking a swift sniff. Vino approved, ordering, "Barkeep. Another," after gulping most of the spinning contents in a swallow, a few wayward dribbles flowing like tears from the corners of his lips, soaked by his spongy beard.

The graying man licked his upper lip as if there was still a functioning head on his beer.

The air in the room was full of smoke, though no one was smoking. A city ordinance took care of that years ago. Yet, somehow, the remnants of snuffed cigarettes remained. Or maybe it was the haze of men's souls with nowhere better to go. King took a sip in memory of them.

The bartender, bottle in hand, asked King, You gonna pay for this? with a glance before tilting whiskey.

King nodded, Go ahead. He pushed himself away from the bar, the stool's legs howling agony. "Bathroom," he informed no one who cared.

King stood at the urinal, relieved. The single, uncovered fluorescent bulb's luminescence waned before amplifying and waning again in a dizzying cycle of light. The floor felt slick, almost glidingly so, indistinguishable between errant piss and soap. The heavy, heavily tagged bathroom door whined company. King peeked over his shoulder, casually, not to wiggle onto his pants. The shadow of the graying man entered the stall.

"Damn useless pecker won't leak," echoed from the shady walls following a grunt and a drip.

King turned his head in the direction of the raspy voice, reading Dark Purple permanently written under Blue Balls. He knew he should respond with some sort of consolation, but he never handled public situations well, so he left without a flush or a wash, hoping the graying man didn't notice his rude and unsanitary bathroom behavior.

The smell of smoke entered King's nose as he rejoined his newfound friend busy swirling a glass and studying the rhythms of the whiskey. Knowing Sir Vino as long as he had, King knew that was new whiskey in the old glass. Vino shot back the drink and shook off the burn. Drops followed the trail laid before them into his beard. King took a sip before sitting.

"Many happy returns to you, sir."

"Obliged."

In the direction of the bathroom, King kept an eye on the air where the graying man was sitting, contemplating an apology of some sorts, simultaneously assuming the needlessness and embarrassment of admitting fault for doing no wrongdoing. He gulped what remained in the glass, and while still to his lips, motioned for another. Hot air fogged the glass under King's nose. The bartender acknowledged King's place next in line on the list of pointless tasks that imitate work.

"How about you?" King asked Vino as the bartender poured. The graying man had returned to his natural habitat at the bar, slumped over his beer like a doctor who'd just lost a patient.

"I shall postpone, for the hour is nigh," Sir Vino said, holding his hand at arm's length, looking past his palm towards the ceiling as if gazing at the stars, romanticizing emphasis. He removed himself from the chair, with a bow complimented, "You're companionship has been most hospitable, this fine evening," and left the bar as if he never was. Even the smoky air never registered a disturbance from Sir Vino. The stillness pulsated a quick shiver through King's being, frightening him without scaring him, passing with a tremor.

He signed the air signaling his check. The bartender nodded in agreement, and King finished his whiskey. Maybe the bar wasn't fantastic. Maybe the fantastic was only among the stars, sporadically crashing towards the plated surface of the earth, keeping the world spinning forward. But, no matter what, King lied hopefulness to himself, yet understood in his heart of hearts there was no spark of magic to ignite the night.

The bartender dropped the folded check facedown.

"I—I hate to do this, but can I have just another?"

The bartender wadded the check off the bar.

"And that guy—over there." King pointed with his forehead. "Can I have his check?"

The bartender followed the direction of King's forehead. "You sure, buddy?"

"No. But bring it anyway."

The bartender complied with whiskey. King handed him his card without looking at the figures, an act of faith when there was nothing to believe in. He didn't waste any time with the glass, setting it drained and upside-down on the stained wood. He was ready to leave and, with nowhere to go, planned to head north to find the fallen star. He planned to go up in smoke.

but then never running it and disappearing in an internet sort of way of maintaining the domain of past content and closed-loop links. I don't know. Always thought it was funny; forever forthcoming. Really added to the overall effect of this book in a stranger than fiction imitating life imitating fiction sort of way. So, I guess thank you to this story, "Spark of Magic," for the adventure of circumstances and for being such a big influence on myself.

And finally to Itoro Bassey, author of *Faith*, Ben Azarte, author of *Music is Over!*, Alex Miller, author of *White People on Vacation*, Eric Williams, author of *Toadstones*, Joey Hedger, author of *Deliver Thy Pigs*, Justin Bryant, author of *Thunder from a Clear Blue Sky*, Susan Triemert, author of *Guess What's Different*, Benjamin Warner, author of *Fearless*, Patrick Nevins, author of *Man in a Cage*, and Roger Vaillancourt, author of *Un-ruined*, and Leigh Chadwick, author of *Your Favorite Poet*, who hasn't read this book because it's not a Leigh Chadwick book. Timing and chance threw together a book club of strangers; what a wild ride.

Until the next time...

Donald Ryan's shorter works have for real appeared in Hobart, Cleaver, Fiction Southeast, Reckon Review, The Daily Drunk, and elsewhere. This is his first "novel." He lives in Georgia.

->Donald Ryan solely exists online dot com.

CPSIA information can be obtained
at www.ICGtesting.com
Printed in the USA
JSHW082117041122
32650JS00002B/8

9 781088 068441